BEASTLY *Lies*

& BEAUTIFUL *Legends*

HARMONY A. HAUN

ISBN: 979-8-9868359-6-9 Paperback
ISBN: 979-8-9868359-5-2 e-book
ISBN: 979-8-9868359-7-6 Hardback

First edition

Author Contact: harmonyahaunauthor@gmail.com
IG: Harmonya.haun_author

Playlist on Spotify

Click Spotify link above

or scan QR Code

SCAN ME

PREFACE & TRIGGER WARNINGS

As an author it is never my intent to hurt or offend anyone, in any way, with what I write. I am hyper aware of content being triggering and do my best to give amble warning. Please understand that this is a work of fiction, and I am but an imperfect human. If you ever feel attacked in any way over something I wrote, please do not hesitate to reach out to me, in a respectful manner, and I would be happy to discuss.

What you can potentially find triggering in this book includes, but not limited to:
Sexual assault, emotional and physical abuse, adult language, adult content, loss of a loved one, mention of death and killing, graphic violent scene and mentions of blood.

If you ever need to talk to someone, please seek help.
National Sexual Assault Line: 1-800-656-4673
Suicide & Crisis Line: 1-800-273-8255

DEDICATION

To all my beautiful readers. The ones who dive into stories as
a way to escape an imperfect reality.

I see you.

I understand you.

But don't forget, or be too afraid to look up from the pages, and
find the beauty in the world around you. I promise you; it is
there if you look.

You deserve your own HEA too, not just our fictional MCs.

BEASTLY Lies & BEAUTIFUL Legends

Prologue

Bella

LONELY BY BILLIE EILISH, KHALID

It's beautiful in its haunting mystery. It stands alone on top of the mountain, so high up that it looks like the tallest towers touch the sky and dance with the clouds. It seems... *peaceful*, but in a magnificent kind of way. As if it knows it's alone and, instead of drooping and feeling sorry for itself, it stands tall and strong, proud of its resilience and solitude. I know, it's silly to imagine a structure having such feelings. Perhaps I'm projecting my own personal feelings onto it.

It's far enough away to stay out of mind for most people, most days, but still close enough for the threat to be felt. Especially on the days when its shadow seems to swallow up this small town completely.

Knightwell Castle.

Or, as the superstitious lot of New Haven like to call it, Nightmare Castle.

There's a legend of a beast residing alone in the abandoned castle. A beast that has been terrorizing New Haven for centuries. It's said that anyone who travels too far into the forest, who gets too close to the castle, is taken by this Beast and never seen or heard from again.

Completely ludicrous!

There's no animal, beast or otherwise, that could live that long. I guess it's possible that this so-called *beast* could have had offspring and taught them to terrorize us too, but it all sounds silly to me. Then again, my mother and I are shunned and accused of practicing witchcraft, so the opinions of these small-minded people don't really mean much to me. They just refuse to see the reality staring them in the face.

People leave.

Yes, people are here one day and gone the next, my own father included, but I'm not in denial. I'm not blaming some mythical *beast* for the decision my father chose to make. He left us because people change, because people are cruel and selfish. He left because he didn't want this life, this family. He left because he didn't want *us*. He wasn't taken by some beast. He wasn't held hostage and tortured to death in that castle. But for the people of New Haven, it's easier to blame some scary beast than to admit the ugly truth.

They were abandoned.

But I know the truth and I'm not afraid of the castle or who might live in it. In fact, it's the exact opposite; I'm intrigued and curious. I find myself sitting on the roof of our little cabin in the woods, staring at the castle more often than not. I feel drawn to it. I can't explain it, but it feels familiar somehow. Especially on nights like this when the moon is full, acting like a personal spotlight for the castle. It seems to glow under the moonlight, which I know is just in my head, just the way *I* see it.

And on nights like tonight, I feel the pull towards the castle deep in my gut, as if a rope is wrapped around my spine, gently tugging at me, trying to pull me forward.

And on nights like tonight, I almost give in because I don't know what the castle holds but I know what New Haven holds, and I want no part of it. I don't fit in. I don't belong here. And I want to see for myself if what they say is true.

Is there really a beast?

Bella

Love The Way You Lie by Eminem, Rihanna

"Wow."

I do a little twirl, my yellow summer dress flaring out around me, showing more of my thighs as I do.

"Do you like it?" I ask nervously, as I stop spinning and face him, fiddling with the fabric.

I'm not sure how he's going to react to the new dress. The pleated bottom hits right above my knees, the neckline scoops, and the straps leave my arms bare, revealing more skin than anything else I've ever worn before.

His dark eyes take their time slipping down my body before he drags them back up. I love when he looks at me like this; like I'm his life-saving oasis in the desert and if he doesn't have a sip of water *this instant*, he may just die.

He stalks toward me, closing the distance between us with long, confident strides. My heart beats in time with each step he takes, beating with excitement and uncertainty.

THUD.

THUD.

THUD.

One large hand wraps around my waist, pulling me into his solid body, while the other hand tenderly tucks my hair behind my ear before tracing my jaw and tilting my chin up so I can meet his gaze. Staring into his chiseled and handsome face, my heart stutters, and my stomach flips, but it feels more like uncertainty and fear than excitement.

"You look absolutely stunning, Bella. I can't wait to show you off on my arm and let everybody know you're mine."

When his lips land on mine, my body finally loses some of its tension and I lean into him. The feel of his tongue on my lips, seeking entry, sends a hot and tingling sensation shooting through my body, and when his tongue slides against mine, I moan my pleasure into his mouth.

He kisses me hungrily, reminding me that I *am* that oasis he's been searching for, that this kiss *is* his salvation. His hands hold me tightly, almost bruising, as if he's afraid I'll disappear into thin air. It scares me sometimes, his need for me, but it also makes me feel so beautiful and so damn special. This is going to be a great night.

He breaks the kiss and I'm left smiling up at him with a more confident smile now. "I think you like the dress."

"I like the way *you* look in the dress and I'm going to like the way you look on my arm in the dress even more." He chucks my chin playfully. "Let's get going. I'm starving."

"'Kay."

I'm still beaming like a lovestruck idiot, clinging to his massive arm as he leads us down the sidewalk in town. My flats allow me to keep up with his large gait, but it's so beautiful out I wish he'd walk a little slower so we could enjoy the fresh evening air. The sun is just starting to set, painting the sky in beautiful pastel shades of pink and orange against a crisp blue background. All the leaves on the trees have turned from green to their beautiful golden hues of oranges, yellows, and reds. I think this is going to be one of the last warm days we have before winter starts to sneak in. It's already been a mild fall compared to what we normally have this time of year, so I'm waiting for the cold shoe to drop.

I release a contented sigh. "Isn't it beautiful?"

"What?" he asks, voice clipped.

"This." I wave my free hand in the air. "The weather, the sky, the fresh air. It truly is amazing how much beauty this Earth creates."

A grunt is all I get in response.

I don't let his lack of appreciation take away from mine, but I'm quickly distracted by my name being yelled loudly and repeatedly. We're forced to come to a halt in front of Main Street Bakery as Chip comes barreling out the front door, wrapping his little body around my legs in a bear hug.

"Bella! Bella! Bella!" He starts jumping up and down before he lets me go. "I need to ask you something. Momma said I could."

I unravel myself from Gabriel's arm before I unravel Chip from my legs. I kneel down in front of him and pinch his still chubby little cheeks. "Chip, Chip, Chip," I mimic. "What do you want to ask me, love?"

"Momma said I was having a birthday party and I could invite whoever I wanted! Will you come? Please, please, please!" He continues to jump up and down with the unrestrained excitement children often have.

I gasp as if I'm in shock although I already know it's his birthday and have already planned to be at his party. "A birthday party? It's not your birthday," I tease.

"Yeah-huh! It is! It's tomorrow! You *have* to come, Bella, you have tooooo," he pleads.

His mom, Mrs. Potts, is the only one in this town, besides Gabriel, who speaks to me. I think the majority of the reason is because, as a single mother, she needs all the help she can get. I've babysat Chip since he was a baby and he's absolutely my favorite person in this godforsaken, rinky-dink, ignorant town.

"Bella," Gabriel huffs his impatience, "just tell the kid you'll be there and let's go. I already told you once, I'm starving."

I ignore him as I continue to give Chip my full attention. "And how old are you going to be? Five?"

He stomps his little foot. "No! Six! I'm not a baby anymore, Bella." He drops his chin and scowls as he pouts, looking up at me through thick lashes.

I laugh and ruffle his hair. "Six! Well, I can't miss such a big birthday now, can I? I'll be there."

"Yay!" He's back to smiling and jumping up and down, clapping his hands in victory.

"Now go back inside and help your mom like a big boy." I gently push him towards the store.

"Ok!" He turns and runs to the door. Before he disappears inside, he turns back around. "Don't forget to bring me a birthday present!"

"I won't," I promise with a chuckle as I stand back up, ready to give my attention back to Gabriel.

He's now standing a few feet away and, surprise, surprise, he's not alone. Something flares up inside of me, but it doesn't feel like jealousy. Then again, maybe it is. I've never experienced it before to know if it is what I'm feeling but it feels more like annoyance. Gabriel and I have been dating for almost a year, mainly because he was so persistent and incredibly sweet that I finally gave in. However, once I did, the honeymoon stage was over rather quickly.

I've dealt with things like *this* happening all the time. Unlike me, Gabriel is loved by everyone in this town. Especially the ladies. Not that I can fault them for their attraction. He's tall with broad shoulders and a body that's packed with muscle to accompany his handsome face. I swear, there's not one soft or squishy part on his rugged body. He's the hottest thing this town has to offer, and he knows it. His arrogance is unparalleled and, honestly at first, I wanted nothing to do with him or it. But he kept showing me another side of him, the side I saw just minutes ago in his arms and, well, he eventually wore me down.

I have to admit that it wasn't that hard to wear me down. Since it's only mom and me, life gets lonely. Don't get me wrong, I cherish every second with my mother but it's just not the same as having a partner to share your life with. That's part of the reason I gave into Gabriel's efforts. I don't want to say it's a lack of options because he has these incredibly beautiful and vulnerable moments where I can see the type of man he *could be* if he wanted to. Those glimpses keep me holding on to the hope that he *will be* that man if I just give him time. Annnddd...ok fine, a big part of it is a lack of options. It's not like anyone else in this town is begging to date me.

However, the sweet Gabriel from earlier is nowhere to be found now as I watch him openly flirt with another woman right in front of me. He's clearly staring at her *very exposed* cleavage as she touches his arm and stands way too close. Hell, who am I kidding? I'M looking at her cleavage, too. His hands fall to her hips as he leans in, whispering something in her ear that causes her to throw her head back and laugh before punching him playfully in the arm. He pulls back with a satisfied grin on his face, and I finally get the nerve to walk over and interrupt their little exchange.

"Lucille," I say sweetly as I approach them, forcing a smile onto my face. "It's so nice to see you. How are you?"

I might as well be a damn ghost for the response I get. Her eyes remain locked on Gabriel as she slides her index finger down his chest. "It was nice to see you, Gabriel. I'll see you later." She practically purrs like a damn cat in heat.

As she steps away from him, she finally acknowledges me

with a sneer. Her eyes take in my appearance, and she scoffs as she prances away in her sky-high stilettos and an exaggerated sway in her hips. I roll my eyes and look back at Gabriel, who is clearly salivating as he watches her walk away. If he was a dog, the drool would be puddling at his feet, and he'd chase after her trying to hump her leg. I look down at my summer dress, the one I thought was really pretty until I saw Lucille. Hell, Gabriel made me feel pretty too, that is until I see the way he looks at *her*.

I cross my arms over my stomach self-consciously and look down at the sidewalk. Gabriel lifts my chin, forcing me to look at him.

"Hey, she approached me not the other way around. If I wanted to be with her, I would be, but I chose you. Don't start with this jealousy shit that isn't warranted."

I can feel the swell of my throat as the tears start to build but I fight against them. I manage to nod and give him a weak smile. He leans down and lays a peck on my lips before taking my hand in his and leading me towards the restaurant.

As we pass by the bookstore, I notice a sign in the window. *Fifty percent off everything! Today and tomorrow only!* I immediately push all other thoughts aside and perk up at the thought of adding a few more books to my ever-growing TBR pile. Anything to take my mind away from this miserable town.

"Look." I point to the sign in the window. "Mr. Stevens is having a sale! Maybe we can stop by after dinner?"

"Yeah, maybe," he says, absentmindedly.

We walk the last minute to the restaurant in silence. At this point I'm just trying to be agreeable until we get food in him. He's no fun when he's hangry. Luckily, there's no wait. Not like Gabriel would ever be left waiting. The hostess leads us to our table and manages to touch him THREE TIMES in a matter of thirty seconds. He smiles easily at her and doesn't seem the least bit bothered by the blatant and overzealous flirting happening in front of me. Since I've been left to quietly follow in their wake, I sigh and roll my eyes, reminding myself that he chose *me*. He's here with *me*. That should be enough, right? Every other woman in New Haven would literally lie, cheat, steal, and probably kill, to be in my shoes. So, why isn't it enough?

Once we're seated and the food has been ordered, Gabriel pulls my chair in closer to him and places his hand on my thigh. He's all smiles and sweet conversation again and, slowly, I start to relax. I push the image of him and Lucille out of my mind, not wanting to dwell on it anymore. It was just a harmless conversation. It's not like anything happened. I'm totally overreacting and I'm not going to be the one to ruin this night. Not when it started out so well.

The waiter arrives with our plates; a huge steak and baked potato for Gabriel and grilled chicken and veggies for me. Gabriel gives his plate all of his attention as he devours his food, and we sit in companionable silence as we eat.

Literally minutes later, he pushes his plate away and leans back in his chair, one hand settling over his stomach, as he sighs with contentment. "That was just what I needed."

I chuckle at his clear obsession with food. I swear, I've never met a person that eats as much as he does. "I'm glad you enjoyed it."

"How is everything this evening?" the waiter asks politely, as he stops at our table again.

"Fine," Gabriel grunts.

"It was all delicious." I offer up more of a response for the poor young guy, who's obviously new to waiting tables and to New Haven. I've never seen him before and he's treating me like a normal human being and not like a freak. That in itself deserves my friendliness.

"You didn't seem to eat much." He gestures to my barely eaten dinner. "Was something wrong with your order?"

"Oh, no, no! Not at all, I promise! Please tell the chef

everything was great."

I feel Gabriel's large hand come to rest on my thigh, the sweet gesture making me smile even more. I like that he wants to touch me, and I also like that he makes it known that I'm with him.

The waiter nods and gives me a nervous smile. "Alright. Would you like me to box that up for you, Miss?"

I continue to smile warmly at him. "That would be great! Thank you. And don't be so nervous. You're doing a great job." I offer him a compliment to help boost his confidence.

My smile immediately turns into a wince as Gabriel's strong fingers pinch the inside of my thigh. He pinches so hard that I squirm in my chair, and I can feel tears starting to well up behind my eyes. I quickly drop my gaze so the waiter doesn't notice. Once he's gone, I try to remove Gabriel's hand from my thigh, but he's too strong and I don't want to cause a scene.

I stare into his dark eyes. They look almost black as he stares back at me with so much profuse anger. "You're hurting me," I whisper, voice cracking from the pain.

"Do you want to go home with that piece of shit nobody waiter, is that it?" His voice is low and controlled but he's speaking through clenched teeth.

"What?" I ask, in total shock. "Gabriel, what are you even talking about? Please, you're hurting me!"

He releases his hold on my leg and abruptly stands. He pulls out his wallet and throws cash onto the table. "Home. Now," he orders, as he grabs my hand and pulls me from my chair.

He leads me quickly through the restaurant, heading toward the front door. I hear our waiter shout behind us about forgetting my food. All I can do is duck my head, hiding my face from everyone as Gabriel pulls me out onto the sidewalk. I'm practically jogging to keep up with his angry stride as he continues to pull me. I look up at him, but his face is hidden in shadows, only illuminated partially as we hurriedly pass underneath the streetlights.

"Gabriel, slow down," I plead, my request landing on deaf ears.

To the rest of the world, I'm sure it looks like we're just walking down the sidewalk together, maybe even like we're in a hurry to get home and take each other's clothes off, but appearances can be deceiving. Gabriel may be holding my hand, but it isn't *lovingly*. He's squeezing my hand so tightly that I'm afraid my bones are going to snap at any second. I don't know what hurts worse, the sting in my thigh or the grip on my hand. No one in this town would ever believe a bad thing about Gabriel though. He can literally do no wrong in their eyes. Hell, I believed his façade as well, but I've since seen behind the carefully constructed mask. They have no idea about the ugly beast he keeps locked up inside.

The second we enter the house my back meets the door roughly and his large hand envelopes my neck. "Is that why you bought this new dress? To get attention from other men like some whore?"

I struggle to breathe as his hand clamps down on my throat. I claw at his hand with both of mine, trying to get underneath his fingers but it's no use. He has more strength in his pinky than I have in my entire body.

"Did you enjoy that? The way he was *flirting* with you? The way he was *looking* at you? Did it turn you on?" His other hand slips under my dress and yanks my panties to the side. He forces a large finger inside, and it hurts because I'm not at all turned on like he suggests.

"This pussy is mine, Bella, it belongs to me. *You* belong to me. And I won't have any girl of mine dressing like a fucking whore ever again." He releases my neck and grabs the collar of my dress, pulling with all his strength.

My body is yanked forward by the force of the dress being

ripped off me. I collide with his immovable body, still impaled on his hand. A strangled scream catches in my throat as I try to scream, gasp for air, and sob all at the same time. I don't even realize I'm crying until I taste the salt of my tears. The dress is now hanging loosely around me, revealing my chest. He pulls my bra down and grips one of my breasts as his finger still pumps inside of me.

"Why do you do this to me? Am I not enough? Is my attention not enough? Is my love not enough?"

My mind can't keep up with his rollercoaster of questions. First, I'm a whore, and now he's upset that I don't think he's enough? What in the actual fuck is happening?

His large hand clamps around my face, lifting it so I have to look up at him. "Tell me I'm enough for you."

"You *are* enough, Gabriel. I don't want anyone else." My voice shakes, betraying my fear. I need to turn this around. I need to somehow quell his anger or else he'll only hurt me worse. I raise my shaking hands until I'm tentatively cradling his face. "I only want you, Gabriel. No one else could ever come close to you. You're perfect and I'm so lucky to have you. Please, forgive me. I promise not to ever hurt you again."

"No one else can make you feel like I do, Bella." He finally pulls his fingers out of me. He's still gripping my face as he forces his fingers into my mouth. I don't fight it, but I choke on another sob. "See how good I make you feel? You're already soaking my fingers."

He pulls his fingers out of my mouth and replaces them with his tongue. This kiss is hungry in an entirely different way than it was at the beginning of the night. This kiss is harsh and claiming. There's no pleasure or desire in it. Despite his words, there's definitely no love. He's kissing me like it's his right, and there's not a goddamned thing I can do to stop him.

He breaks the kiss and spins me around, forcing my face into the door as he aggressively pulls my panties down my thighs. I hear the clink of his belt buckle, the snap of the button on his jeans, and the slide of his zipper. It's as if the sounds are being played on loudspeakers at a concert. I'm hyperaware of everything he's doing behind me and I'm absolutely dreading what's about to happen, but the best thing I can do right now is NOT fight it.

A whimper leaves my lips as he pushes his dick inside of me in one hard thrust. More tears fall down my cheeks as he angrily pounds into me. His hands move to hold my hips as he continues to fuck me, with no regard for anything or anyone else besides himself and his own pleasure.

"Fuck," he grunts. "Do you feel that? No one else is going to make you feel this good. No one."

My heart and my mind are both screaming in protest, but my body is betraying me. I can feel myself growing wetter and wetter as he continues to ruthlessly fuck me, as if I'm nothing more than his fuck doll. His possession. I'm not a person in his arms right now. My tears are of no consequence.

Luckily, it's over before I have to endure it for long or fake any type of pleasure of my own. He groans and slams into me one last time. I can feel his dick pulsing, releasing his orgasm inside of me. His head falls to my shoulder as he pants, trying to catch his breath. I squeeze my eyes closed and try to disappear. How I wish more than anything that I could just evaporate into thin air right this second.

He finally pulls out of me and turns me around to face him. He cradles my face, sweeping his thumbs across my wet cheeks, drying them from the tears that have fallen.

"I know," he says softy, as he looks into my eyes with the same reverence he had earlier. His forehead drops to mine and he closes his eyes and sighs in relief. "I love you too, Bella." He leans down and kisses me softly before pulling away. "I'm gonna go shower and then

I'm going to hold you all night, I promise."

He leaves me standing at the door, completely fucking confused and just as misshapen and torn as my dress. I pull the top of my dress over my exposed breasts and slowly slide to the floor. I hide my face in my knees and let the agony silently pour from my eyes again.

How did I end up here?

How has Gabriel fooled so many people for so long?

How is this now my life?

And most importantly…

How the fuck do I get out of it?

Bella

GIVE ME A REASON BY EVA UNDER FIRE

Sunlight streams in through the window, rousing me slowly from sleep. My body is relaxed, and I let out a contented sigh as I enjoy the beautiful song the birds are singing in the trees outside. I'm only allowed a few minutes of peace before I feel the covers rustle and the bed dip, seconds before Gabriel's strong arm slides over my waist and pulls me into his chest. He nuzzles the back of my neck before laying a soft kiss on my shoulder.

"Mmmm, good morning." His voice is groggy with sleep.

The sweet display of affection would have once brought a smile to my face, but last night's events have barely left my mind. Sleep couldn't even take the fear and anxiety away from me as Gabriel haunted me in my dreams.

"Morning," I croak out, clearing my throat.

It's tender and sore from his vicious grip. He's been aggressive with me before, hurtful with his words, but he's never physically hurt me like he did last night. I feel like last night was a small step in a new direction and *not* one I want to explore with him. I've read enough about abuse to know that this is only the beginning. Things will only escalate until I'm not just bruised and scared but making excuses for broken bones.

The only problem is, where do I go? I can't hide from him. I can't escape. And I know for a fact that he won't just *let* me go. It's not in his nature to be denied. Or at least it's not in his nature to accept it. Gabriel gets everything he wants and, unfortunately, that includes me.

"I'm starving," he says, as he gently bites into my shoulder. "I'll make us breakfast. What would you like, sweetheart?"

After what he did to me last night, the nickname, sugary tone and attitude make me sick to my stomach. How can he just forget about what happened?

WHAT. HE. DID.

How can he act like nothing's wrong?

I close my eyes and count to ten. I have to remind myself that today is a new day and the last thing I want to do is wake the beast before we've even gotten out of bed. If we can have a lighthearted and easy day, I'll take that any day of the week. So, I push everything else down deep inside and prepare myself to fake it until I make it out of here.

"Hmmm...," I contemplate. "I definitely need coffee. And...eggs and bacon."

"Lots of bacon," he agrees. "Coming right up." He kisses my shoulder again and I feel the bed release his weight as he slides out.

"And pancakes!" I yell, as he heads into the kitchen. Might as well take advantage of his clear attempt at an apology.

He chuckles. "You got it, babe!"

God, why can't he be this version of himself all the time? Why does he have to be so self-centered and cruel? Doesn't he like it when we're like this? I just can't wrap my mind around his different personalities and I've yet to figure out exactly what sets him off. It can be something as harmless as it was last night at the restaurant or absolutely nothing at all. I have no idea what goes on in that overreactive imagination of his.

I give myself another few minutes to enjoy the comfort and

peacefulness of bed before I toss the covers aside and get up. I head into the bathroom to pee but stop as I get a glimpse of myself in the mirror. I walk to the counter and lean against it, staring at my reflection.

My eyes take in the bruises ringing my neck and I tentatively brush my fingertips over the sensitive skin. You can clearly make out the fingers of a hand. My throat starts to swell as the emotion builds up inside of me. I try to swallow, to force the thick ball of emotions back down, but that only causes my throat to hurt again. I swipe at the tear that escapes my eye and hurry over to the toilet, eager to take my eyes off the brutal reality and truth around my neck, only to find myself staring at the darkest bruise I've ever seen gracing my inner thigh. It's the size of a fucking golf ball and it's puffy and swollen. I wince when my slight touch sends a shock of pain into my thigh, and it feels like he's pinching me all over again.

I pull my pajama shorts back up, leaving the bruise in full view. Good. He needs to see what he's done to me. He needs to see the proof on my skin that *he hurt me*. Maybe that will shock him more than any talking can. I stop at the vanity again, grab a hair tie out of a drawer, and pull my long hair into a ponytail. There will be no hiding or downplaying his abuse. He's going to see it and face the truth of his actions head on.

I walk into the kitchen with my shoulders back and head held high. I'm not going to start a fight but I'm not going to cower away from him either. I'm not going to act like what he did last night didn't happen when the truth of his cruelty is coloring my skin.

"Smells delicious already," I announce myself. "Can I help with anything?"

"No, no. You just relax and let me spoil you with breakfast for a change," he says, as he continues to work over the stove.

I move to stand next to him, leaning back into the countertop as I watch him flip the bacon. Once he's done, his eyes finally land on me. I watch as his eyes take in my neck and slowly travel down until he sees the bruise on my thigh. It's glaringly obvious against my fair skin and, honestly, it doesn't even look real. It looks like I colored myself with a purple marker.

His eyes make their way back up to mine, stopping on my neck for a few seconds before he approaches me. One hand settles on my hip and the other gently tilts my chin up. His dark eyes meet mine and I'm happy to see that there is some regret. Maybe last night was a fluke after all. Maybe it was a one-time mistake, and now that he's faced with his actions in the light of day, he realizes how badly he fucked up.

"I didn't mean to hurt you. I had no idea how sensitive your skin was." He shakes his head and chuckles. "Your skin is so fair it shows every little blemish, unlike my thick skin. I'm sure they look worse than they are."

I'm pretty sure I'm staring at him like he just sprouted a second head. Is he seriously making this MY fault? My skin is the problem here?

"You do believe me. Don't you, Bella? I love you and I would *never* do anything to hurt you on purpose. I swear. It won't *ever* happen again. I promise," he says, with such conviction and sincerity in his eyes that I'm having a hard time NOT believing him.

When he looks at me like this…God, it makes me feel everything I've ever wanted to feel. I'm so confused. He leans down and claims my mouth with his. I'm too fucking astonished to react. I kiss him back solely out of habit, but it turns into a heat-filled kiss of pure desire.

When he kisses me like this…it feels special. He makes me feel special when he's this way with me; soft and tender and loving.

The shock and confusion I've just experienced in the past minute has turned my brain to mush because as his lips pull away, I hear myself saying, "They look worse than they are. I'll be ok."

"That's my girl." He chucks my chin and returns to the stove. "Let me make it up to you. How 'bout we go to the bookstore later and you can pick out a few books, my treat." He looks over and delivers a heart-stopping smile and winks at me.

Am I being crazy? Am I being too hard on him? I mean, we've been together for nine months and he's never put his hands on me like that before. Maybe last night was an accident. Maybe that was a one-off situation. Because I know he *does* love me. You can't kiss someone the way he kisses me without having real feelings behind it. And every couple fights, right? I mean, I've never really been exposed to relationships or love before. It's always just been mom and me, and she's never had a relationship of any kind after my father as far as I know. So, maybe I'm being ridiculous. Maybe this is completely normal and something all couples go through.

I can either push back and fight or I can trust him. I can trust when he says he didn't mean it and that it will never happen again. And, since he's never done this before, I decide to give him the benefit of the doubt. I'm going to trust him.

"If I have time later that would be great!"

"Time? Why wouldn't you have time?" he asks gruffly.

"It's Chip's birthday party. I need to get ready after breakfast and head over."

He rolls his eyes. "I don't know why you're going to a child's birthday party. He's probably not even going to remember it anyways."

"He's six, Gabriel, not three," I laugh. "He will absolutely remember it. And I've babysat him his entire life, he's not just any kid to me."

"Fine," he grunts. "Just don't stay too long and come home early so we can go to the bookstore, ok?" He places a peck on my lips. "Grab the plates. Breakfast is ready."

・ ・ ・

When no one comes to answer the door, I let myself into Mrs. Pott's house. There are several voices coming from the kitchen, so I head that way, only stopping to deposit my gift on the table in the living room along with the others. As I enter the kitchen, a few eyes flick my way but quickly look away. Within seconds, the kitchen is cleared out as everyone heads out the back door and into the backyard, where I can hear even more voices and the screaming and yelling of happy kids.

"I don't know why she even bothered to come."

"No one wants her here."

"I don't know what he sees in her."

"She's put a spell on him, obviously. You know Matthew saw them dancing naked in the forest, right?"

"Who knows what they have in that garden they grow."

Their remarks are whispered, but not quietly enough. They clearly don't care if they're overheard. I roll my eyes and ignore them, something I've learned to do well enough over the past twenty-four years. Still, no one is perfect or impervious to hateful words. As strong and uncaring as I may appear to be in front of their faces, I have my moments of weakness when I'm alone.

"Mrs. Potts." I smile as I approach her. "Is there anything I can help you with?"

"Oh, Bella, dear, thank you for coming. Chip is going to be so happy to see you. He's running around somewhere in the backyard if you want to find him and say hello. Just check the snack table and see if anything needs refilling. I've got it handled in here at the moment."

"Alright, well, holler if you need me."

I take a deep breath and reluctantly walk into the backyard. I swear, you'd think I had a contagious, flesh-eating disease the way these people flinch and flee from me. You know, I've never understood their logic. If my mother and I were in fact, *witches*, you'd think they'd be doing everything in their power to stay in our good graces. I mean, if my mother and I really practiced witchcraft, every single person here would know it. For one, I would delight in giving Lucille a huge, hairy mole on her face. The thought makes me smile to myself.

As I scan the crowd, I'm immediately relieved to see that Lucille isn't here. In fact, none of her bitchy little clique is. Thank God. I walk over to the snack table and see that it has plenty of plates, napkins, and cups. There are still plenty of sandwiches, chips, and finger food. The punch is still half full and the tub next to the table, full of ice, still has plenty of drinks as well. The kids are too busy playing to eat at the moment, but once they stop, they're going to be little tornadoes and rip through this food.

"Bella!" I hear Chip's voice over the noise when he spots me and comes running.

I kneel down and he crashes into my arms, never once slowing down as he approaches me. His arms wrap around my neck, and he buries his head in my chest, but just as quickly he lets go and stands back.

"You came! I knew you would! Did you bring me a present?"

I laugh. "Of course, I did, silly! You only turn six once!"

"Ok," he says. "Can I open my present now?"

"Well, what did your mom tell you?"

He hangs his head. "Mom says I can't open the gifts until later, after we eat and have cake."

"Well, what your mom says goes. You better listen to her or else she may not let you have any more parties. You don't want that to happen, do you?"

"No!"

"Chip!" Another kid calls from across the yard. "Come on! We're gonna hit the pinata! They said you have to go first since it's your birthday."

Chip grabs my hand and pulls me forward. "Come on, Bella! Watch me hit the pinata! I'm gonna break it and get all the candy!"

I manage to stay through singing happy birthday and cutting the cake, but everything has taken longer than I expected, and I do want to take Gabriel up on his offer of going to the bookstore. I absolutely deserve some free books for all the shit I put up with. I slip out as everyone is getting their cake. The only one who will even notice I'm gone will be Chip, but he's too preoccupied right now to care. I don't take it personally. At his age, I'd prefer some cake and gifts, too. Who am I kidding, at this age I'd still prefer cake and gifts. The fact that he even wanted me here to begin with is enough for me. He'll soon grow into the *girls have cooties stage*, so I'll take this time while I have it.

As I'm approaching Gabriel's house, I see the front door open, and my heart simultaneously explodes and plumets inside my chest. I duck behind a tree before I'm seen, my heart pounding so loudly I'm afraid it's going to give me away. I'm close enough that I can hear what's being said.

"When can I see you again?" Lucille's voice purrs like a satisfied cat.

"I don't know, I'll text you."

"You're sure we don't have time for one more round?"

"No." Gabriel's voice is hard, leaving no room for argument. "She'll be back soon. You need to leave."

"I don't understand why you're even with her if you obviously want to be with me."

"You don't need to understand what I want, Lucille, just keep fucking me when I tell you to. Now, go."

I hear the front door slam and the clicking of her heels along the flagstone as she gets closer to where I'm hiding. I hold my breath and slowly maneuver around the trunk of the tree, careful not to make any noise as she continues past me and down the driveway, heading towards town.

I'm left leaning against the tree, staring at Gabriel's house. The house I've pretty much been living in for the past six months. Other than my racing heart, I feel completely numb. I don't know how to process what I just witnessed. Am I surprised? Honestly, no. I've seen the way he looks at her, hell, the way he looks at every woman. I've seen the way he openly flirts with women in front of me, as if it means nothing, and then makes *me* feel crazy for thinking that it does.

Before I even have a plan in mind, I'm storming into the house. I slam the door behind me as I barge in. I find him in his bedroom, removing his boxers, shower running in the bathroom. He's clearly getting ready to wash off any traces of Lucille.

"Don't bother," I say, as I stop in the doorway, crossing my arms. "I saw her leave and I heard what you said. In fact," I laugh sarcastically, "I never in a million years would have ever thought I'd be saying this, but I'm with Lucille on this one. Why are you even with me if you're fucking her? And God knows who else you're sticking your dick into."

"It's not what you think—"

"Not what I think?! What I think is you're an arrogant piece of shit fucking asshole and I never should have ever said yes to dating you!"

He storms toward me, and even though he's completely naked, he still manages to look absolutely terrifying. He's easily twice my size and ripped with muscle. Somehow, my stubbornness and anger allow me to hold my ground. I don't know if it's a smart thing to do or incredibly stupid, but the adrenaline spiking in my blood wants this fight. This isn't something he can excuse or lie away. I saw it with my own eyes. I heard it with my own ears.

"It doesn't mean anything. She doesn't mean anything to me. I don't love her. I don't want to be with her. I told you; I chose you!"

I scoff. "You chose me? You chose me to be what? Be your fucking doormat? Your fucking fool? Well, fuck you!" I push him in his chest as hard as I can.

He staggers backwards, unprepared for the attack, but he recovers quickly. His large hands wrap around my wrists, holding me tightly. "Don't be a fucking stupid bitch, Bella. You know damn well no one else fucking wants you. Who else is going to fucking love you if not me?"

"If this is what you call love then I don't fucking want it! Not from you! Not from anyone!" I push and pull, yanking at my hands locked in his grip.

"Stop fucking fighting and listen to me! Do you have any fucking idea how badly Lucille and every other woman want what you have with me? I gave you a piece of myself that I've never given anyone!"

"I don't care!" I scream in his face. "I don't care! I don't care! I don't care! You're a fucking pig! You're a piece of shit and I don't fucking want *any* piece of you. Let me go you fucking assh—"

It takes a few seconds to register the floor underneath me and the pain erupting across my face. My hand instinctively touches my cheek, which is hot to the touch and pounding. It feels like my heart is in my mouth and not in my chest. There's something liquid dripping down my chin. I wipe it off with the back of my hand.

Blood.

Gabriel is kneeling in front of me. "Shit, Bella, I'm so sorry. I didn't mean to...fuck! Are you ok? Hey," He grabs my chin and forces me to look at him. "You're ok. It's just a busted lip, nothing bad. You're ok."

I wrench my face out of his hands as I scramble to my feet.

"Don't touch me," I say calmly, even though my entire body is shaking and I'm beyond fucking terrified, as I start to back out of the bedroom.

"Bella, come on, wait. It was an accident. I didn't mean to hurt you. I love you, baby. Come and shower with me. Let me take care of you and we can put all of this behind us. I promise I won't ever see Lucille again. Come on, baby, you're the only one I want."

I try to shake my head but that just makes the room start to spin and sends a shooting pain across my cheek. "I'm going home, Gabriel. I'm not staying here another night with you."

"Baby, please, don't do this. It was just the heat of the moment. We'll look back on this tomorrow and laugh at how silly we're both being. Come on, don't leave. Not like this. Let me make it up to you. I love you, Bella."

"I'm going home, and unless you plan to tie me up, gag me, and keep me hostage, you'll let me leave."

He sighs and hangs his head in defeat. "Ok, baby, I understand. You need some time alone. But I'll come check on you tomorrow and we're gonna talk about this. We're gonna fix this, ok? I don't want to lose you. I'll do whatever it takes, I promise."

I don't turn my back on him as I continue to make my way across the living room and fumble for the doorknob behind me. He remains across the room, hands held up in front of him as if to show me he's harmless, but those hands are far from harmless.

I manage to get the door open, and once I'm through it and it closes behind me, I turn and run. I run as fast as I can, every hard thud of my shoes on the ground sending a shockwave of pain splitting across my skull. The pain only helps me run faster.

I make it across town and through the forest by sheer muscle memory. I've walked this path a million times since childhood and could navigate it blindfolded if I had to. I come to a stop right before the clearing, where my house sits like a lonely soul, a fitting reality for both of its residents.

The thought of walking inside and facing my mother like this makes me nauseous. She warned me about Gabriel. She always told me he had an ugly energy about him. It's not that I didn't believe her or that I wanted to ignore her warning, but it was nice to be seen for once. It was nice to be coveted. And I let his attention, and the opportunity to experience love, wear me down. I liked the idea of being with someone, of not being so fucking alone, more than I feared the potential downfall. And now that I'm standing here, bruised and beaten and completely fucking broken, none of it was worth it. None of the so-called love was real. No, I can't face my mother just yet.

So, I continue to run.

I run further into the forest. I run away from facing the consequences of my actions. I run away from my mother's pitying eyes and the *I told you so's*. I run away from the hateful people of New Haven. I run away from Gabriel. I run, and run and run, away from everything.

But no matter how far or how hard I run, I can't outrun myself. I can't outrun my embarrassment. I can't outrun my naivety. I can't outrun my weaknesses.

Tears come and my vision blurs. There's only a half-moon starting to climb into the sky, and it isn't penetrating through the thick trees. The darkness seems to be closing in around me and I stumble.

I fall.

I roll.

I tumble.

I feel the hard impact of rocks, sticks, and branches as my body is thrown down the side of a hill. I can't make out which way is up, and which way is down. At some point I realize I've stopped moving. My entire body is one big ache, from my toes to my fingernails, and every damn inch in between.

And underneath all of this pain I'm still here.

I can't outrun myself.

Mercifully, darkness takes pity on me and covers me in a heavy, black blanket of nothingness.

BEAST

Monster by Fight the Fade

There's nothing on this Earth less graceful than a human. Standing on my balcony, I can hear it crashing through the forest like an elephant, interrupting my attempt at enjoying a peacefully night. Comparing this human to an elephant is unfair; even elephants are far more graceful than what I'm hearing at the moment. That is, unless they're driven by fear with no care for caution. Perhaps this little human is also being driven by fear. I close my eyes and take a deep whiff of air. It takes a few seconds to pinpoint the scent but it's not fear I smell.

It's desperation.

And it's female.

Typically, the only thing that drives people this far into the forest is there lack of navigational skills, which one hundred percent of the time leaves them dripping with fear when they realize where they are. Once in a while I get the young kids only out here on a dare by their friends, if you can call people who bully you into doing something *friends*. However, on rarer occasions I get the human that has given up on life. The one who chooses to walk through this forest, to *my* castle, because they no longer fear death. They crave it. Those lost souls come in search of me specifically, *The Beast*, as I've been so generously titled, in hopes that I'll accept their sacrifice and take their life.

Well, they're not wrong.

All who have found their way to me have only ever met one fate. As for me, well I'm still here, aren't I? So, I guess in a sense that does indeed make me a beast. If not a beast, then a monster at the very least.

And this beast is currently extremely confused by this new human so dangerously close to my home because there's no fear, rather there's an overwhelming will to live. So, it doesn't make sense why she's running so wildly and desperately through my forest.

Her scream pierces the night...and my chest...gripping my heart with its agony. She's in pain. I'm over the balcony rail and plummeting to the ground below before my mind has a chance to process my actions. I don't know if it's the need for another human or simply concern that drives me. Surely, it's the former. This human has come to me exactly when I needed her; therefore, I need to capture her while I can. I don't have time to ponder it as I follow her scent and quickly make my way to her.

The forest allows me through effortlessly. No roots cause me to stumble, and no branches reach out to cling to me and halt my progress. One would think the forest is alive and moving around me, afraid to touch and awaken The Beast, but the truth is I've prowled this forest floor for longer than I care to remember. The forest and I may as well be one with how intimately we know each other.

The trees suddenly clear and I stop at the top of a ravine. Her scent is strong now, and the intoxicating sweet scent of blood fills my nose and makes me shudder. I haven't smelled anything so sweet in centuries. I allow myself a moment to close my eyes and enjoy the delicious fragrance, my mouth watering, anxious for a taste. Thank God I've already been satiated for the evening and I'm able to push The Beast aside.

When I finally open my eyes and look down, there she is,

sprawled at the bottom, completely unconscious. Even though it's dark, with only a dim light illuminating from the small crescent moon, my vision allows me to see her just as clearly as if the noon sun was high up in the sky. Her face is mostly hidden by her disheveled copper hair. Her jeans and top are filthy and torn from her race through my forest. No doubt she tumbled down into the ravine.

Ungraceful indeed.

"Well," I sigh.

It's so much easier to capture and hold someone hostage when they have no idea what's happening and they can't fight back. Not that anyone has been successful in fighting me off. For some reason, I don't want her to *have to* fight me. I don't want her to be scared of me, even though it's inevitable. She'll wake up in my castle and I'll be nothing more than her captor.

Nothing more than a beast.

Sighing in defeat, I descend into the ravine. I kneel down beside her unconscious body and gently brush her hair out of her face. She's lying face down, only half of her face revealed, and I immediately see the swelling and bruising gracing her cheek. I see the tracks of tears through the layer of dirt on her face, and dried blood on her lips and chin. Even with the injuries and dirt, I can tell that she's beautiful. And young. What does a beautiful young woman have to run away from? What caused her enough inner pain that it was forced to escape down her cheeks?

"Why are you here?" I ask out loud, not expecting an answer but eagerly wanting one.

I find I'm eager to know her story. Eagerly wanting her eyes to open so I can see what color they are. Eagerly wanting her mouth to open so I can hear her voice. Eagerly wanting to touch her skin so I can find out if it's as soft as it looks. Eagerly wanting to taste her lips, her skin…and her blood.

I should just leave her here. I should turn around and walk back home and act like I never saw her. I don't want anything she has to offer me. In the end, she will only cause me pain. And I'm so tired of the fucking pain. But what choice do I have? What choice does The Beast have?

I shake my head and pick up her limp body as gently as I can. I don't know where else she might be hurt, and even though she won't feel it I don't want to cause her any more pain. My concern for this stranger confuses me. I'm not without feelings, but there's only been one other time I felt this and that was a lifetime ago. That was before I became The Beast. Before I became numb and empty. And these feelings… they're definitely not a good thing considering what I need to do. What I *have* to do to survive.

For the first time in centuries, I find myself hesitating. I find myself questioning what I'll do next. I find myself not thinking about my needs. But my needs are *exactly* what I need to be thinking about. Because if I don't do what I need to do, if I don't hold her hostage and take what I need from her, I'll do unspeakable things. *Monstrous things.*

I'll be forced to be The Beast everyone fears.

Bella

Lost by Maroon 5

My body feels heavy.

My muscles are sore.

My head is foggy.

My entire face is throbbing. My cheek and lips feel ten sizes too big. I almost let out a groan, but it gets caught in my throat as the sound of voices makes me freeze.

I push through my grogginess, eavesdropping on the conversation, trying to recognize the voices.

"This is a *good* thing, Master, and just at the right time," a male voice says. "You and I both know my remaining days are limited. You'll need her."

"Look at her," A deep male voice demands. Even though it's a whisper, his commanding tone is unmistakable. "She can be no more than twenty-five if that. She has her entire life ahead of her. I won't take that away from her. I won't keep her here against her will."

"Master—," the first male voice starts.

"Did you see her face and neck?" the deep male voice continues. "She wasn't running from something, she was running from *someone*, and I won't be another person who hurts her."

"Master, you have to think about yourself. What will happen if you don't and I'm no longer here? You don't have a choice, you have—"

"I do have a choice!"

The outburst makes me jump then I freeze again and hold my breath, praying they didn't notice. There's silence for a moment and then they start to whisper again, this time in hushed voices I can't make out. Who are they? And what on earth are they talking about? Keeping me against my will? Oh my God, has Gabriel done something? Did he find me and kidnap me? But that's not Gabriel speaking.

Where the fuck am I? Who are these men? I need to find out, but I'm terrified I'm about to realize I'm chained up in some damp, dark dungeon. I slowly crack open my eyes but make every effort not to move any other muscle in my body. An enormous, dark pit stares back at me. The fire charred brick of a cold and empty fireplace takes up the entire wall before me. I move my eyes, trying to take in as much of my surroundings as I can without moving my head. I'm lying on a plush sofa, a cozy blanket draped over my body, but that's all I can see. The rest of the room is hidden in darkness. Only dim light from flickering candles illuminates the area around me. My heart starts to race as I realize, that while I'm not chained up somewhere, I am somewhere I don't recognize, I have no idea where that somewhere could be, and I have no idea whose voices those are.

"Shh, she's awake," the deep voice says, loud enough for me to hear.

Shit. How the hell does he know that? I haven't moved a muscle and from what I can tell, they can't see me from where they seem to be standing behind the sofa. Well, there's no use trying to fake being asleep. I start to push myself into a seated position, but as soon as I move my entire body screams in protest.

The groan I held back earlier comes out with a vengeance. The next thing I know, two old, wrinkled hands are on me, assisting me.

"There, there, now. Move slowly. You've been through quite the ordeal, my dear."

I have so many questions, but the only thing I can think about at the moment is the pain radiating through my body.

I groan again. "Everything hurts."

"Yes, yes, you took quite the tumble tonight. I'm no doctor but based on the bruises I'd say that's one very twisted ankle though I don't believe it's broken." He points to my bare right foot peeking out from beneath the blanket. "Same goes for the wrist," he motions to my left wrist, "and the bruising on your torso suggests a fractured rib or two, but again, I'm no doctor."

I look down at my body and the adrenaline starts to push past the pain. I pull the blanket up and look underneath, revealing that I'm no longer in my jeans and blouse from earlier, but in a loose flowing, silk gown. I immediately clutch the blanket closer to my body to shield myself.

"How did I get into this? Where are my clothes? Where am I and who are you?"

He chuckles. "Apologies, dear. We do not wish to startle you. You're completely safe here, I assure you. Master found you passed out in the forest, pretty banged up, so he brought you here to help you. My name is Louie Lumineux, and the master of the castle is Alexander Knightwell. I must admit, I did undress you solely to take stock of and clean your wounds, my dear. Modesty will do you no good if you die from an infection now, will it?"

Lumineux. That name seems familiar. Like a word that's on the tip of my tongue but I can't quite remember what it is or how to pronounce it and my brain is too tired to try. The adrenaline seeps out of my body at his reassuring words, so I let his name go for now, along with my embarrassment. It's somehow oddly NOT embarrassing considering his age and, honestly, I'm just too damn tired to really care about anything at this point. The important thing is I don't need to fight or run. At least not at this very moment. If they wanted to hurt me, they would have done so while I was unconscious. Instead, they took care of me and made sure that I'm ok. Still, I can't quite wrap my head around what's happening. *Alexander Knightwell* was the name of the last-known owner of the abandoned castle; the last-known owner who lived *centuries* ago. I suppose this could be his descendant.

"Wait, so you're telling me that I'm *inside* Knightwell Castle?"

He nods slowly. "That's correct."

"But...I thought this castle was abandoned. I mean, well...," I struggle to get the words out as my brain tries to keep up and make sense of everything, "it's just that there's a legend...about a beast that lives here. Not that I've ever believed it but—"

"Oh, you better believe it." His misty blue eyes sparkle with humor. "There is definitely a beast that lives here though he's pretty tame most of the time."

I scrunch my eyebrows in confusion. "But *you're* here. And you don't look...*tortured.*"

He chuckles again, apparently amused by me. He shuffles over to one of the side tables and comes back with a glass of water and a couple of pills.

"What are they?"

"Just something for the pain, my dear. Trust me, they'll help you feel better."

I take them from his open palm hesitantly, reminding myself that if they wanted me unconscious and locked up, I would be. I toss the pills in my mouth then take a big gulp of water. It's crisp and refreshing and exactly what I need. I continue drinking until it's gone.

"Thank you," I say with a sigh, as I relax back into the cushion behind me. "I know I just woke up but I feel exhausted."

"That's not surprising. I'm going to freshen up a room for you, give you somewhere comfortable and private to lie down. In the meantime, I hope this will do."

"I don't think I even have the energy to move to any other room. This is perfect." I drop my head on the back of the sofa and close my eyes, praying for whatever drug I just swallowed to hurry up and kick in.

"Very well, dear, I'll be back to check on you."

"Wait," I jerk my head up. "I have so many questions."

"All in good time. All in good time." He smiles warmly, his face crinkling with years of smile lines, and pats my knee in a very grandfatherly gesture. "Rest. There will be plenty of time for questions."

I nod in agreement and give him a weak smile. "Thank you, Mr. Lumineux."

I'm not sure how I manage to get into a somewhat comfortable and painless position, but I do. And despite being in what everyone calls *Nightmare Castle* with a man I've never met or even seen, and with the knowledge that there *is* a beast lurking around here somewhere, as the drug-induced sleep starts to slowly pull me into its grip, I fall asleep feeling comfortable and safe.

For the first time in months.

I feel completely safe.

BEAST

DROWN BY TYLER CARTER

She looks so peaceful when she sleeps, so innocent. How could anyone lay a hand on her? Was it a drunken father? A jealous lover? A strict mother? No. No, those bruises around her neck are from a man. A large man by the looks of the handprint. What kind of man would hurt a woman that can't fight back against his strength? What did she do to anger him? Is that why she was running in my forest? Was she trying to get away from the same man that hurt her?

So many questions run through my mind as I sit on the stone bench in front of the fireplace and watch her sleep. The pain pills Lumineux gave her seem to have done their job and freed her from pain, even if only temporarily. At least she can get some sleep and start to recover, start to heal. But what happens once she's healed? What if she demands to return to her home as soon as she wakes up? The thought of her going back to whatever situation she escaped from makes my stomach flip and my blood boil. *Fucking hell! What is wrong with me?!*

Standing up to walk away, I somehow end up standing directly over her. She seems so small, so fragile. I slowly lower my body until I'm kneeling beside her. I know she won't wake up, not with the pain pills in her system and her body's sheer exhaustion.

Still, the thought of her waking up and catching me staring at her makes me nervous.

I feel excited.

I feel anxious.

I feel absolutely fucking ridiculous. I haven't felt these types of feelings in quite some time. It all feels new and exciting.

Dangerous.

It's dangerous to lean into these feelings because I know where they inevitably lead. It's why I've strictly avoided them for so long. Hell, I've avoided them for so long that I can't even trust what I feel right now is real and not just a reaction to her simply because she's a woman. Still, this realization solidifies my decision.

She can't stay here.

There's still debris from the forest tangled in her hair. I reach for it, running her hair through my fingers, amazed at how silky it is. I raise it to my nose and take a deep breath of her scent into my lungs. She smells warm and comforting. Like wildflowers dancing in the breeze in a quiet, sun-drenched meadow. I want to lie down next to her and get lost in the warmth of her body and scent.

No, Alex. No, you don't want to do that. You know damn well you can't get close to ANYONE. It never ends well. Not for you. Not for The Beast.

If she demands to go back home, I won't deny her. I already told Lumineux I refuse to keep her here against her will. Yes, I could make her want to stay. I could make her believe it's her choice to stay and she would never know different, but I won't do that to her. I don't know why but something inside of me will not allow it.

She needs to leave.

There's something about her presence though, her energy, that has already seemed to change me somehow. I've never decided to let someone go, EVER, much less the instant I see them. I have no idea what's happening to me, and I don't want to acknowledge the danger that this decision puts me in, the danger Lumineux tried to remind me of. I know damn well what will happen if he dies and I don't have his replacement. Still....

She needs to leave.

I shake my head and stand up, beginning to pace. "No, Alex. She's not special. It's not her, it's *you*. Snap the fuck out of it."

The truth is, I need her to stay to satiate The Beast. But more than that, I WANT her to stay. In the same breath, I want absolutely nothing to do with her.

She needs to fucking leave.

Bella

It's still dark when I wake up. I have no idea how long I was asleep or how to gauge the amount of time that's passed. Considering it's still dark it couldn't have been long, but I feel extremely well rested nonetheless. Whatever Mr. Lumineux gave me sure did the trick.

I could lay here forever. I *want* to lay here forever and forget the past two days ever happened. I want to stay here and continue to hide from my life because I have no idea how to face it. How to face Gabriel. How to face my mother. I just want to turn back time and never say yes to Gabriel in the first place but, since that's not possible, I guess the next best thing is to do what I'm doing.

Hiding.

Unfortunately, my bladder doesn't agree with me. The pressure is intense and screaming at me to get up and find the bathroom. I slowly move my legs over the edge of the sofa and push myself into a seated position. My entire body is still tight and sore, protesting any type of movement. I guess the pills and the sleep only helped my energy levels.

"Ugh," I groan out loud. "Why is this my life?"

I can't think of any bad karma I have coming to me. I've kept to myself my entire life. Even over the past nine months with Gabriel, I've done nothing but try to be *nice* to people. Not that it ever did me any good, but I tried when I could have easily been a royal bitch instead. I should have just been a bitch. Maybe that would have at least felt good. Hindsight and all of that.

My bladder is about to explode so I push all thoughts of Gabriel and New Haven aside for now and start to stand.

"Ahh! Shit, fuck, fucking shit!" I whisper yell, as I fall back onto the sofa which causes my bruised or fractured ribs to send another wave of pain rushing through me.

I remember Mr. Lumineux telling me I was basically beat to shit as pain radiates through my entire body and steals the air from my lungs. I'm left wincing and gasping for air, trying not to move a single muscle that would only send more pain shooting through my body.

After I finally manage to relax and breathe normally, I try standing again. This time, I put the majority of my weight on my left leg and barely set the toes of my injured foot down on the floor to give myself some balance. I glance around and for the first time since waking up here I feel lost and overwhelmed.

There's an antique lantern on the side table. It's my only source of light in this immense space. I can feel the darkness of the castle creeping in as if it's interested in who's disrupting its peace. I swear I can feel eyes on me. My body senses it too, the hair raising on the back of my neck and arms, followed closely by goosies. I shudder at the thought of what might be lurking in the shadows.

The Beast.

But again, if anyone wanted to hurt me, they would have already. *Unless this beast likes the chase. If it likes to hunt its prey and not have a helpless and pathetic meal.*

I shake my head. "Get a grip, Bella. Mr. Lumineux wouldn't have left you here *alone* if you weren't safe."

Hobbling over to the side table, I take hold of the lantern and raise it up above my head, trying desperately to penetrate the shadows to no avail. I turn around in a complete circle, having no idea which way to go. I need a bathroom ASAP, or I'll pee my damn panties. My heart is suddenly in my throat at the thought that I might not even be wearing panties! My free hand reaches for my hip, and I sigh in relief as I feel the panty line.

"Thank God." I let out a heavy breath. "Alright, well, this castle is big enough to have more than one bathroom. I'm sure I can find one in either direction." I decide talking out loud to myself isn't the strangest thing that's happened recently so why not.

I push the eerie feeling of being watched away. I'm sure it's only my imagination; a beautiful thing when you're getting lost in worlds written in black ink on a cream-colored page, but not so great when you're in a dark, semi-abandoned castle with the legend of a monstrous beast that kills people potentially lurking in the darkness.

I limp along, leaving what seems to be a sitting room of sorts, and enter an enormous hallway. Even if it is a bit scratchy, I'm thankful for the rug that seems to go on forever underneath my bare feet. The air isn't necessarily cold due to the mild weather outside, but it is a bit cool and I imagine the stone floor would be even cooler. I shiver as I imagine how cold this castle must get in the winter. There's no possible way to keep something of this size comfy and cozy all the way through.

I approach a closed wooden door and hesitate to reach for the handle. Who knows what could be on the other side of it. I'm guessing it's not going to be a monster jumping out at me, but one can never really be sure. Too bad because I'm out of options. I need to find a bathroom like, now! I reach for the handle and turn it. The creak of the door as it starts to swing open sounds too loud in the eerie quietness. I hold my breath waiting for something, anything, to happen. Nothing attacks me. There's no sign of anyone or anything else being anywhere in this damn castle.

I take a wobbly step into the room and out of habit I search the wall for a light switch, completely shocked when I find one. Flipping the switch, the room is immediately flooded with a soft white glow. I'm frozen in place as I take in the huge and immaculate space.

"Thank God," I whisper to myself, as I shut the door and lock it behind me.

I managed to locate the bathroom on my first try. *Kudos to me!* If that's what you call a room with a sofa, chair and ottoman, a counter with not one or two but three sinks, and what looks to be bathroom stalls across from them. The room is bigger than my bedroom and bathroom combined at home. I place the lantern on the counter, no longer needed, as I hobble into one of the stalls. I hold on to the walls and gently lower myself onto the toilet seat. When I manage to sit with very minimal pain, I slouch into myself and let my bladder unleash.

"Ahh," I sigh with instant relief.

How can peeing feel so good? The body is a strange and wonderful thing. It's strong enough to grow an entire human being inside of it, provide food for the baby, and yet, one little tumble down a hill and I feel like I'm never going to walk again.

I complete my business and stand up, the toilet automatically flushing as I step away from it. How in the hell am I standing in a bathroom with electricity and a sensor toilet, but I was left with a lantern for light? Maybe the bathroom is the only thing updated and the rest of the castle is still...outdated?

I contemplate all of this as I wash my hands. I'll ask Mr. Lumineux as soon as I find him. That, along with a million other questions. Once I'm done, I finally look up and gasp at what I see in the mirror.

I look even worse than I feel. My hair is a tangled bird's nest on my head, literally. There are twigs and leaves stuck in it. My right cheek is puffy and the nastiest shade of green and yellow I've ever seen. My lip is swollen too, and there's a smear of dried blood on my chin, along with a thick layer of dirt covering it all.

"Oh, sweet baby Jesus. I look like hell."

I grab the cloth I used to dry my hands, run it under hot water, and then start wiping my filthy face. My cheek and lip are sensitive, but I manage to get the caked dirt and blood completely off. I pick out all the twigs and leaves I can find in my hair, but it's a lost cause without a brush. *To hell with a brush, I need a shower. Better yet, I could go for a long soak in a hot bath.*

A knock at the door has me practically jump out of my skin. My hand flies to my chest, attempting to hold my heart still, as I let out a pathetic little scream.

"Dear, are you in there? It's Louie."

Oh Bella, you're such a scaredy cat. Who else would it be? The Beast coming to murder you in the bathroom?

"Yes!" I call back, voice shaky. "Just a second."

I struggle to make my way across the large room quickly. When I manage to finally make it to the door, I'm out of breath and exhausted from the effort. I open the door and I'm greeted with a smiling Mr. Lumineux, graciously holding out a pair of crutches.

"I thought these would be useful until your ankle is healed."

I return his smile. "Mr. Lumineux, you're a life saver! To say I'm struggling is an understatement. Thank you so much." I take the offered crutches and place them underneath my arms, letting my weight fall on them, immediately grateful for their support and the relief on my body.

"Please, call me Louie. I'm afraid I didn't get your name, my dear."

"Oh, my goodness, what terrible manners you must think I have. My name is Bella. It's a pleasure to meet you, Louie. Really, thank you for everything you've done for me."

"The pleasure is mine, Miss Bella. I'm sure you can imagine

we don't get many visitors," he laughs softly. "Your presence is just the breath of fresh air this old stale castle needs."

"No, I don't imagine you do," I laugh nervously.

"Allow me to gather the lantern." He motions to the counter still visible behind me. "We'll need it."

I step aside to allow him into the bathroom. "Why is it that you use lanterns when there's electricity?"

"There's only electricity in some areas of the castle, not all. Besides, the legend is that this castle is abandoned with only a ferocious beast around, is it not?" He continues without waiting for an answer; it's not like he doesn't know the legend. "We like to keep it that way and a bunch of bright lights on would defeat the purpose."

"I see," I say, although I don't know that I do.

I mean, what does it matter if there are lights on or not? No one would voluntarily come to this castle either way, abandoned or not. Well, not the closed-minded people of New Haven anyway.

"Come now, Miss. Bella, let me show you around the castle. I'm sure you'll need to know your way around while you're here healing. At least I'm assuming you'll be staying until you're well enough to travel?"

"Honestly, I hadn't really thought about it, but I don't suppose I'm in any shape to be traipsing through the woods," I say, as I clank along beside him on my crutches, thankful for his slow, hunched gait.

"Indeed," he chuckles softly.

"It's such a shame that it takes something drastic to make you realize how much you take for granted. Like *walking*."

"And eating, my dear. You haven't had anything in at least twenty-four hours, you must be starving, yes?"

"Twenty-four hours? No, I had food this past afternoon but, now that you mention it, I *am* starving."

"Oh, no, no dear. You slept through an entire day. It's now the evening on a brand-new day that's come and gone. You last ate yesterday."

I stop hobbling along as his words sink in. "What? I slept an *entire* day?"

"Yes. The pills helped but you must have been completely exhausted. Please, don't worry, you can stay as long as you like. I assure you, your company is much appreciated by this old man," he says sweetly, patting my arm.

"It's just that my mother, she's probably worried sick about me. Unless she thinks I'm with Gabriel," I say, more to myself. No, Gabriel said he was going to check on me after I had some time alone. If he went to my home, he probably told my mother some lie about me being upset for no reason and running off. She's probably *definitely* worried.

"If you'd like to write your mother a note, the Master can deliver it for you, if that will make you feel better?"

"Yes, please! That would be greatly appreciated, thank you!"

"No worries, dear. Now come, let's get you to the kitchen and then into a bath."

I smile genuinely at the old man who's everything I'd ever want in a grandfather. I never knew my grandparents from my mother or father's side. My father left when I was too young to really remember him. I have pieces of memories that I think may be of my father but could be nothing more than dreams I've held onto, wishing for them to be memories. Like I said, it's only been my mother and I for as long as I can remember. So, I'm happy to be around Louie. To experience what could have been if I had a different life.

"Whoa!" All thoughts come to a complete stop as the hall emerges into a gigantic entryway. "It's exactly like I expected it to be," I whisper in awe. "Just like a fairytale castle from the movies."

Louie chuckles as he stops and allows me to take it all in. "Yes, yes. I had the same feelings when I saw it for the first time, too. Now, the most important thing to remember is that this side of the castle...," he points down a darkened hallway, "the South Wing, is strictly off limits."

I turn to face where he's pointing. I hear what he said but my focus is pulled to the huge stair case that ascends up to a second floor, its stone steps covered with a red carpet fit for royalty. Tilting my head up, I can see a glorious chandelier hanging far above us. Of course, it's dark and lightless, the dim light from our two lanterns that Louie carries leaving it more to shadow than light, but I can still see that it's marvelous. I can only imagine what it must look like lit with hundreds of flickering candles.

I turn around and am faced with the biggest wooden doors I've ever seen, framed by windows just as big. They're easily three or four times as high as a normal door and just us wide. I can't imagine how heavy they are and how much strength it must take to open them. I look down at where my feet are spinning me in slow circles and gasp at the beautifully intricate design in the floor. I'm no longer standing on grey stone or carpet, but what looks like immaculate white marble with an impressive and perfectly symmetrical and elaborate arabesque design.

"Wow," I mutter to myself. "Wow, just wow."

"Beautiful, isn't it?"

"This is beyond beautiful. It's one of the prettiest things I think I've ever seen. I can only imagine what it looks like flooded in warm light."

"You can get a good look at it tomorrow. These doors face east, and when the sun comes up it lights up this room quite magically. When I first came here, I found myself in here often."

"When *did* you first come here?"

He sighs. "I'm afraid this is going to lead to many, many more questions. Let's get some food in you and get you cleaned up. Then we can relax, and you can ask all the questions your little heart desires."

As much as I want to argue because I'm impatient and dying of curiosity, he's right. I feel weak and my stomach is literally grumbling and feels like it's eating itself. Let's not even talk about how absolutely gross I feel being so dirty and not showering in two days. So, I follow him across the entryway and down another hall. He leads me into an enormous dining room with a table that could easily seat twenty, maybe thirty people. Entering the kitchen through the dining room, he flicks a few switches, and the entire kitchen lights up in a bright white light; nothing warm and dim in here. Even the stainless-steel appliances gleam in the bright light.

Once again, my jaw hits the floor as I take in a space that would fit my entire house. There's a huge island in the middle of the room, one side lined with stools for seating even though there's a dining room next door. This is something you would expect to see in a fancy, upscale restaurant or hotel kitchen. There's a stove that's bigger than a sofa against the far wall, more burners than anyone could ever need. Then again, if you were entertaining a castle full of hundreds of people, I suppose all of them would be needed. Two large sinks sit next to an industrial dishwasher on the wall to my right, and to my left, what I'm assuming are the walk-in refrigerator and freezer stand side by side.

"Holy...moly...," I say in shock. "This is like...I can't even...wow."

The stone walls fit in with the modern look better than I would have thought, giving the space a little more warmth and homeliness.

"Now, what would you like to eat, dear?"

"Well, I know technically it's probably dinner time but I'd love some breakfast if you have anything for that."

"I could go for some breakfast too," he nods with a genuine

smile, and walks over to another door I hadn't seen.

He opens it and I see a large walk-in pantry. He comes out with his hands full, and I feel bad that he's doing all of this for me.

"How can I help?" I ask, feeling completely useless.

"Nonsense! You're our guest! I've always loved cooking and haven't had anyone else to cook for in ages. This is my treat. You just kick up your feet and, when the time comes, eat, eat, eat! That's the best compliment you can give an old amateur chef like myself."

"If you insist," I concede. "But once I'm back on my feet, literally, it will be my turn to treat you."

"I very much look forward to that, my dear. Now, pancakes or waffles?"

A huge grin splits across my face as I get comfortable on a stool at the island. All thoughts of my true reality, Gabriel, New Haven, and my mom, slip away into the far reaches of my mind. Right now, I'm inside Knightwell Castle with the sweetest old man I've ever met who's about to make me breakfast. I feel comfortable and safe. I feel like I'm truly wanted here and, oddly, I feel like I belong here. Like I could be happy here.

After all, I'm used to being alone most days. The emptiness doesn't bother me. Quite the opposite actually. Another solitary soul at home in an abandoned castle with a mysterious Master and a legendary Beast. What more could a girl want?

"Waffles, please!"

Bella

I don't think I've ever eaten so much in my entire life. Not for birthdays, not for holidays, never. Louie cooked up a storm for the two of us, and every single thing he prepared was mouth-watering and delicious. He's officially a magician in my mind.

After we ate, he led me to the room I'll be using while I'm here. It's on the second floor, and the hundreds of stairs I had to navigate to get here took about a hundred years to climb. He was nothing but gracious and patient as I slowly worked out how to crutch myself up the stairs.

My room, like everything else in this castle, is spectacular. It's once again bigger than my entire home. There's another large fireplace in this room with a chaise and sofa in front of it. A large vanity and a huge wardrobe take up space on the opposite wall. Everything is decorated in black and gold and fit for a damn queen. The canopy bed that sits against one wall has to be a California King, not that I've ever seen one, but the sheer size of it blows my mind. There's a beautiful and delicate golden veil-like fabric hanging off the canopy that's been tied back, just like you see in the movies.

The bathroom is connected to the bedroom and I about damn near lose my mind when I walk into it. The walls are made of the same stone that the entire castle seems to have been built with; however, this room has been renovated as well. The floor and counters are a beautiful marble in a neutral sand color. All the accents match the bedroom, but what takes my breath away is the bathtub. It's a huge, black, claw-foot tub with a gleaming gold faucet and handles. I've never seen anything like it, not even in movies.

I'm standing here, in awe of it all, and I feel like I've been transported to an entirely new world. Better yet, a daydream. Hell, *better* than a daydream. Everything about this place is perfect. I could stay here forever and never once not be taken aback by its beauty. Even the parts of the castle that haven't been renovated are breathtaking. It's clearly still cared for, and it makes me wonder why it's basically been abandoned.

One of the many questions Mr. Lumineux has offered to answer, but first, this glorious bathtub is calling my name. I prop my crutches up against the wall then hobble over to the tub. Taking a seat on the side, I lean over to get the hot water started. Holding my finger under the stream, I wait until it starts to warm before putting the stopper at the bottom. I turn on the cold water, evening out the hot, and then pull the gown over my head and toss it on the floor. Swinging my legs over the edge, I test the water out with my feet first. It's perfect, so I lower myself in and lay against the cool porcelain, letting my head fall back, eyes closed, as the hot water slowly starts to claim my body inch by inch.

I know I should be more cautious and alert. I should be worried that my poor mother has no idea where I am. I should be nervous and frankly terrified that I'm in an abandoned castle with such a dark legend attached to it. I should be so many things right now, but I can't bring myself to care about a single one.

I sit up to turn the water off then sink back into the comforting embrace of the hot water. "Ahh." I release a heavy sigh, along with all the tension my injured body has been carrying.

It's been so nice to be here and not have to be on edge every second of every day, worrying that I'm going to somehow set Gabriel off. Granted, I have been asleep almost the entire time but...still, it feels good not to have anyone watching me or expecting anything of me. It feels good not to have the weight of the world on my shoulders for once, even if I have only set that weight aside temporarily. At the end of the day, my life is my life, and I can't run away from it forever. Things might be different if my mother wasn't alive, not that I want her gone, but if I was truly alone I'd leave New Haven and never look back. The world is a very big place and I'm sure I'd be able to carve out a beautiful life for myself...*somewhere*. Or maybe that's just an optimistic storybook, happily ever after that's nothing more than a work of fiction.

Well, all you can do is focus on the here and now and right now you should be enjoying this bath. I slide underneath the water, the tub big enough that my entire body is submerged, leaving me feeling completely weightless. Letting my limbs relax, they bob along in the water to a soundless beat when a shadow suddenly moves over my closed lids and blocks out the light. I open my eyes and shoot out of the water, gasping for air, and frantically searching the bathroom for any signs that someone else is here.

"Who's there?" My voice shakes slightly and the beat of my heart pounds in my ears. "Mr. Lumineux?" I wait a few seconds, holding my breath, and straining to hear his shuffled steps across the floor. "Louie? Are you there?" I ask, a bit louder.

Silence.

I let my breath out slowly and sink back down into the water, trying to relax. "It was nothing, Bella. No one is in here. No one is spying on you." I say the words out loud to comfort myself.

It's just that sixth sense kicking in. The feeling of being watched. Sometimes that gut feeling is right and warns you of dangers lurking in the shadows, and sometimes it's nothing more than your mind giving into your fear. The idea of a beast living in the castle is no doubt adding to my subconscious fear and overactive imagination.

My reprieve interrupted, I hurry and clean myself up, shampooing and rinsing my hair with the products that were already here. No doubt Mr. Lumineux set this all up while I was asleep for an entire day. I wonder how he managed to have all of this though. The products. The gown I was wearing. Considering it's just the two of them here, and I can't imagine they get many guests, I wonder how they seem so prepared for one?

I get out of the tub, feeling so much better than I did when I got in twenty minutes ago, and manage to wrap a luscious gold towel around my hair and another one around my body. I crutch over to the gigantic wardrobe, curious to see what's inside. Louie said they had stocked it up with clothes they believed would fit me. Again, how they've managed to do all this within twenty-four hours baffles me.

I open the large doors, and for the millionth time I'm left standing in shock and awe, my jaw on the floor. Inside are rows and rows of clothing, most hanging but some folded on shelves that run down the middle, on top of several drawers. There's everything from elegant gowns to casual dresses to jeans and blouses, shorts and T-shirt to leggings and sweatpants. Literally, more clothes than I've ever owned in my entire life right here in front of me, for my choosing. And don't even get me started on the shoes lining the bottom.

I shake my head. "I'm dreaming. That's the *only* explanation. I ran away from Gabriel, fell and hit my head, and am lying somewhere in the forest, dreaming."

I open one of the drawers to find underwear inside. This is insane. This is literally everything I could ever want or need. And it all looks brand-spanking-new! *Where in the hell did all of this come from? I'm so fucking confused.*

I grab some clean underwear and a bra, then decide on leggings and a long, casual and comfortable looking shirt, paired with flip-flops. Since I don't plan on leaving the castle today, and I don't want to try jamming my swollen ankle into shoes or boots, I opt for relaxed and practical. Besides, who am I going to see or try and impress? Mr. Lumineux? The Beast?

I've never cared about impressing anyone before, until Gabriel, and look how well THAT turned out. No, there will be no caring about anyone but me, myself, and I. And what I want right now is comfort.

After dressing, I return to the bathroom to comb my hair. I plait it in a loose side braid that hangs over my shoulder and out of the way of the crutches. There's still very clear bruising on my neck but, thankfully, it's no longer tender. The bruise on my thigh, however, is still painful. He must have damaged the nerves or something. My cheek and part of my lip are still just slightly puffy with discoloration of a bruise, but overall, I do look refreshed and well-rested. It's painful to move and breathe deeply from the injuries of falling in the woods, but despite all of that, despite what my body has to say, my eyes are shining brighter than they have in a long time.

I feel free.

I don't have to pretend to be something or someone I'm not here. Louie doesn't know me. He doesn't know I'm an outcast and I doubt that he would even care if he did know. I don't know what the master of the castle will think of me but, again, I doubt that he has an opinion one way or another. Here, I get to just be *Bella,* and it feels amazing.

Finally leaving my room, I walk down the hallway towards the staircase. I stop at the top of the stairs, looking down over the rail into the immaculate entryway beneath me. The lantern I hold does nothing to pierce the darkness below, but I look through the darkness nonetheless, imagining the beauty of what lies beneath the shadows of night. I desperately want to see this castle not only in the light of day, but also illuminated in all its glory at night. I imagine it takes on two completely different versions of itself in the day versus the night. Although the emptiness doesn't bother me, the darkness does. Not in the way that it probably should. I'm not afraid of the darkness, or what may be lurking in it, but it makes me sad. I feel like the castle has been forced into darkness, forced into hiding, when it deserves to be seen. Even if it's only being seen by myself, Louie, and this elusive Master. When I finally see him and get to speak with him, I'm going to ask him why he chooses to live in the shadows. I can't imagine anyone *wanting* to walk around in the darkness all the time.

I feel a presence behind me and quickly turn around, sending one of my crutches clattering to the floor in a loud ruckus.

"Hello?" I speak into the darkness around me, my lifted lantern only casting light a few feet around me. "If you're there, you can come out and talk to me."

Silence.

"I know that if anyone wanted to hurt me, it would have happened already. I'm not afraid of you."

At this point I have no idea who I might even be talking to. The master of the castle...*what was his name again? Gah, I can't remember.* I could very well be speaking to The Beast or to nothing more than shadows, hiding no one at all. I'm met with only more silence. I let out a disappointed sigh as I lean down to retrieve my crutch.

"Ahh," I hiss in pain, my ribs protesting the movement.

Once the crutches are solidly back in place under my arms, I continue toward the staircase but stop short of taking the first step down. I stare into the darkness opposite me. *The South Wing*, Louie called it. According to Louie, that entire side of the castle is strictly OFF

LIMITS. It belongs to the Master and apparently he likes his privacy. I can't help but feel a little inkling calling me into the darkness. Calling me into his space. It feels like the same pull I've always had sitting on the roof of my cabin, staring at Knightwell Castle for hours, longing for something more.

I sigh, knowing there's nothing for me in that darkness. There seems to be nothing for me anywhere. I shakily make my way down, taking each step painfully slowly but not wanting to risk another mishap. I don't think my body would be able to handle a tumble down a thousand steps.

By the time I reach the bottom landing, I'm worn out and once again out of breath from the effort. I'll be grateful once I make it back to the sitting room Mr. Lumineux said he'd meet me in. I make my way back down the same hallway I came out of earlier, still unable to really see my surroundings but heading towards a beautifully glowing light.

As I enter the sitting room, the first thing I notice is that a small fire has been started in the fireplace. Mr. Lumineux is seated in one of the chairs in front of the fire, facing me.

He smiles when he sees me. "Come dear, relax by the fire. I've made us some tea. I hope you like rooibos. I find it's the perfect remedy for these old bones."

"I love tea!" I exclaim, returning a bright smile. "Black tea and rooibos are actually my favorites. Thank you for making it and for…well, everything you've done for me."

"It's been my pleasure, dear, truly. Your presence here has given me new purpose and, I must admit, it feels great to be needed again and to have such lovely company."

"Surely the master of the castle…umm, I'm sorry, what's his name again?"

"Alex, dear. Alexander Knightwell."

"Yes, Alex. Surely, he needs you just as much and must be

great company if you've stayed here with him."

Louie chuckles as he pours our tea. "He has been my closest companion and best friend for most of my life. Honey and cream?" he asks.

"Yes, please."

He nods then continues. "He does need me, yes, but for much different reasons than you do. Here you are, dear." He hands me a cup of gloriously steaming tea before he takes his cup and returns to the chair opposite me.

I take a tentative sip, testing just how hot the water is and get a taste of delicious, sweet flavor across my tongue. "Mmm," I moan my pleasure. "What flavor of tea is this? I've never had tea this flavorful before."

"Toasted brown sugar. One of my personal favorites."

"Wow! Well, Mr. Lumineux, I'd have to agree with you. This is absolutely delightful, thank you."

"Louie, dear. Please, call me Louie."

"Well, Louie...," I smile again, his presence bringing me much needed ease and comfort, "I have so many questions, but I have no idea where to even start."

"Start wherever you like. We have plenty of time, I assure you."

"Alright, well, I guess we can start with a question I've already asked, which is how long have you been here? And how did you come to be here? And, I guess, I want to know why you've stayed, considering it seems...*lonely*."

He nods, crossing one leg over the other, settling in for the long conversation to come.

"I've been here for fifty-five years," he starts, but before he can continue, I'm already interrupting him.

"Wow, really?! Holy moly, that's a really long time," I say in shock. "I don't know what I expected to hear honestly, but fifty-five years? Wow," I repeat.

Louie laughs joyfully. "Yes, yes. It's quite a long time. Double the length of life you've experienced, I assume."

I nod. "Yes. I'm twenty-four."

"Ahh, such a young woman. You have a long life yet to live. I hope that you can spend it as happily as possible, with less heartache than I've had to endure."

I take another sip of my tea, not really knowing exactly what to say. I want to ask about his heartache, but I also don't want to overstep. I also don't want to tell him that I've already lived a less than happy life. Luckily, I don't have to think of anything to say as he continues to answer my asked, and unasked, questions.

"I used to live in New Haven," he explains.

"Really?"

He nods again. "Way before you were born. I owned a hardware store called Lumineux's."

"That's it! That's why your name sounded familiar when you said it the first time. I've heard people in town say the name. The hardware store is still there but the name has been changed and it's now owned by a man named Bradley LeFou, a pathetic excuse for a man actually."

The thought of Gabriel's disrespectful and handsy best friend makes me nauseous. I tried to tell him that his friend made me uncomfortable, but he never believed me. Of course, he never did anything in front of Gabriel. It was always when we were alone and he knew he would get away with it simply by being Gabriel's best friend. Ugh. The whole town seriously makes me sick.

"Well, it's a bit unfortunate to hear that the store went to someone foul but it doesn't mean much to me these days."

"The whole town is foul, honestly. You're not missing anything and you're lucky to have gotten out. I guess if I was you and had the choice to stay here, I would take it in heartbeat rather than be forced to live in that pathetic town."

"I'm sorry to hear that. The town used to be pretty decent. From what I recall, at least. I left for much different reasons." I watch as Louie slips further into his memories. "I had a wife, Claire. She was my high school sweetheart and my soulmate. You know, it's not often people actually find their soulmates, but Claire was mine and I was hers."

I smile as I listen to the way he talks about his beautiful wife. He speaks about her so many years later as if his love for her is just as strong, if not *stronger* now than it was back then. He speaks about her the way I want someone to speak about me one day. This is the love that I'm so desperate to feel. This is the love I was hoping to find by giving Gabriel a chance, but he doesn't even come close to what Louie is describing and reliving.

"Claire was pregnant with our first child, a baby girl, Chloe. A little mix of both of our names; Claire and Louie." He smiles at his own memory but it's a sad smile, and I'm suddenly dreading hearing the rest of his story. "It was a difficult childbirth. We lost Chloe only minutes after she was born. She was born with an irreparable hole in her heart and left an irreparable one in mine that day, too. I lost Claire hours after Chloe. The day that should have been one of the happiest days of my life ended up being the worst."

His watery blue eyes are still haunted with the memory as if it was only yesterday. I can see the pain on his face and hear it in his words. My heart breaks and tears flow down my cheeks as I listen to his story. I feel guilty that I've made him talk about this, bringing back all of these painful memories.

"Louie, I'm so, so sorry for your losses. And I'm so sorry for asking you—"

"Don't be sorry, my dear. If I didn't want to talk about it, I wouldn't. It's an honor to share my life and their memory with you. I'm ashamed to say, I haven't spoken their names out loud in far too long. So, thank you for bringing them back to me."

I swallow, words evading me as my feelings overwhelm me. How can I possibly accept his gratitude? How can he even be this kind and wonderful? I've never experienced any sort of kindness from anyone other than my mother, and briefly from Gabriel, but his facade doesn't count. I feel like I don't deserve Louie's kindness, especially after what he's been through. If I was in his shoes, I couldn't guarantee that I wouldn't be angry and bitter as hell.

"After that day, I tried to pick up the pieces of my life, I really did. I knew that Claire wouldn't want me to waste the rest of my life mourning them, but...living life is often times easier said than done and I just couldn't function without them. I wanted desperately to follow them into death and live a beautiful eternal life with them, but I knew I couldn't do that by taking my own life. So, one night I left. I walked through the forest, toward Knightwell Castle, praying and hoping that the legend of a beast was true. I came willingly, with nothing in my heart except the irreparable hole, expecting to meet my end."

"But you didn't."

"No, my dear, I didn't find my end that night but I'm closer to it now. I can feel it calling to me and...," he nods his head, "I'm ready. I've made the best of what was left of myself and my life, here, with the Master. I've been a companion to him these past fifty-five years and he's been mine."

"You've mentioned him before. Why haven't I met him yet? Does he not want me here?"

"Alex is...," he struggles to find the right word, "complicated, my dear, but he truly means well. He's a good man and we've both come to care for each other deeply. He's just...different than you and I. He doesn't open up or experience life the way you and I do. He likes his solitude, and he can be a bit cold and standoffish. But if you're patient, once you get to know him, he's one of the best and most selfless people you'll ever meet."

"But he doesn't want me here," I repeat.

"Don't you worry yourself with that. You're welcome here for as long as you'd like to stay, I promise."

His answer and attempt at reassuring me doesn't quite work, and I change the subject. "How is it that you seem so prepared for guests? I mean, where on earth did the clothes and shoes even come from?"

Louie smirks and takes a sip of his tea. "The Master has his ways."

"Well, that's not at all cryptic. I thought you were going to answer all of my questions."

"Some answers are not mine to give."

"Alright," I reluctantly concede with a sigh. "You also mentioned I could write a note to my mother and that Alex would deliver it. How will he manage to do that if he's up here hiding and pretending as if he doesn't exist?"

"He has his ways," Louie repeats.

"Wow, Louie. I like you, I really, really do, but you're being awfully frustrating at the moment."

"I don't mean to be, truly, but some answers are best explained by the Master and the Master alone."

"Can you tell me anything about this beast that lives here?"

"He's vastly misunderstood. As you can see," he motions to himself, "he doesn't just kidnap people to torture and kill them."

"No, maybe he doesn't, but most legends start based on some truth."

"Indeed. Once upon a time, The Beast may very well have been *exactly* what the legends suggest, but I can't speak to that. I can only tell you what I know of it, and I know that The Beast *is* capable of terrible and monstrous things, but I've never witnessed them. Now, just because I've never seen it and don't believe he would ever resort to such vicious and animalistic acts, one can never be sure. I can't make any promises that The Beast won't ever lose control."

His words make me slightly uneasy. I've felt eyes on me on more than one occasion. I know there's something lurking in the darkness of this castle, and perhaps that's *exactly* why it's kept in darkness as often as possible. To give The Beast more places to hide.

"Knowing this truth, you still believe I'm safe here?" I ask, nervously.

"I may not know much, my dear, but one thing I know for certain is, above all else, you will never be safer than you are here. I can guarantee it."

And I don't know why, maybe I'm crazy and the people of New Haven have been right about me all along, but I believe him. I've always felt drawn to this place, even from far away, and now, being here, I feel…at peace. Maybe it's all the times I've sat on the roof staring at the castle, imagining its peacefulness. Maybe my imagination and optimism are folly. Maybe they'll even get me killed. But I haven't once sensed any kind of terror or dread being inside this castle.

I've already suffered at the hands of one beast, hiding in sheep's clothing. Now I'm faced with taking my chances on The Beast of legend or the beast of reality. The thought of what I have to look forward to when I return home is enough to make me take my chances here. At least for now.

"I'd like to write that letter to my mother, please."

Bella

I THINK HE KNOWS BY TAYLOR SWIFT

The gardens on the side of the castle are breathtaking. Not that I would have expected anything less. As I walk down the uneven flagstone path, it's hard to believe I'm still in New Haven. It feels like an entire world away. My life and the problems I ran away from feel like another lifetime. There's no sense of time here. No worries. No stress. No exhausting people. Thank God.

I limp over to the bench I discovered yesterday, almost hidden under an arbor overrun by unruly, beautiful, and fragrant white roses. I lean the cane I've upgraded to against the bench and then set down the items I've been carrying before I sit. Unfolding a small blanket, I drape it over my lap then reach for my book, settling in. I could sure go for a glass of wine too, but I couldn't carry everything since I'm still relying on a cane to alleviate the pain in my ankle. My body is doing much better but I still have a ways to go before I'm back to normal.

It's been five days since I woke up in Knightwell Castle. The master of this beautiful castle still eludes me, and I have yet to run across any ferocious beast. I'm beginning to wonder if either even exists or if they are both simply stories of legend. Then I remember that deep, angry voice from the night I woke up here and know that at least the Master is real. Unless I imagined it. Regardless, it has been five days of peace, relaxation, and the best talks and cooking lessons with Louie. For the first time in my life, I have a little idea of what it would be like to have a family. Well, a family beyond just my mother. It's not often that the grass is actually greener on the other side, but in this instance, I think it definitely is. I truly envy those that have the kind of family I never will.

I wonder, do they even realize what they have? Or are they looking across the fence at someone else's grass, too? It's such a shame that most people spend their lives looking at what others have, constantly comparing themselves to others, without knowing the full truth of what they're comparing. *Isn't that what you're doing, Bella?* I have to remind myself that even though others may have the kind of family I don't, that doesn't mean it's a *good* situation. I'm all too familiar with how well people hide behind their masks, only portraying the best versions of themselves and their lives for others to see and envy.

I'm not going to fall into that spiral. Gabriel sure helped with shattering any rose-colored lenses I may have owned before. No, I will simply appreciate the time I have with Louie, counting it as the blessing that it is, while also appreciating how happy my mother and I are with the life we have. Because I may not have everything that I want but...does anybody?

Unnecessary and useless things won't satisfy me. Dwelling on what I don't have won't help either. The only way that I can be truly happy is if I find it with what I already have. *Making some choices with yourself in mind wouldn't hurt either.* True, but I also need to focus on what's inside of me and all around me. Like the beautiful pink and purple sunset currently painting the sky for my viewing pleasure. Like the first glimpse of night slowly sneaking onto center stage. Like the strongest of the stars making their appearance earlier than the others, fighting against the setting sun, determined to shine.

It's up to me, and me alone, to shine. I need to have determination, to make my own choices, or fall victim to the world around me. Fall victim to the Gabriels of the world.

"What are you doing here?"

The deep voice shatters my contemplation and I jump, sending the book that had been laying open and forgotten in my lap to the ground.

"Sweet baby Jesus!" I exclaim, grabbing at my chest, my pounding heart frantic beneath my touch. "You scared the shit out of—" I swallow my words as I'm finally met with the owner of the deep voice. The same voice I heard talking to Louie the night I woke up here.

The sun has fallen below the horizon, but the light of twilight still lingers, giving me just enough light to make out a sweep of midnight hair over silver eyes that sparkle just as beautifully as the stars in the sky. I can also make out a dangerously beautiful and chiseled face, and generous lips which are currently pressed into an unapproving thin line.

His scowl should deter me from any type of conversation. The angry look he's giving me should make me pick up my book, grab my cane, and walk away from him as fast as my injured ankle will let me. But I'm currently mesmerized by the man I'm staring at. I thought Gabriel was the most handsome man I'd ever seen, but it's clear now I only thought that because I'd never seen *this* man before. Even in the dim light, there's no mistaking his alluring perfection.

I ignore the daggers being thrown my way by those silver eyes and slowly peruse the magnificence of his body. Broad shoulders, check. Biceps bulging as his arms cross over a massive chest that stretches his black T-shirt, check. Tapered waistline, check. Strong, thick legs that seem to go on forever and ever, check.

Sweet baby Jesus.

"I asked you a question." His voice is an irritated growl now, snapping me out of my unwarranted desire-filled brain fog.

I shake my head, embarrassment heating my cheeks. "Oh,

umm," I mumble. I don't even remember what the question was. *Way to go, Bella! React as if you've never seen a man before, you big fucking idiot.* To be fair, I have *never* seen a man this gorgeous before. Gabriel is good looking, sure, but in a very standard and *normal* way. This man is NOT normal. This man is…*surreal.*

"I'm sorry. What was the question?" I briefly meet his expectant gaze before flicking my eyes down to watch my nervous hands picking at a loose thread in the blanket.

"What are you doing here?" he repeats.

"I was just reading…," I start, but then realize the book in question is on the ground and I hadn't been reading at all. "Actually, I was just appreciating your beautiful garden and the beautiful sunset and…umm, I was just…thinking," I say nervously, my answer more of a question than a statement.

"That's not what I mean." He sighs heavily, as if he's already tired of dealing with me after only a minute of speaking with me. "What are you doing *here*?"

"Oh, yes, of course. I've been running around your castle like I live here and I'm sure you're not very happy about that considering you're not used to visitors, and I'm sure you enjoy your space, and the peace and quiet, and well, then here I come and ruin all of that for you and…," I trail off, realizing I'm rambling like a damn lunatic, not even stopping for a breath! I seem to have forgotten how to speak like a normal fucking human being. *Get it together, Bella!*

I dare a glance in his direction, and I think I see the beginnings of an amused smirk, which eases my nerves just a tad, but when I give him my full attention his face is back to that menacing scowl. Ok, maybe I totally imagined the smirk. Shit.

"Sorry," I say again, through a nervous chuckle. "You're Alexander Knightwell, I'm assuming? The master of the castle Louie has mentioned?"

He nods once, silver eyes never once leaving my face.

I clear my throat, my heart still beating way too fast in my chest. Geez, this man makes me nervous in a million different ways. "I'm Bella O'Brien. Louie said that you're the one who found me in the forest." I clear my throat again and sit a little straighter on the bench, trying to settle my nerves. If he was going to hurt me, he would have never brought me here. Or, he would have brought me and kept me locked up. *He's not The Beast.* "Thank you for...umm, bringing me here and taking care of me. I really don't want to intrude or overstay my welcome. If you want me to leave I—"

"You're welcome." He interrupts.

He uncrosses his arms and slides his hands into the pockets of his dark blue jeans, his rigid stance easing *slightly*. How is it that such a mundane motion, such a normal stance, can be so fucking sexy?! How is it even translating to *hot* in my mind? Maybe I have been way more sheltered than I thought.

"How are you feeling?" he asks, voice low and deep, sinking like a stone to settle dangerously low in my belly.

"I'm good." My voice is a breathless sigh. Just talking to this man has me practically melting.

His eyebrows raise at my response. No doubt he noticed the fact that I can barely even speak. Surely this is an amusing, if not rather annoying, conversation for him. Especially considering he doesn't exactly converse with people on a day-to-day basis and now he's stuck with me. A blubbering and melting mess of nonsense. He probably can't wait to get out of this interaction.

So...why is he walking towards me?

And, oh God, why is the way his body moves so damn sexy? Walking isn't sexy! I sit up even straighter, body tense, breath locked tight in my chest as he approaches. He places his hand on the bench, inches from my blanket covered thigh, and kneels down to pick up the book at my feet.

"Hmm...," he hums deep in his chest, as he picks up the book and examines the cover, "*Alice in Wonderland*."

"I'm so sorry," I say, as I tentatively reach for the book but then hesitate and pull my hand back. "I promise I don't normally treat books like this. I would never purposefully let a book fall to the ground, especially one as beautiful as this. I've never seen that edition before."

He's still crouched down beside me, his face just a little lower than mine causing him to look up at me. The light is hanging on by the thinnest thread, fighting fiercely against the night, and I'm thankful for it as it allows me to just make out his features. They're even more pronounced and impossibly perfect up close. His lips are no longer pressed into a thin line; they're full and the lightest shade of pink I've ever seen. They lend the perfect amount of softness to his otherwise hard features.

I pull my eyes away from his lips to meet his intense silver gaze. I've never seen eyes the color of his; like liquid mercury. And just like mercury, I know this man has the potential to destroy me...slowly, from the inside out. I can almost feel him starting to sink into my skin. His Adam's apple bobs in his throat and for the life of me, I don't know why that's hot. How did the most random and normal things suddenly become turn-ons?

He breaks our eye contact, and his eyes sweep over the lingering bruises on my neck. The hateful and ugly bruises that seem intent on reminding me of my last encounter with Gabriel every time I look in a damn mirror. I can't wait until they finally fade, and I no longer have to be reminded of them, even though I know I'll never forget that night and how his hand felt, squeezing my throat and inching me closer to death with just the strength of his fingers.

His eyes heat with anger and the muscle at the back of his jaw twitches violently. I close my eyes, not wanting to see his expression or let him see the tears starting to well in mine. I self-consciously reach for my throat, trying to hide the embarrassing truth even though I know it's futile. He's seen them. And even when they do finally fade away, he'll still know they were there. He'll know the truth.

"Keep it." His voice startles me out of my thoughts for the second time tonight.

I open my eyes and find him still kneeling next to me, still looking up at me. "I'm sorry?" I ask, confused.

He gestures to the book he's laid back in my lap. I hadn't even felt him place it there. "The book," he clarifies. "Keep it."

"Oh, I couldn't possibly—"

"I insist," he says, voice deep and hard, leaving no room for argument.

I watch, befuddled and in awe, as he stands in one fluid motion and walks away from me, his sexy body disappearing into the darkness. Actually, it's like the darkness enveloped him in a warm embrace, eagerly taking him in.

I stare into the space where his body disappeared for a long time. I'm not really sure how to process my first encounter with the master of the castle. At first, he seemed so angry and irritated that I'm here, but then the way he looked at me, and the anger I saw in his eyes when he saw the bruises, and the generosity of his gift...I don't know. I don't know what in the hell to think about it.

About him.

About the way he made me feel.

The chill in the air makes me shiver and I come back to reality. It's colder up here on the mountain and I can feel the change from fall to winter happening quickly. I gather the blanket and book in my hands, then reach for my cane as I stand. I slowly make my way across the flagstone path, barely able to see through the blanket of darkness that has fallen around me. When I finally make my way back inside the castle, I head to the sitting room that Louie and I use every night. Since being here I've adapted to their schedule, which means I'm awake during the night and I sleep most of the day. According to Louie, it's safer to be up and moving around when the people of New Haven are asleep. I suppose it makes sense if they're trying not to be seen.

Before entering the sitting room, I glance behind me, down the hallway that leads to the entryway and the stairs that lead up to the other floors of the castle. I feel the familiar tingle down my spine as if someone is watching me. I wonder if Alex is there, somewhere in the darkness, watching me.

The thought sends a thrill racing through my body. I *want* him to watch me. Even more, I want to see those silver eyes on me. On my body. Hell, who am I kidding, I want that man's hands on my body. I want everything I never wanted with Gabriel. Because I was never interested in Gabriel until he started pursuing me. Until I thought, what the hell, give it a chance. And sure, there were moments when it felt beautiful and loving with the possibility of something great, but now that I've stepped away from the situation, now that I can be honest with myself, I know I was never more than a possession to him. It pisses me off that I actually did opened my heart and gave him a piece of me. I gave him a piece I can never get back and he didn't deserve it. He never deserved a kind word from me, much less nine months of my life. He didn't deserve me.

Does Alex deserve me?

Or is he another man who sees what he wants and takes it?

If I've learned anything from my experience with Gabriel, it's that a man will do and say anything to get what he wants. They're the perfect fucking actors and liars when they need to be. Just because Alex genuinely seemed to care about my well-being and gave me a book doesn't mean he's any different than Gabriel.

Perhaps the only beasts that exist in this world are men.

Period.

I shake off the feeling of Alex's eyes on me along with the excitement that it brings and walk into the room, smiling as I see the only man I trust sitting in his normal chair before a small fire. The only man who isn't interested in taking anything from me.

The sweet and wonderful Louie Lumineux.

ALEX

ON MY MIND by MNQN

Her presence has filled these empty halls and rooms for a week. Even when I don't see her…I feel her, I smell her, I sense her. It's like she's infiltrated every breath and space of this castle, but unlike an enemy that snuck in under my nose, I let her in. I brought her here against my better judgement.

Why?

You know why, I taunt myself. I feel so torn. It's like listening to an angel and demon fighting for a voice in my head. I know what I *need* to do, and I also know what I don't *want* to do. And those two choices do not go hand in hand. I need to make up my mind but it's so hard to do when she's so goddamn distracting.

Her scent lingers in the spaces she's been and when I lose it, I find myself seeking it out. Seeking *her* out, like I'm doing now subconsciously. But again, why? It's not like I'm actually going to do anything. I've only approached her once, in the garden. I had intended to tell her to leave as soon as she could. I had intended to tell her that her presence here wasn't needed *or* wanted. I had intended to be an asshole and maybe even scare her into leaving.

What I hadn't intended was to be thoroughly taken by how incredibly sweet and pure she is. When she started rambling on and on, completely flustered, it was amusing, but also…endearing. I know she wasn't faking her reaction to me, and it stirred something inside of me. Something poked and prodded at the empty, dead space inside my chest. I found myself eager for more. More of her words and more of her voice spilling out of her luscious lips, soft and sweet as honey. More of her crystal-clear blue eyes, sparkling with life, aimed in my direction and sparking my own fuse to life. She was shy and nervous, but when I knelt by her and she locked her sky-blue eyes with mine, I may as well have drifted up to Heaven. And the light smattering of freckles across her nose and cheeks had me aching to touch them with my fingertips, to count them, no matter how long it would take. She was beautiful when I found her lying in that ravine, covered in dirt, blood, and tears, but I never could have prepared myself for her true beauty. Her undeniably pure and simple heart.

I find her alone in the sitting room, curled up in the chair by the small fire, book open in her lap. It seems to be one of her favorite places to be. She's either cooking up a storm with Lumineux, laughing brightly, or cozy in the sitting room or in the garden with a book always in hand or close by. I have the strongest urge to show her my library because I know it would not only impress her, and I want to impress her, but it would also bring her joy. The only reason I don't is because I'm trying to keep my distance from her, and the library is *my* domain. It's my safe space where I let all of my walls down and face my ugly truths. I don't want her to see me that way and I don't want to lose my safe haven.

So, I linger in the shadows, quiet and utterly still like the predator I am, watching her. I'm only a little ashamed to admit that I've watched her read, for hours, on more than one occasion. I get lost in the expressions that show freely on her face. I get lost in her soft gasps of surprise, her small bursts of uninhibited laughter, and the quiet tears that fall down her cheeks. I get lost watching her get lost in the stories.

Of course, I've also been listening to her and Lumineux,

eavesdropping like a creep in the shadows. I can't help it. I'm curious about her. I'm *drawn* to her. I want to know more about her and what happened to her. I want to know why she was running through my forest and what caused the bruises on her face and neck. Unfortunately, they haven't discussed what happened to her. She holds her cards close to her chest, even with Lumineux, and fuck, that just makes me even more curious as to why. What does she have to hide?

Or maybe I'm only seeking her out, chasing her, because she seems to have a key that will unlock the feelings deep inside of me. I felt it that night when her scream punched its way into my chest.

Perhaps that was part of the reason I approached her in the garden, to *feel* something. Perhaps I'm lying to myself, and I didn't even need a reason to approach her but used it as an excuse. I hadn't planned on dropping my guard even a fraction of a millimeter, but being in her presence, actually talking to her, made me feel...*happy*. And I haven't felt happiness for a long, long time. Life has numbed me so thoroughly that I didn't even think I was capable of feeling anything anymore. That's not entirely true. I know pain, sadness, and loss *intimately*. I constantly feel the aching hole of longing. Longing for something that I can never have, no matter how fucking hard I try. This is why I have to stay away from her. It only ever ends one way.

Her, dead.

Me, alone.

Bella

Break My Heart by Dua Lipa

I think this castle, or maybe Louie, has magical abilities. All I have to do is mention something and POOF there it is as if just my thought alone manifested it. Ok, maybe not that instantly but it does feel like magic. The other day, Louie was asking me about books, a topic I'm always more than happy to discuss, and he asked me what I like to read. Of course, I went off on a tangent about all the different genres I enjoy reading, I was only a little embarrassed to tell the old man I enjoy reading…ahem…*romance*. Keeping it on the safe side, I mentioned how much I love a certain author and how I'm on a mission to read ALL of their books. Literally, when I woke up the next evening, there were a stack of their books on my nightstand.

Magic.

I don't know how he does it, or how the master of the castle does it. All Louie will say when I ask him about it is, *"Master has his ways,"* like that's not at all cryptic and unhelpful. Since I'm not really being an open book myself, I don't push the issue. Besides, does it really matter? I mean, do I really care how all of this is even possible? This castle not completely falling apart? All their supplies? My clothes? Books? I know I should care but I just don't. I have zero cares being here. It's like the outside world doesn't exist and I'm content to just live here, in this castle, and in my own world. I know it's not a long-term option, but for now I'm enjoying my freedom.

"Ha!" I can't help the snort that escapes as I think of the irony. I'm literally locked up in a castle, hiding, and I feel *free*. That's not at all concerning for the state of my mental and emotional health.

"I would say that must be a funny book, but it doesn't look like you're actually reading it."

His amused voice immediately captures all of my attention. My entire body seems to snap awake, my blood humming in my veins at the mere sound of his voice. Alex is standing only a few feet away from where I sit, hands casually slid into the pockets of his dark jeans, a plain red t-shirt pulled tightly across his chest. He looks like a damn snack, making my mouth water. How had I not noticed him? This is the second time he's managed to quietly sneak up on me. Both times I had been attempting to read but instead was lost in my own thoughts.

"Oh," I say, as I look down at the half-opened book in my lap. "No, I *was* reading but just got lost in a thought there for a second."

"Must not be a very good book then."

I scoff. "On the contrary. This is shaping up to be a perfect five-star read, thank you very much."

I'm trying to sound offended, in a joking kind of way, but all attempts at being light and silly fade when I finally lift my eyes away from my book and meet his. He's standing just at the edge of the lantern glow, his face half lost in shadows and half illuminated by the dim light and the flickering orange flames of the fire. Shadows dance across his face, highlighting his incredible bone structure and square jaw, but fuck...those eyes. They are haunting and beautiful, shining brightly and trained directly on...*me*. No one has ever looked at me like he does.

Intently.

Fully.

As if I am the only thing to look at in a bare, stark-white room.

As if I am the only thing of consequence. The only thing in this world that matters. The room could be burning down around us, and he wouldn't notice. All he would notice is *me*. That's how he looks at me and it makes my blood hot, and my insides melt, and I can't help but break the eye contact and squirm in my seat, licking my suddenly dry lips. I feel the heat rising up my neck and into my cheeks, embarrassed that I showed him *very clearly* just what his presence does to me.

I'm flustered. It's suddenly too hot by the fire and I simultaneously want to meet his silver gaze again, to get lost in him instead of my book, and to run from the room, taking my embarrassment with me. I do neither. I sit in my chair, gripping my book so tightly my fingers ache and I try to get control of my racing heart.

"Which one is it?"

I swallow. "I'm sorry?" I ask, confused, as I make myself meet his steely gaze.

There's that hint of a smirk again. A slight twitch of his lips right at the corners. "The book. Which book are you reading?"

Déjà vu hits me hard, remembering our conversation in the garden, and how it went almost the same way; me blubbering and an awkward mess, him all calm and controlled sex appeal.

"Oh, I doubt you'd know it." I try to laugh but it gets caught in the tightness of my throat, coming out strangled and awkward. *Come on, Bella! You have got to do better than this.*

"Try me," he demands, voice dropping lower and doing things to my insides.

"Ok," I concede and hold up my book, showing him the cover.

He takes a few steps, closing the distance between us and reaches for the book. His long fingers gently brush over mine and the simple touch sends a shiver down my spine. My skin tingles where his skin touches mine. Such an innocent touch shouldn't affect me like this. What's wrong with me?

He turns the book around and takes a minute to read the blurb on the back. I watch as a beautiful eyebrow arches. "Interesting. Perhaps I can borrow it after you're done."

Now I do laugh. "Yeah, ok. Like you have any interest in reading this sappy, sad, yet beautiful *romance book*."

"And why wouldn't I?" He sets those damn intense silver eyes on me, challenging me, and I have to take a deep breath, trying to settle the butterflies suddenly stirring in the pit of my stomach.

"Because," I say, simply, "you're a *guy*—"

"Really? I hadn't noticed," he interrupts.

I give him a deadpan glare. "And guyssss…," I continue, "don't read this type of stuff."

Another arch of his eyebrow and he returns his hands to his pockets. "And what is it that *guys* read?"

"I dunno…," I shrug, "like, sci-fi stuff. Action books, maybe thrillers?"

"Hmmm," he hums, the sound caressing my skin like the gentle touch of a feather. "Well, you're right. I do read those."

"See!" I say, smiling victoriously.

"But I do read romance as well. I think the way women tend to write men is…a bit farfetched but," he shrugs his big, broad shoulders gracefully, "I understand the appeal."

I literally have to pick my jaw up off the floor. It's not often I'm left utterly surprised and speechless. At least not in a good way.

I clear my throat. "You're not at all what I expected." I have to crane my neck to look up at him from my seat. I hadn't realized just how tall and imposing he is.

"Do I dare ask what you expected?"

I let out a heavy breath, laughing softly, a little embarrassed of what I'm about to admit. "A beast, obviously."

"Ah, the legend."

I lift one shoulder. "I never really did believe the legend of some rabid and dangerous beast living up here, but when Louie mentioned a master of the castle, I have to admit I did picture someone more...like him."

"Old, you mean."

I laugh again, this one coming a little easier as I see the humor in his eyes. "Yeah, old," I admit. "And I dunno, I guess like a weird shut-in, paranoid, and maybe a bit...*looney*."

"Well, I'm sorry to disappoint you."

"What? Oh God no! Trust me, you are *not* a disappointment like, *at all*. How could you even think that you're a disappointment? I mean, look at y...." I realize I'm rambling again and about to make a complete fool of myself basically telling him I think he's God's gift to women. I clear my throat and slow down. "I just mean, you're not what I expected but definitely not a disappointment."

"Well, *I'm* a little disappointed."

I scrunch my eyebrows together. "Why?"

He takes his hands out of his pockets, placing one on the arm of the chair, the other on the back for support, caging me in as he leans down towards me. I press further into the back of the chair as if I can somehow move away from him even though I don't really want to. His sudden closeness takes me by surprise, and I catch my breath and hold it as he comes face to face with me. His molten gaze travels slowly across my face, stopping for a few seconds on my mouth. I return the favor and take in his full lips, achingly close to mine, which lights a flame of desire inside of me starting right between my legs. How can a complete stranger bring out such intense and wanton need in me?

"Because you're a reader, Bella."

Oh God, my name on his lips is going to give me a damn heart attack. I feel like I'm going to pass out, but that's probably because I'm still holding my breath, desperately trying not to move and ruin this moment. Whatever this moment is.

He leans in further, his smooth cheek just barely grazing mine as he whispers in my ear. "You should know better than to judge a book by its cover."

And then he's gone. Leaving behind the scent of his clean, fresh detergent and…cinnamon?

I take a deep, shaky breath. His absence is way more noticeable than it should be, leaving me shivering by the fire, goosebumps erupting across my skin.

Holy hell, who is this man?! I feel so far out of my depth, desperately searching for solid ground underneath me as I barely keep my head above the water. I have no experience for this. I have no experience for *him*.

"Good Lord," I whisper to myself. "I'm going to fucking drown."

ALEX

I hadn't meant to approach her again, but I couldn't help it. My mind screams at my feet to stop moving and at my mouth to stop speaking, but it's like they have a mind of their own. I'm being led by an unseen force and that force seems determined to destroy me. Because each time I speak to Bella I want more. I want more conversation, more connection. I want to be in her presence. I want to be the one she gives all of her attention to. And fucking hell, I want to give her all of *my* attention, too.

With my hands and lips and tongue and...teeth.

I want to stop her rambling and leave her speechless. I want to drown her in so much pleasure that she's only capable of making gasps and moans and whimpers. I want her so far gone that she can only form one word in her mind.

Alex.

Just imaging her squirming beneath me as I bring her to orgasm, screaming my name, has my pulse racing and my cock growing inside of my jeans. I palm my hard dick and groan. The smallest touch has me aching for more. I've never felt this sensitive or desperate before. Well, maybe back in my teen years once upon a time, but those memories are long gone, which leaves me with nothing to compare this new situation to.

Nothing to compare *her* to. There's only ever been one woman I thought I could love, but we were never given the chance to explore what was between us. I don't want to lose that chance again because no one else in my long history has ever garnered my interest so quickly before. With nothing more than her scent on the breeze and a scream that crawled under my skin and embedded in my veins.

When she looks at me with those sweet, doe eyes, I feel all my steadfast control coming undone. One look from her and I feel stripped bare in an unsettling, yet exciting, intoxicating way. Every time she licks her lips, it sends a bolt of desire crashing through me. And the way her skin smells...damn. I had to stop myself from letting my lips fall to her neck when I leaned in to whisper in her ear. It's been so long since I've felt this alive, this *aware* of somebody else. I knew having her here was a bad idea, but I can't bring myself to leave her alone much less ask her to leave.

The sound of her slow, soft footsteps snaps me out of my fantasies. I reach for the book I brought with me and place it in my lap, hiding the evidence of my desire. Her footsteps hesitate at the entrance to the sitting room, but I pretend I'm reading, acting like I'm unaware of her presence when I'm anything but. I'm acutely aware of where she is almost every second of the damn night.

She slowly makes her way to the chair opposite me, the one she usually occupies, but she doesn't immediately sit.

"Umm, hi." Her voice is low and hesitant. "I don't mean to intrude. This is normally where I meet Louie."

"Louie is resting," I say, as I keep my eyes glued to my book, still pretending to read. The book may as well be written in Latin because I can't comprehend a single sentence with her here, distracting me.

"Oh. Is he ok?"

The genuine concern in her voice makes me look away from

the page and I'm met with wide, worried eyes searching mine for an answer. She's only known Louie for a week but she's acting like he means more to her than some random stranger. Her heart is so deeply *good*. It's so clear to see that I find myself, once again, wondering how anyone could hurt her.

The thought has my eyes drifting to her neck. She's wearing an off the shoulder t-shirt and the light from the flames of the fire dance across her smooth skin. I want to trail my lips across her shoulder and down to her collarbone, before I kiss my way up her neck and claim that sweet mouth. I want to know what her skin tastes like, what her mouth tastes like, and what her skin feels like under my touch.

My dick is fucking hard again and I have to clear my throat before I speak. "Louie is perfectly fine," I assure her. What I don't tell her is that I told the old man to scram because I wanted some more time alone with her. He had given me a very arrogant, *I told you so,* look before graciously disappearing for the night.

"Oh, thank God." She breathes a sigh of relief and touches her chest over her heart. "You scared me there for a sec."

"Apologies. He's just taking some well-earned personal time. Although he argued quite fiercely about leaving you without someone to talk to. I assured him I'd see to it that you were taken care of and…entertained."

She smiles lovingly and it brightens up her entire face. I have to force myself to keep my ass in my chair and not get up and claim that smile as mine.

"He really is the sweetest man I've ever met. He's so thoughtful, but I'm perfectly fine being on my own. I don't need anyone to entertain me. I'll leave you to your reading." She starts to turn, and panic rises in my chest.

"That's not necessary," I rush out. "I know this is where you enjoy being. In fact, I feel like I'm the one intruding. Perhaps I should leave you to it." I close my book and start to stand.

"I don't mind." She smiles again, this time more shyly. "I mean, I don't mind being alone, but I'd like the company. That is, if you're up for it? Because if you're not then I completely understand. I know that you're not used to guests, and Louie said that you like your priv—"

"Bella."

"Mhmmm?" She swallows and looks embarrassed. It's fucking adorable and I have to fight the smile tugging at my lips. I don't want her to think I'm laughing at her.

"Would you like some tea?" I motion towards the teapot and cups sitting on the coffee table between us.

"Oh. Yes, please. That'd be great," she says, as she finally takes her seat.

I busy myself making her tea, adding honey and cream just the way she likes it. When I hand her the cup, she briefly meets my eyes before quickly looking down at her hands as she takes it from me. I can't help but notice the beautiful, long lashes framing her eyes and the touch of pink staining her cheeks. There's not a drop of makeup on her face and she damn near takes my breath away. I have to remind myself to breathe.

"Thank you," she says quietly, brushing the hair away from her face and behind her ear.

"You're welcome." I force my feet to move and take me back to the chair across from her.

I shouldn't even be here right now. I shouldn't want to spend time with her. I shouldn't be trying to get to know her, or impress her, but the thought of letting her go and not seeing where this could lead is overriding my common sense. What's that saying? Something about experiencing love and losing it is better than never having experienced it all? *What in the actual fuck, Alex! Are you seriously already throwing around words like love?* Jesus Christ, what in the hell is wrong with me.

Anyway, I don't know how I actually feel about that saying. Before Bella, I would have said absolutely fucking not. I don't want to experience love only to lose it. Again. Because at the end of the day, I *am* The Beast, and I will lose it. *I will lose her.* But after Bella, I'm no longer certain I know where I stand on the matter. And that's not a good thing for me *or* for The Beast.

"Mmmm."

Her moan makes my eyes snap in her direction. She has both of her small hands wrapped around the mug. I have the filthiest thought of wondering how they'd look wrapped around my hard dick and have to shake my head to clear the image. She brings the cup to her lips again and closes her eyes, sinking into her chair, and finally relaxing.

"This is my favorite tea," she explains. "How did you know to make it with cream and honey?"

"Louie may have mentioned it," I lie. *Or I may have been watching and listening to every single little thing about you.* I keep that stalker thought to myself as I sit back in the chair and cross ankle over knee, attempting to appear casual and unaffected. "You seem to be doing better. You're not using a cane anymore."

"Oh, the ankle is much better. Still a bit sensitive, and I have a slight limp." She shrugs in a carefree way. "And I still can't put a lot of pressure on my wrist either, and the ribs still hurt when I take too deep of a breath or lay a certain way." She laughs softly. "I guess I'm still pretty banged up but much better than I was."

"That's good. I imagine you'll be heading home soon then?" I ask, trying to keep the nervousness I feel out of my voice.

"Oh, umm....," she holds the cup in her lap, and starts lifting and dunking the tea bag. I wonder if she's just as nervous as I am. "I hadn't really thought about it, honestly. But I'm sure you want your castle and privacy back. I should be well enough to travel back to town in a day or two." She glances up at me and gives me a weak smile.

"Bella." I drop my leg and rest my elbows on my knees, leaning toward her, giving her all of my attention. I want to make sure she understands what I'm saying.

Her eyes slowly look up and meet mine. Her chest rises and falls in shallow breaths. I can hear her heart pounding in her chest. "Yes?"

"I only asked if you planned on heading home soon. Don't put words in my mouth and don't assume you know what I want. I'm not asking you to leave, and you don't have to leave if you don't want to."

She swallows and looks relieved. "Oh. Thank you."

I know I shouldn't press, that it's none of my business, but I've been dying to know what happened to her. I've been dying to know what caused her to run so wildly and carelessly into my domain. Especially since she knew about the legend.

"Who were you running from?"

Her eyes shoot up to mine, wide and caught of guard. "What makes you think I was running from someone?"

My eyes drop to her neck. There's no longer any discoloration there, but I had seen the bruises. She knows it, too. Her hand comes up and rubs her throat before she returns it to the cup, gripping it tighter than before. She drops her gaze again, looking embarrassed. I feel like an ass for making her feel this way when all I want to know is who he is and if I need to fucking find him and make him hurt for what he did to her.

"Who is he?" I prod.

She shakes her head. "No one that matters."

"He scares you."

She nods and my entire body sings with rage. I don't know why I have the overwhelming urge to protect her, to keep her safe. Ever since the first night I heard her scream in pain and fear, I've been compelled to protect her. The fact that a man has hurt her physically and emotionally, leaving behind a scar that will never heal, has me ready to unleash The Beast. *I want to make him bleed.* I'm clamping my teeth so tightly my jaw starts to ache. The only thing that pulls me out of my very bloody thoughts is her soft voice.

"I've only recently found out that he's not a good guy. I think I've known all along that he isn't, but he didn't actually do anything to prove it to me until recently. I didn't even *do* anything wrong he just...snaps. I thought it was love but...," she laughs sarcastically, "I was soooo wrong. I don't want anything to do with him but he's not the type of man you say no to. He won't allow it. When he wants something, he gets it, period. And for the life of me, I can't understand why he wants *me*, but he does and...," she sighs heavily, "I don't know what to do."

I want to tell her that I know *exactly* what the fuck to do. I want to tell her to take me to him. To let me have a...*talk* with him, man to man. I want to tell her that I can guaran-fucking-tee he'll never lay a finger on her again. But I can't tell her that because then she'll be scared of me, too. Then she'll see that I am truly The Beast, and I don't want to see her look at me any differently than she does now.

So, all I say is, "You can stay here. Stay for as long as you'd like. He'll never find you here, and if he does, I swear he won't lay a hand on you as long as you're in my care."

Her beautiful blue eyes finally meet mine again. In place of her earlier embarrassment, I see gratitude and relief. I want to go to her, to kneel in front of her and hold her face in my hands while I look into those stunning eyes. I want to watch them flutter closed as I whisper promises of safety against her skin. I want to make her forget he ever existed.

"Thank you, Alex. Truly."

Fuckkkkk. Why did she have to say my name like that? Why

does she have to look at me the way she's looking at me? Like she sees me as much as I see her. Like she feels this...*thing* between us, too. But I don't want to rush this. I don't want to scare her off or push her when she's not ready. She just had a traumatic experience at the hands of someone she thought loved her, I doubt she's ready for anything more with a stranger.

So, I sit back in my chair and open my book back up, knowing full well that I won't be able to read one damn word as she sits across from me, but content to pretend like I am for hours just to be near her.

"You're welcome, Bella."

Bella

NEW SENSATIONS BY SUNSLEEP

"So, how was your evening last night, dear?"

I can't hide the blush that creeps into my cheeks at Louie's innocent question. I don't even know why I'm blushing. It's not like anything happened between me and Alex. All we did was talk a little bit and the rest of the time was spent reading in companionable silence. Although, if I'm being honest, I maybe read one whole page the entire night. Our silence was comfortable but also extremely distracting. We kept sneaking glances at each other when we thought the other wasn't looking. I sat as still as I could in my chair, but inside was a riot of hummingbird wings fluttering franticly against my chest and stomach.

That man's eyes heat me up from the inside out in ways I thought were only possible in romance books. If just his gaze on me makes me feels this way, what would it feel like for him to actually *touch* me? Does he want to touch me as badly as I want him to? No, no way. A man like Alex, all good looks and sexy and everything my imagination has ever pictured while reading one of my fictional book boyfriends, does not want a woman like me. A blubbering, inexperienced mess.

"Perhaps I shouldn't ask," Louie teases with a chuckle.

"What? No! No, nothing happened…geez." I laugh nervously.

"We just talked a bit and then we both read. It was completely innocent and quite...*nice*, actually."

"Mhmmm, I see. That smile is definitely a new one. A *nice*, new one," he mocks, sweetly.

I slide my hands under my thighs, swinging my legs in the air, feeling like I'm flying and not just sitting on the kitchen island. I bite my lip in an attempt to dampen my god-awful cheesy ass grin, but I fail miserably. Of course, this is when Alex decides to walk in.

"What's going on in here?"

God. His voice alone is an aphrodisiac, running along my skin and coaxing out the desire that seems to have bloomed deep in my belly.

He was MIA the first handful of days I was here, but after the garden encounter, he's been making an appearance every night and I am *not* complaining.

"Were your ears ringing, Master?"

"Louie!" I hiss under my breath. I do not want him to know we were talking about him.

"As a matter of fact, they were, Lumineux."

I glance at Alex as he approaches. His eyes are locked on me, one eyebrow cocked in curiosity, his lips pulling to one side in a smirk that wakens those damn hummingbirds in my chest.

"But the question is...," he stops about two feet away from me and leans his hip into the island, crossing his muscled arms over his chest, never once taking his eyes off me, "were you saying good things about me or..." He drops his eyes to my lips and speaks in a tone I've never heard before. It's so low and deep, it's almost a growl in his throat. "Bad things?"

And just like his eyes and voice have dropped, I'm tempted to drop my damn panties. Right here, right now. The cheesy grin has been wiped completely off my face and I think I've forgotten how to speak. It's not like I could even if I tried. My mouth is dry, and I swipe my tongue across my bottom lip, pulling it between my teeth before letting it go slowly.

Alex leans in closer to me and whispers in that deep, husky voice. "Bad things then."

I blink and mange to pull my eyes away from his lips, which are pulling into that damn sexy smirk again. "What? No." I shake my head and laugh nervously. "We weren't talking about you *per se.* Louie just asked how my night was and I was simply telling him that we basically just sat in the room and read together, and nothing, I mean *nothing* happened, and—"

"I think Alex is just teasing you, dear." Louie pats my knee, thankfully stopping my word vomit.

I know my face is bright red, showcasing very clearly how embarrassed and flustered I am. I look over at Alex and he's still standing casually against the island, but his smirk has turned into a full-blown smile revealing beautiful straight teeth that could be in a toothpaste ad, and a deliciously deep dimple in his right cheek. I think my heart literally stops beating. I've never seen a smile so damn disarming before. I'm hypnotized.

He dips his chin and looks up at me coyly, his silver eyes shining with mischief.

He's flirting with me.

Holy shit!

He's flirting…with *me.*

My mind goes blank and the only thing that comes out of my mouth is, "Louie was teaching me how to make bread." *Really, Bella? That's the best you've got? This gorgeous man is flirting with you and all you've got to say is something stupid about bread?!* Jesus, Mary, and Joseph, I'm pathetic!

I hear Louie mumble something about leaving and the dough

needing time to rise, but I can't focus on anything else because Alex still hasn't taken those devious eyes away from me, and now he's moving even closer. I watch as he takes the last step between us, and I swear he's moving in slow motion.

"I can tell," he says, as his hand reaches out toward me, ever...so...slowly. "You have a little bit of flour..." I gasp as his fingertips graze my jaw and slide under my ear to the back of my neck, his thumb wiping gently across my cheek. "Right here."

He rubs his thumb across my cheek twice before his hand stills, cradling my face. His head moves toward mine and all I can do is think *he's going to kiss me! Oh my God, oh my God, he's going to kiss me!* His lips stop dangerously close to mine. I feel his warm breath on my lips and smell the cinnamon on his breath when he speaks.

"You're cute when you're nervous. And if you keep licking and biting that lip, *tempting me*, I won't be able to stop from tasting it for myself. You've been warned."

His fingertips linger on my skin as he pulls away. My body sways slightly as I lean forward, chasing his touch. He leaves me sitting on the island, complete stunned, and aching with need, watching him walk out of the kitchen.

I throw myself back to lay on the island with a heavy sigh. I place one hand on my stomach and one on my chest, trying to settle the flurry of wings inside of me. My heart hammers hard against my palm. What is this feeling? It's scary as all hell but I kinda love it, too.

"Oh, Alex Knightwell, where have you been all my life and what are you doing to me?" *More importantly, whatever it is, please don't stop.*

ALEX

ANIMALS BY MAROON 5

It took every ounce of willpower in my body not to close the distance between our lips. The urge to taste her, to claim her as *mine*, was profound. I don't know how or why I feel this way, but it's impossible to ignore. *She* is impossible to ignore. The only thing that has ever come close to rivaling how I feel about Bella is the hunger that calls to The Beast inside of me.

The Beast that I will never be free of.

I came to terms with who I am a long time ago, but that was before the goddamned curse. The curse that has left me utterly alone for far too long, with nothing but an eternity of pain, heartache, and longing left in front of me.

And I'm forced to face this curse every single day because my hunger can never entirely be satiated. I can't just seclude myself in my castle, alone. I *have* to feed The Beast. Of course, I've tried to distance myself as much as possible from The Beast, to be detached. That only led me to become The Beast of legend, something to be feared. It did absolutely nothing to disguise the cold-hard truth that I'll forever be alone in this world no matter what I do. I can't hide or outrun what's inside of me. And I've tried for centuries to break this fucking curse. I thought that perhaps it would fade over time, but it hasn't.

This is why I should keep my distance from Bella. I'm no

fucking good for her. I don't deserve her, and she doesn't deserve this cursed life. She deserves to live a long, beautiful life full of love and experiences and adventure. She deserves everything I can never give her. And everything that she can give me will only destroy me further. It will only make The Beast that much more vicious.

I keep reminding myself, almost every damn second, of all these things but I can't stop myself from acting on my impulses. My mind is telling me one thing and my heart is telling me something completely different. It seems that currently my fickle, bleeding heart is fucking winning.

I honestly have no clue how I got here, but I'm standing in front of her door. I've been standing in front of her door for...minutes? Hours? I have no fucking clue because time doesn't exist when Bella is involved. It's like my entire world evaporates around me and all I see are those two cerulean eyes pulling me under their depths and I'm all too happy to sink into them.

I'm about to walk away when the sound of my name stops me in my tracks. I take a step closer to the door, not that I need to in order to hear what's going on, but I want to get as close to her as I can. I hear the rustle of fabric, covers being shoved aside, and the deep, heavy breaths of her panting. Her heart is beating so loud I can practically feel the rhythmic beat in my own body.

Her loud, drawn-out moan lands like a shockwave on my skin, awakening every damn nerve ending, making my cock stir to life. *You're a fucking pervert, Alex. Walk away!* But I don't walk away. My hard cock keeps me rooted in place as I close my eyes and focus on the sounds coming from behind this godforsaken door. I want to *see* her. Is she lying on the bed with her hand shoved down the front of her panties? Is her shirt pulled up to reveal her full breasts, nipples tight with the need for contact? Or is she completely naked, legs spread wide with her beautiful body on full display?

I unzip my jeans and pull out my aching cock. I drop a generous amount of spit directly onto my hard length and begin to pump myself in time to her heavy breaths. I place my palm on the door, holding myself up as I hang my head, close my eyes again and focus on every little moan, whimper, and groan coming from Bella. I imagine it's me in there with her, my head between her legs, bringing out these intoxicating sounds.

I imagine slipping my tongue up her slit, parting her lips, and finding her wet and ready. Fuck, I bet she tastes like sweet Heaven and feels like warm sunshine. I stroke my dick harder, faster, matching her panting breaths as she slowly brings herself closer and closer to climax.

I reach behind me and tug my t-shirt off, over my head, gripping it in my fist. The pressure of my own orgasm is building, making my balls ache with the need for release. Not yet. I grind my teeth and lean back into the door, hyper focused on what's happening on the other side.

"Oh God, right there." Her voice is shaky and breathless. "Don't stop, Alex, that feels so good."

A growl rumbles deep in my chest at the sound of my name on her pleasure filled lips. Jesus Christ, I want to be the one making her come for real and not just in her fantasies. I feel like I'm about to explode and don't know if I can hold back the flood a second longer.

"Fuck, I'm going to come." She groans and then starts to scream her pleasure, but I hear the smack of her hand over her mouth, muffling them.

I have to clamp down my own jaw to keep my own pleasure quiet as I release my orgasm into my t-shirt. I gently lean my forehead against the door, my chest heaving with the exertion and the experience of coming with Bella for the first time, even though she's completely unaware of it. Son of a bitch. I've never done anything like this before. I tuck my exposed dick back into my jeans and can't help but feel like a damn creep. A beast in an entirely different way but just as insatiable.

Insatiable for her.

I stay still, listening to every little sound, the rustle of covers again, and then finally her deep, even breathing lets me know she's asleep. I slowly turn the doorknob and push the door open one slow inch at a time. Once it's wide enough to slip through, I enter her room and walk soundlessly to her bed.

I can smell her arousal in the air, and it sinks low in my gut and tightens my balls. Even though I just had a release, I can feel my dick stirring again, begging for more. Begging to slide inside of her and feel her tight little pussy, slick and warm, instead of my own hand.

She looks so peaceful, and there's a small smile on her lips, and I wonder if her fantasies of me followed her into her dreams. She's so damn beautiful, I could watch her sleep for hours. *Yup it's official, I have become a certified creep.* Still, I stay looking down at her and gently tuck her hair behind her ear. She hums unconsciously at the touch. How is this woman making me fall so helplessly without even trying? Without even having touched her or kissed her? What's going to happen to me when I finally swim in her soothing waters?

Pleasure and pain.

Pleasure for a fleeting moment in time.

Pain that will last a lifetime.

Is she worth it?

Yes. Yes, she is.

Bella

I wake up feeling equally satisfied and starved, and for once I'm not talking about food. As much as I love to eat, I'd gladly give up everything, even chocolate, to be sustained instead by Alex. Well, at least the Alex in my dreams who is absolute perfection. The Alex in real life is…well, physically he's perfect. Well, shit. I mean, he's perfect with clothes on. I wonder what he looks like without his clothes. Of course, I've dreamt of what he looks like, but I have no actual evidence to go off. What if he's super hairy? I'm not a fan of chest hair. Eww, what about back hair? Or what if he has a micro penis? Not that there's anything wrong with that but…ok, who the hell am I kidding, that would suck!

Why am I even thinking about his penis?

Because I'm a horn-dog all of a sudden, that's why. It's like all those intense hormones I felt as a teen that were never explored or satisfied have come back with a vengeance. I was never this horny with Gabriel, even when we were having sex. I guess it felt good, but it was never mind-blowing. Then again, maybe that's all sex is. I don't know because I don't have anything else to compare it to. What if what I felt with Gabriel is the best it gets? What if all those romance books are nothing more than what they are; works of fiction? Mind-blowing, body-exploding, soul-soaring fiction.

But even if sex doesn't get better, I've still never felt quite this...*aware* before. Aware of my own body, every inch of my skin sensitive and aching for contact. Aware of someone else's body, their heat, their scent. No, this is definitely different. Alex is different.

The way those silver eyes burn into me in the sexiest way. God, he barely touched my face and I practically combusted on the spot. Just the image of his sexy smile, that damn dimple, has my hand traveling south again. I've been awake for literally a minute, and I already need to satisfy my craving for him. My body is speaking loud and clear about what...no, *who* it wants.

I was dying for him to kiss me but also terrified he would. What if I'm no good at kissing? What if I'm no good at anything? Ugh, I'll be mortified. I will literally die inside if I embarrass myself like that in front of Alex. *And now the mood is ruined. Way to go, Bella.* I remove my hand from underneath my panties with a heavy sigh. Probably for the best anyways.

I throw the covers aside and slide out of bed, the cold air hitting my exposed skin, making me shiver. It's always a little bit cool inside the castle but this isn't just cool, it's cold. Walking over to the window, I the sun already sitting low in the sky, only a couple of hours left in the day before night comes sweeping in. The sky is clear and bright, and there's a light dusting of white on everything for as far as I can see.

"What in the world?" My breath fogs up against the cold glass.

We're barely at the tail end of October. We typically don't get snow until around Thanksgiving. Then again, I've never been up here in the mountains, so maybe this is completely normal. The mountaintop always has a white peak long before and after New Haven sees snow.

I rush over to the wardrobe and pull a pair of sweats over the boy-shorts style underwear I like to sleep in, grabbing a sweater to throw on over my tank top, forgoing a bra in my excitement to get outside. I slide my feet into some Uggs and shuffle quickly to the restroom to pee and brush my teeth. I'm out of the room in under five minutes, half jogging, half limping out into the garden.

There's really hardly any snow on the ground but it's deceptively slippery. I slow to a walk after almost biffing it on the stone steps. It must have gotten pretty cold in the early morning hours, causing some of the moisture to freeze underneath the fluffy powder. I make it to my bench in one piece with no new bruises or scraps added to my healing body. The beautiful white roses are finally starting to wilt under the weight of the snow and the cold weather. A few petals have fallen onto the bench, and I pick them up, smelling them before rubbing my fingertips across their silky petals.

Brushing the bench off before I sit, I wish I had brought something to lay on it. Shrugging, I sit anyway, the cold moisture immediately sinking into the fabric of my sweats, but I don't care. I look out into the garden and beyond. The castle sits on the side of the mountain, and I have a clear view all the way down and into the town of New Haven far below. The town is reduced to no more than specks of buildings in a clearing with homes scattered between the trees.

Looking at the town from this far away, with the fresh white powder of snow covering everything, giving it a look of purity, I can almost believe it's a nice town. There's no doubt it's beautiful and charming. It's a crying shame that it's populated with the nastiest people I've ever met. I have to believe that the world is better than what I've experienced at the hands of my neighbors. The world has to be filled with more Louies and Alexes, it just has to. I refuse to believe that we're alone up here in this castle, the only three genuine souls in the whole wide world. Well, there's my mother of course. And Chip. Then again, would it be so bad if it was just us; Alex and Louie, and Mom and me, alone together? I could think of worse things.

I close my eyes and let the warmth filtering down from the

sun sink into me. It's definitely not as powerful as the summer sun, but it's helping to keep the cold at bay. Once it dips beyond the horizon it's going to get way too cold to be out here in just wet sweats and a sweater, but I want to at least see the start of the sunset before heading back inside.

My fingers and toes are numb by the time the sun touches the horizon, blessing me with vibrant shades of red and pink, like oil paint spread across the sky. I will seriously never get tired of seeing sunsets. No matter how many I experience, not one has ever been the same as the one before. And that's a miracle of creation if you ask me.

"Bella! Are you out here?" Louie calls from the castle.

"I'm here, Louie! In the garden! Come watch this beautiful sunset with me!" I yell back.

I keep my eyes on the sky, not wanting to miss a thing as I wait for Louie to join me. Several minutes go by and Louie still hasn't made his way to where I'm sitting.

"Louie?" I call out.

Nothing.

"Louie, are you ok?" I ask, as I start walking toward the castle, a nasty little seed of worry rooting into my gut, my sixth sense telling me something is wrong.

I start to jog lightly across the flagstone path, still careful of my healing ankle but needing to make sure Louie is ok. As I round the bend, the large sprawling stone steps come into view and my heart drops like a stone in my chest.

"Louie!" I scream.

I forget about the twinge in my ankle and rush to where Louie is lying, crumpled on his side on the steps. A red stain of blood rivals the vibrant colors of the sunset. I storm up the steps and fall to my knees at his side, the warmth of his spilled blood sinking into my sweats. There's so much blood!

"Louie! Oh my God, oh my God."

My hands frantically hover over his body, desperately looking for an injury but terrified of moving or hurting him further.

"Louie, can you hear me? Louie, please open your eyes." He doesn't answer. He doesn't open his eyes. "Oh, dear God." I swallow my panic, somehow managing to remain somewhat calm. It's like I'm in the eye of a hurricane and any second a storm of emotions is going to overtake me. I gingerly reach my fingers to his neck and close my eyes, focusing on his pulse.

There.

It's light and slow but it's there. I move my fingers lightly across his scalp and when I get to the back of his head, I feel it. A huge gash, gushing blood. *Oh my God, it's too much blood. What do I do? What do I do?* Alex. I need to get Alex!

"Hang on Louie, I'm going to get help," I whisper, as I reluctantly pull myself away from his prone, unconscious body.

I have to take the steps slowly because of the ice. No doubt that's what caused Louie to fall, and I'll be no good to him if I end up beside him. Once I make it into the castle, I sprint down the hall towards the entry way like an antelope being chased by a lion. I take the stairs up to the second floor two at a time My heart is beating too loud in my ears, my breath is coming in tight, painful bursts, in my lungs, and my watery eyes are blurring my vision. Louie can't die! He can't!

I hesitate for only a split second once I reach the landing before launching myself to the right. Towards the secluded and off-limits portion of the castle.

The South Wing.

I have no idea where I'm headed, but I let my feet carry me anyway. I follow my gut and run, yelling at the top of my lungs as I fly through the darkness.

"Alex! Alex, where are you! Please, you have to help! Alex!"

I approach the first door I see and don't hesitate. I turn the doorknob and push it open, barreling inside. There's a small amount of light, barely enough to see anything, filtering in through a high window. There's nothing except old, dusty furniture covered in creepy white sheets. I turn and continue down the hall, yelling for Alex.

I come to another door and after a few seconds inside know he's not here either. The room looks like my insides feel. Everything is flipped over, topsy-turvy, and completely destroyed. It's a room full of nothing but broken things. The remnants of chaotic anger. The result of a beast. A cold shiver runs down my spine, but I ignore my rising fear and continue on.

At the end of the hall, I come to a huge, black wooden door with some kind of carving on it. It's too dark to make out and I'm in too much of a hurry to inspect it. Luckily the door opens, and I burst inside, yelling as much as my winded lungs will allow.

I know I'm in the right room now because there's a huge four-poster bed sitting smackdab in the middle of the room. I can't see much else because the light from dusk is all but faded now.

"Alex, please! Please, you have to—"

My ragged breath is suddenly forced out of my lungs as my back slams against a wall, and a heavy weight wraps around my neck, dangling me above the floor. Flashbacks of Gabriel rush behind my eyes before the image clears and I'm left staring into the eyes of The Beast. Red, glowing eyes stare at me from inches away, and long, sharp fangs snarl in my face. Blood. Is that blood on his lips? A guttural, vicious growl sends fear rocketing through my body and I'm so damn terrified, I can't move.

I can't think.

I can't breathe.

I can't focus.

I see spots. I blink and blink and blink, but it's no use. I'm about to pass out, but before I do, my body drops to the floor. My hands instinctively reach for my throat as I gasp for air. My breaths feel like knives slicing down my throat, stabbing into my air-starved lungs.

"What are you doing here?" an angry voice yells. "You were told never to come to this side of the castle!"

I recognize that deep voice. Only this time, there's nothing sexy about it. It doesn't slide over my skin like a teasing lover's touch. It's angry. And it terrifies me. *He* terrifies me.

"Shit!" he exclaims in frustration, his hands running through his hair as he paces in front of me. "Blood." He stops and stands in front of me. His face is tense with aggravation, but his voice is no longer an angry yell. "Why are you covered in blood?"

I try to speak but my voice is lost. Fear still races through my body, causing me to seize up. Alex, because he looks like Alex again, all traces of The Beast gone, moves towards me. My mind starts working again and I scramble backwards, trying to keep distance between us but the wall is immediately at my back. I sink to the floor and pull my knees to my chest, hiding my face behind them, trying to be as small as possible. My entire body is shaking uncontrollably, and my heart feels like it's going to explode.

Alex kneels in front of me but doesn't attempt to reach for me. I peek over my knees and see silver, regretful eyes staring back at me, but I can't stop seeing the red eyes and animal fangs that were seconds away from ripping out my throat.

"Bella...," he starts, running his hands through his hair again and closing his eyes briefly, "I'm so sorry. I'll explain everything, I promise, but first you have to tell me why you're covered in blood."

All I can manage is a small shake of my head.

"It's Luminex's blood. Is Louie hurt?" He speaks calmly and slowly, treating me like a scared child. Or better yet, like a scared little rabbit trapped in a corner.

I nod.

"Where is he, Bella? Tell me where he is so I can help him."

"He's on the steps. By the garden." My voice sounds hollow and far away. I don't recognize it.

Alex is out of the bedroom before I even finish my sentence. I hesitate for only a second before I'm on my feet and running out of the room, too. Only I'm not following him. My heart aches for Louie. I don't want to leave him. I want to know that he's going to be ok, but I can't stay here. I can't stay here with *him*. With The Beast.

I descend the main staircase in record time and race across the entryway towards the huge front doors. I grab the large handle and pull with all my strength. Surprisingly, the door swings open easily then I'm bounding down more stairs, careful not to slip on the snow-covered ice. I make it to solid ground and head straight for the forest and my home down below.

It's completely dark out, only the very tip of the moon visible over the mountain top, leaving me to navigate unknown territory at a pathetically slow pace. My adrenaline is starting to fade, alerting me to my injured ankle and sore ribs, but fear remains locked onto my heart in a death grip, pushing me forward. I trip over rocks and roots. Low branches and bushes claw at my clothes and skin, attempting to hold me captive. I push on, desperate to get as far away from Nightmare Castle as possible. I don't know how long I've been blindly running through the woods, but it feels like hours.

A haunting howl splits the night sky. A few seconds later, others erupt in response. *Oh shit! Oh shit! Get the hell out of here, Bella!* Another burst of adrenaline urges me back into a run, and I ignore the pain rocketing up my calf. I still can't see where the hell I'm going, and it doesn't take long before the uneven ground sends me sprawling to the frozen ground. Another howl, closer this time, has me clawing at the forest floor, desperately trying to get back on my feet. I make it another few steps before I'm thrown to the ground again.

I'm out of breath, my body is in bad shape, and I can feel all my injuries, including the new ones peppering my skin and sinking into my muscles. I try to push myself up again, but my arms collapse beneath me. My cheek hits the icy forest floor, my chest heaving for air. I just need to take a minute to catch my breath. Just a minute and then I'll keep going.

A low growl alerts me to the presence of danger. I push up onto my knees and my heart rate spikes again. Glowing eyes surround me.

Coyotes.

This is it. This is how I die.

ALEX

I should have never reacted that way. I haven't been uncontrolled in a long, long time. It's not like me to lose control of The Beast like that but she caught me off guard. And the thought of her seeing me...seeing what I had been doing...I panicked.

But I can't think about that right now as I carry Louie inside. He needs all of my attention and I'm going to give it to him, even though the look of fear in Bella's eyes is playing on repeat in my head. I push the image of her out of my mind as I lay Louie down on the kitchen island. I rush to the sink, start the hot water, and then run around the room gathering supplies. I fill a large bowl with hot water and set it down beside Louie, then dip a clean cloth in it and begin to clean the gash on his head. Once I've removed as much of the dried blood, snow, and dirt as I can, I press another clean cloth to the wound and apply steady pressure. I need to get it to stop bleeding so I can stitch it closed.

I feel like it's taken hours to get Louie patched up and settled on the couch in the sitting room, the same spot we brought Bella to not long ago. In reality, it's been about twenty minutes. I'm thankful that The Beast allows me to move and react much quicker than a human.

Louie woke as I was bandaging his wound and I was able to give him pain pills before settling him in front of the fire. I'm reluctant to leave him, but he's going to be asleep for a while and I need to find Bella. I need to find her and make this right. The last thing I ever wanted was for her to be afraid of me, for her to look at me and see my absolute worst quality. The Beast. This is not how I wanted her to find out.

I quickly make my way to her room and knock on the door. "Bella? It's Alex. Can we talk?" I hang my head as I'm met with silence. "Bella, please. Allow me to apologize and to explain." No response.

I close my eyes and listen for any signs that she's there on the other side, listening to me, but I can't sense anything. I slowly twist the knob and push the door open. "I'm coming in."

My eyes quickly sweep across the room before I walk into the bathroom. She's not here. I turn and run back the way I came. Maybe she's in the garden. I pass the blood on the steps, the moonlight making it look black and disturbing. I need to clean it as soon as possible. I don't want Bella to see it.

She's not at her usual spot on the bench either. "Fuck!" I mutter to myself. *How could I let this happen?* I pull at my hair and pace in front of the bench, my mind frantic. *Where is she?* My eyes dart to the forest sprawling down the mountainside and I don't even have to try and track her. I know she left. She's running as fast and as far away from me as she possibly can, and I don't blame her. The sound of a coyote's howl echoes up the mountain and I'm crashing through the trees before the rest of the pack responds.

The moonlight barely illuminates the forest floor which means Bella must be running blind. There's no way she's getting out on her own, especially with coyotes on her trail. It doesn't take long to find her, crouched on the ground, a huge coyote prowling towards her, lips pulled back, snarling, and ready to attack. The rest of the pack waits at her back. I can hear her heart hammering in her chest, the fear she felt for me earlier nothing compared to what I sense now.

I jump at the same time the coyote does. I tackle it in midair and we come crashing to the ground, rolling, and trying to gain dominance. Even though this coyote is large and insanely strong for a predator, he's no match for me. I wrap my arms around his massive neck and twist. The coyote lets out a pained whine before the crack of his spine meets my ears.

Bella's scream punches me in my gut and I'm by her side in an instant. The rest of the coyotes attack together and it's impossible to keep them all at bay without getting hurt. Claws and teeth sink into me as I fight to keep them off Bella. A large coyote manages to jump on my back, staggering me to my knees. I reach behind me, grip a handful of its fur, and rip it off me, slamming its back into the ground. It immediately goes limp. There are dead coyotes scattered around me as the final two limp off and disappear back into the woods.

I'm left standing in the middle of a circle of death. I close my eyes and slow my breathing, gathering what's left of my strength because I'm going to need it to face Bella. I just displayed The Beast yet again and I don't know if I can handle the look I'm about to see on her face. I take a deep breath and turn to face her.

She's pushing to her feet, her legs shaking, barely able to hold her, but she remains standing. Her eyes lock with mine and I see the fear, clear as day, shining through her wide blue eyes. What I didn't expect to see is a little bit of awe and, is that...*curiosity?* Whatever it is, I'm grateful for it. I'm grateful that it isn't just straight fear and hate staring back at me.

"Bella." I take a very slow, cautious step towards her. Her eyes widen but she doesn't move away from me. "Are you ok?" I ask, as I reach my hand towards her. My heart falls to the floor as she flinches away from my touch. I drop my hand in disappointment and regret, but again, I can't blame her.

"You're hurt." Her voice is low and raspy, and her eyes quickly skate over my body. My forearms are cut badly, my shirt is torn almost to shreds, showcasing more gashes on my chest and stomach. I'm practically covered in blood, both mine and coyote. I don't even want to know what my back looks like.

"I'm ok," I assure her. "Are you ok? Are you hurt?"

She shakes her head. "Nothing too bad."

"Let's go back to the castle, let me—"

"Louie," she interrupts, as if just remembering that he's hurt. "Is Louie ok?"

"He's ok at the moment. I took care of his head wound but he had a bad spill. I don't know what more may be wrong. He's resting now but we need to get back to him."

"We?"

"Yes, we. Please come back to the castle and let me explain everything. I...," I let out a heavy sigh, not once looking away from her, "I don't want you to leave."

I see the hesitation in her eyes. I know that she's in the same position she was in when I found her a week ago. She was running from a man that hurt her, a man that scared her. And now, that man is me, and I hate myself for it.

"Bella, please." I take a step toward her.

She backpedals quickly but then cries out in pain and falls to the ground. I don't think about it as I rush to her, kneeling beside her but not touching her. "What's wrong? You said you weren't hurt. Where are you hurt?"

"My ankle mostly. I think I hurt it again."

I slowly reach for her, and again I'm met with fear. I hang my head and run my hands down my face. "Bella." I look at her beautiful blue eyes and hold her gaze, pleading with her to hear me. "The legend is true, there is a beast that lives here. *I am The Beast.* But that's not the only thing I am. You've seen *me* for who I truly am. I may be part beast, with urges I can't deny, but I *can* control them. I will never lay an unwanted hand on you, much less a hurtful one. I'd never be that kind of monster."

"You already did." Her voice shakes and her eyes tear up.

My heart sinks in my chest. "I didn't mean to. You caught me off guard and I reacted terribly. I panicked. And it's not your fault, and there's no excuse for what I did to you." I sigh, exasperated and desperate for her to believe me. "I'm far from perfect and not above making mistakes. I can apologize until I'm blue in the face, but apologies don't mean shit. Let me prove it to you. Let me show you that you can trust me. Let me show you that you're completely safe with me and I will never, *ever*, hurt you. Please. Come back to the castle with me."

"Well, you did just save my life. And I don't think I can make it home now, even if I wanted to, and I want to make sure Louie is ok."

"Ok." I smile, trying to reassure her that this is the right choice.

"Ok," she whispers back.

I get to my feet and wait for her to join me. She struggles to stand, and it takes every ounce of my control not to help her, but I refuse to continue digging myself into a hole. I'm not going to do anything to scare her any more than she's already been. I'm not going to do anything to make her think any less of me. I already have my work cut out for me but I'm up for the challenge. For her.

She manages to take a couple of steps before she winces in pain and leans against a tree.

"Bella, please, let me help you."

"You're hurt, too," she argues.

I shake my head. "Trust me, I'm fine." I approach her slowly.

"I'm going to pick you up and carry you. Is that ok?"

She looks at me for a long time. I can practically see the wheels turning in her mind, considering all her options before she nodding, giving me consent. I lean down and slide one arm behind her back. Her arm hooks around my neck as my other arm catches her behind the knees and I scoop her into my arms. Once again, I'm carrying an injured and dirty Bella in my arms through my forest. Only this time she's awake and I can hear how hard her heart is pounding in her chest and I can feel her eyes on me. Her uncertainty.

"I'm not going to hurt you." I meet her gaze, hoping she sees the genuine truth to my words. I've said them before but I need her to believe me. I pull her tighter to my chest, needing to feel her next to me. She gasps and her lips part, and I can't help but let my eyes fall to her full, luscious lips. Her tongue swipes across her bottom lip and I have to close my eyes and clench my jaw. My warning to her rings in my ears.

And if you keep licking and biting that lip, tempting me, I won't be able to stop from tasting it for myself.

I don't know if she remembers and is testing me, or if she genuinely licked her lips unconsciously. Either way, as much as I want to capture her mouth with mine, now is definitely not the right time. I've ruined everything that was building between us, and I have to restart from square one. No, I have to start from beyond square one now. I need to regain her trust, which is not going to be easy.

I use this time while I have her in my arms, where she's forced to listen to me, to say what's weighing heavily on my mind. "I know that you were hurt by someone who claimed they loved you. I know this person did exactly what I did, and I know how scared you are. You have every right to be, and I hate myself for being the one to cause you this pain and fear. I promise, I'm not like him. I know you don't believe me, how can you?" I scoff, incredulously. "Yes, I'm a beast, but I'm not a beast you ever need to fear, Bella, and I'm going to spend as long as it takes proving to you that I'm different."

"Why?"

"Because I've met a lot of people in my lifetime. I haven't always been alone, hiding out in a castle. I know a beautiful heart when I see one, and yours is the most beautiful one I've ever seen. I should let you go. I should let you walk away but…."

"But what?"

"I don't want to let you go," I say, in a pained whisper.

I'm being vulnerable when I said I never would be again. I'm opening up my heart to this woman knowing she's only going to take it with her to the grave. I'm now playing an active part in my own destruction, and I can't seem to help it. If anyone is going to destroy me one last time, I want it to be her.

I want it to be Bella.

Bella

BLINDFOLD BY SLEEPING WOLF

Once again, I'm soaking in a hot bath, my body aching all over. My skin has several knicks, scratches, and bruises from my escape attempt. Honestly, how freaking reckless was that? What was I thinking running into those woods, alone, and with absolutely no light to see by? I'm lucky I survived one trip through the forest much less two. And if Alex hadn't come after me, I wouldn't have. Those coyotes were literally attacking when he showed up and saved me.

He saved me.

Twice.

That has to count for something, right? But what happened in his bedroom refuses to be forgotten. The eyes. The teeth. The voice. He was sooo angry at me. And when his hand wrapped around my throat, it was Gabriel all over again. I know it's unfair to compare him to Gabriel. He's nothing like him. He's not arrogant and self-centered. He's not trying to chase after me in hopes of claiming some prize he can display on his arm. I really do think his interest in me is genuine. Then again, that's what I thought when Gabriel first approached.

"Gah! Why is my judgement complete and utter shit?"

I don't know what to do and I don't know what to believe. All I know is that I want the truth. I want to know everything about Alex and how it's even possible for him to be The Beast. I don't understand what that even means. I always thought The Beast was an actual monster of some kind. An animal. Now I come to find out he's a six-foot-two, sexy, charming, well-read man, that brings out a desire in me so deep and strong it physically affects my body in ways I don't even understand.

Seeing him fight off those coyotes with his bare hands called to some deep, dark kink I never knew I had. Jesus…it was hot. I mean I was scared shitless and afraid he was going to be killed, but…holyyyyy…I simultaneously wanted to care for his wounds and jump his bones right there on the forest floor. *There is something definitely wrong with me*. And then when he was carrying me in his arms, he held me so tightly, so close to his chest, it was almost as if he couldn't get close enough to me. And I'm ashamed to say, I felt the same way. When his eyes dropped to my lips, I desperately wanted him to kiss me. Nothing else mattered except for the want in his eyes.

Not The Beast.

Not the coyotes.

Not my injured body.

Nothing mattered to me in that moment except for the man I've come to know in my short time here. Alexander Knightwell. And hell, maybe I don't know him at all. I *don't* know him at all, clearly. But it feels like I do. I want to get to know him on *so* many different levels. But is how I'm feeling genuine? Or is it because there's never been anyone outside of Gabriel even remotely interested in me? Am I attracted to Alex because he's new and different and seems to be equally attracted to me? Am I attracted to the idea of him being my escape from New Haven? No, the butterflies in my stomach and heat between my legs when he looks at me has nothing to do with New Haven and everything to do with him.

I sigh as I move to get out of the cooling water. The answer is, *I just don't know*. I don't have answers for anything I'm thinking or feeling. What I do know is that I want to be there when Louie wakes up. I limp over to the wardrobe and find more leggings, a sweater, and some thick, slipper-like socks that come all the way up my calves. It's comfortable and cozy...and cute. Just in case I see Alex.

I take my time walking to the sitting room. I've done a number on my ankle, it's almost as bad as it was the first time. So much for taking time to heal. *Seriously, that was so stupid,* I chastise myself. When I get to the door, I hesitate. Alex is here. My heart immediately takes note and reacts to his presence. *Damn foolish heart.* He's sitting in the same chair that he occupied last time. Louie is laying on the sofa and it looks like he's still fast asleep. I decide that right now my attention needs to be on Louie and not on everything that's swirling in my mind when it comes to the distractingly gorgeous man intently watching me.

"How's he doing?" I whisper, as I approach them. Instead of taking my seat, I kneel down beside the couch and take Louie's hand in mine, settling in on the floor by his side.

Alex's intense gaze never leaves me. "Honestly, he's a bit touch and go. It was a serious wound and at his age...."

I swallow my sudden tears as I look down at the old man who's become so special to me in such a short period of time. He looks so old, so fragile. So completely different than the vivacious and lively old man I've gotten to know. It's terrifying to see him like this and I'm holding onto everything I have not to fall to pieces next to him.

"This is my fault. If I hadn't been outside...if I hadn't told him to join me..."

I gasp when I feel Alex's warm fingertips on my chin, gently pulling my face away from Louie and forcing me to meet his beautiful silver eyes. "Bella, if you never believe another word I say, I need you to believe this. This is not your fault. It was a terrible accident, nothing more."

My chin trembling in his gentle hold, his eyes imploring me to believe him, and I want to. I want to fall into his eyes, into his arms. I want him to make everything better. I want to erase the last two hours and start over. As if he can see my thoughts written on my face, he slowly wraps his arms around me and pulls me into his chest.

I keep one hand wrapped around Louie's delicate one, and the other I wrap around Alex's body. He falls to the floor and drags me into his lap. I'm straddling him and it's nothing like I fantasized it would be. My head is buried in his chest, my hand fisting the back of his shirt as I cling to him and Louie for dear life. I let all the tears that have built up from my last days with Gabriel, my near-death experience in the woods, and Louie's uncertain condition pour silently down my cheeks. I don't make a sound but my body shakes, betraying my tears.

Alex's strong hands firmly cradling my head and back, holding me tightly to him as he whispers reassuring and comforting words in my ear. All thoughts of The Beast I saw just hours ago are gone. How can the Alex I'm experiencing now be the same Alex from earlier? I push the thought out of my head and just fall into his hold, feeling completely and utterly safe.

I don't know how much time goes by, but Alex never lets me go. He seems perfectly content to hold me as long as I need him to. And God, I never want to leave his arms. They feel so good wrapped around me. It dawns on me that I've never been held like this before. I've never been comforted by anyone other than my mother, and mostly only when I was a little girl. I've never realized how incredibly lonely I am. Because being alone and being lonely are two incredibly different things. Even when I was with Gabriel, I was still lonely. I think I always knew his interest in me was one-sided and selfish. It wasn't real. It wasn't deep. Even when we were having sex, it was never intimate. Not like this, not like what I'm feeling simply being held by Alex. Just being in his lap, completely innocent, feels better than anything I ever felt with Gabriel. *How can this feel so right?*

I finally pull away from him and he lets me go, his hands falling softly to my hips. There's a huge wet spot on the front of his shirt from where my tears soaked through. I feel the blush creep into my cheeks, and I hang my head as I mumble, "I'm so sorry."

Once again, Alex's fingers find my chin and lift my face up to look at him. His eyes search mine, darting back and forth. "What on earth are you apologizing for?"

"You're shirt. I ruined it. I didn't mean to—"

"It's just a shirt, Bella, you didn't *ruin* anything. It will dry, and even if it doesn't, or has some stain...," he moves his hands to cup my face, his thumbs gently drying my cheeks, "there's not a shirt in this damn world I would care about more than you."

I stare into his eyes, inches away. How can one man be so fucking beautiful. How can a pair of eyes be so damn captivating? "You're so different than anyone I've ever met."

He returns his hands to my waist, still apparently content to let me sit in his lap. "What do you mean?" His brows gently furrow, and he tilts his head to the side, studying me.

"You're...*nice.*"

His brows furrow even more. He almost looks a little angry. "Are you saying no one's ever been nice to you before?"

I shrug one shoulder. "I mean, sure. Some have, here and there, but it's never been genuine. It's always been when someone wants something from me. The only one who's ever been honestly kind to me is a child." I scoff. "If I had done this...," I gesture to his wet shirt, "to the guy that claimed he loved me, I would have never heard the end of it. How I ruined his shirt and how I'm too emotional and need to grow up and get thicker skin."

"He sounds like a fucking idiot." His voice is low and deep, angry. His hand is back on my chin, holding my face so I can't look away. "You never have to apologize to me and you never have to try and be someone you're not. If you need to cry, cry. If you need to scream, scream. If you need to break something, break it. I will never condemn you for *feeling* and being who you are."

I let his words sink in as his stare does the same, sinking into me, into my chest and into my goddamned traitorous heart. I want to believe him. The way he's looking at me, the way he's holding me, it's everything real that I never knew existed. My eyes drop to his lips, and I realize a second too late that my tongue wets mine. Alex lets out a pained groan and his hand on my waist tightens, his fingers digging into my skin as he pulls me harder against him. I feel his dick stir beneath me and I instinctively grind my hips, pushing against him. Time has stopped. In this moment, nothing exists but us.

"Bella." His strangled voice pulls me out of my desire-filled brain fog, and I meet his eyes again and gasp.

I've never seen him look at me like this before and it's everything I ever thought it would be. It's hot and intoxicating, blazing a trail of desire right through my chest, settling between my legs. I can feel myself getting wet, responding to the subtle grip at my waist, the hardness between my legs, and the heat in his eyes.

His thumb trails along my bottom lip. "Bella, I really want to ki—"

Before he can finish, my eyes snap to Louie as his hand twitches in mine. "Louie." I completely forgot I was still holding onto his hand and this situation with Alex suddenly feels so wrong. This is not the time or place to be seconds away from embarrassing myself to the point of no return.

I feel the heat of the blush on my face as I start to move off Alex's lap. "Oh my God, I can't believe I did that. I was practically dry humping you and I just finished bawling into your chest, not to mention you're hurt, and I must have been hurting you even worse, and Louie is right here and oh my God, you must think I'm a complete nut job. I don't even—"

"The Master is teasing you again, I see." Louie's voice comes out low and weak but amused nonetheless, making me smile.

"Louie!" I whisper yell. His eyes slowly open and he turns his head, wincing in pain, as he searches for us. I feel Alex at my back, looking over me to see Louie.

"How are you feeling, old man?" Alex asks. His words are teasing but he can't hide the worry in his tone.

"I'm afraid to say I've been better. I feel like I took a tumble down some stone steps."

"You *did* take a tumble down some stone steps! I was so scared," I say, voice shaking. I blink back tears and force a smile. Now is not the time to cry. I need to be strong for Louie's sake right now. "But you're ok. You're going to be ok." I squeeze his hand.

"What can I get you? What do you need?" Alex asks softly.

"Something for the pain would be good, Master."

"You can't have more pain meds on an empty stomach. How about I get you some soup to start?"

Louie moves to nod his head then winces and stops, laying as still as he can. "Alright. And some of my favorite tea if you don't mind."

"Not at all, my friend." Alex stands to leave. "I'll be right back but you're in good hands."

"Prettier hands than you, I'd say," Louie teases, once again making me smile in the worst of situations.

"I can't argue with you there," he agrees, and then heads out of the sitting room, leaving us alone.

"How are you feeling, really?" I ask, watching his face closely.

He sighs. "I'm tired, my dear. So very tired. If I'm being honest, I don't much feel like fighting anymore."

"Oh Louie, don't say that." I have to fight to speak around the growing lump in my throat.

"Don't cry, dear. I've lived a longer life than I'd ever intended. You know this."

"I know." I sniff, wiping at my wet cheeks. "It's just that I've only just come to know you and… and well, I'm selfish and I want you here for a long time yet."

"You've really made my last days such a pleasure dear, truly, but my sweet Claire and Chloe have been waiting on me for fifty-five years, and I've been waiting to reunite with them. I can hear them calling to me," he says in awe, a smile spreading across his face. "I'm ready, Bella. I'm ready." He pats my hand, still gripping his.

I can't speak. The sorrow at the thought of losing Louie has taken my voice and damn near all the air in my lungs. I've never been close to anyone other than my mother, and I've never had to face losing anyone like this. I've never had to experience the death of someone I love. And wow, that truth comes out of nowhere. I love Louie.

"I love you," I declare quickly, as if I need to say it now, before it's too late.

"I love you too, dear. May I ask a favor of you?"

"Anything," I insist.

"Stay here with Alex. He's going to need you now more than ever. Even if he doesn't want to ask, or to even admit it, he needs you, Bella."

"But without you here, how can you know I'm safe? Because I, umm… when you got hurt, I went looking for Alex. I found his room and…," I swallow, remembering what happened, "and he…*attacked* me."

Louie's eyes widen slightly. "Tell me what happened."

I tell him how I went running through the South Wing, finding the abandoned rooms until I found him, and about The Beast.

"I'm honestly surprised. He hasn't lost control…well, ever. You must have really spooked him."

"Me? Spooked him?!" I scoff. "I think it's safe to say it was the other way around."

"What I'm trying to say is Alex hasn't opened up to anyone, even me, like he has with you. As much as he'll try to deny it, you matter to him already and whatever he was doing when you went running into his room, he didn't want you to see."

"What could he possibly have been doing that I wouldn't want to see?"

Louie closes his eyes and sighs. He really does look extremely tired, and I feel bad being so selfish, needing to know everything about Alex instead of simply caring for Louie.

"The Master's story is not mine to tell."

"Louie, you have—"

"But…," he interrupts my arguing, "there are some journals. He keeps them in his desk in the library on the third floor. Read them before you judge him, and what you saw. He is not like you and I in a lot of ways, but he has one of the biggest, most genuine hearts I've ever known. His feelings for you are pure, and he deserves a little happiness, dear. Trust me. And trust your gut. I think you know what I'm saying to be true."

"What are you two whispering about in here?" Alex asks, announcing his return.

"Why you, of course."

"Louie!" I chide.

"Ahh, once again I'm the topic of conversation between you two busybodies, huh?" he chuckles, not at all caring that we were discussing him. He sets the tray down on the table and I reluctantly move away, allowing him access to Louie.

I watch as Alex helps Louie into a sitting position, my heart squeezing with worry at every wince and whimper that leaves Louie's lips. I can't believe this is happening. He went from fine one second to talking about letting go the next, and I'm not ready to let him go. But it's not fair to Louie for me to be so selfish when this is what he wants. He wants to reunite with his family, and I don't blame him. I would want that, too. I was just thinking about how lonely I am in my life, and I can't imagine how lonely Louie has been for most of his. If he chooses to let go, I need to accept it. I need to support him.

I stand and go to the fire, stirring the logs to give myself some kind of distraction as I try and get a hold of my tears. I don't want Louie to feel any kind of guilt because of me. He absolutely deserves his happy ending.

After some long, pained minutes, Louie manages to eat a bowl of chicken noodle soup, take a few sips of his favorite toasted brown sugar rooibos tea, and then swallow another pain pill. He remains on the sofa, in front of the fire, content to not let us fuss too much over him.

"He'll be out for the rest of the night and probably most of the day." Alex sighs as he sinks into the chair. "I don't want to think the worst but...."

"But it doesn't look good," I whisper.

"No. It doesn't." He stares off into the flames, a faraway look in his eyes.

"Oh my God," I say, in shock.

Alex's eyes snap to me. "What? What is it?"

"I'm such an idiot." I laugh a bit maniacally. "Louie said he's been here, with *you*, for fifty-five years."

"He has." His eyes are steady on me.

"He's an old man. And you...," I gesture to him, "you are most definitely *not*. I don't know why that didn't register until now. Wow! Maybe I also hit my head harder than I thought because this is crazy!

How are you not an old man, too? What the hell is going on here? *What are you?*"

"I suppose now is as good a time as any for this conversation. I just ask that you please have an open mind, hear me out, and don't judge me too quickly."

He seems just as pained as Louie as he sits across from me, about to tell me everything I need to know about him, about The Beast. I'm suddenly extremely nervous. Do I really want to know? Do I want this idea I have of Alex to be twisted and turned upside down in a way that will ruin everything I feel for him?

No.

Yes.

Damn it. Yes! I need to know the truth. I need to see him for everything he is before I end up in another situation like the one with Gabriel, where I thought I knew the truth and was so horribly wrong.

I take a deep breath and let it out slowly. "Alright. I'm ready."

Bella

"I am The Beast you've grown up fearing," he starts. His tone is matter-of-fact, disconnected from his story and his feelings. "I've been The Beast of legend that has been passed down from one generation to the next for centuries. It has always been me."

"How…," I clear me throat, "how is that possible?"

"There are things out there, in the world, beyond what you know. Beyond what most people know. People…*beasts* like me, used to be far more common, but evolution and fear have all but destroyed that world. And honestly, it's for the best. We were…*monsters*. It was either destroy or be destroyed. We were arrogant and narrow-minded. We thought we were better than humans and never even considered a world where we could live alongside them. And so, we did what we did best, we killed. Each of us determined to be the strongest, the most feared." His eyes look past me, haunted with memories I can't even begin to fathom.

"I'm sorry, but I'm not following," I say slowly, confused, and trying to understand what he's telling me and failing miserably. "Who, or what, are you talking about? What don't I know about the world?"

"Legends, lore, fairytales, they all start somewhere. Sure, they can be exaggerated over time but mainly they're true."

"Alex, please. What are you talking about. Just tell me. What are you?"

"Do you honestly have no idea? Have you not put any of the clues together?"

I rub my forehead, tired of the runaround and vague information. "I honestly don't kn—"

"The nightly schedule. Not aging. I survive off the blood of others."

What? What did he just say? He survives off the blood of others? If that's true, how can Louie think I'm safe here? I can feel the fear starting to climb back up my chest, my heart racing as if it can run away for me and keep us safe. The red eyes, the fangs, and the blood on his lips all makes sense now.

"Vampire," I whisper, my voice barely audible, breathless, and scared. My eyes widen as I stare at the seemingly harmless man sitting across from me and, suddenly, I see him for what he is. A predator. His grace and strength. The way he was able to rip coyotes apart with his bare hands. It all makes sense now and yet it can't be real. "Vampires aren't real."

"We are." His voice is still calm and controlled. He's sitting incredibly still, as if one wrong move will have me racing toward the door and out into the forest again. I can't say he's wrong. "I can hear your heart hammering in your chest, I can hear the blood running through your veins, and I can taste your fear on my tongue," he says flatly, until he finally breaks a little, revealing his own emotion. "And I *hate* that you're afraid of me. It kills something inside of me to see the way you're looking at me right now. They way you looked at me in my bedroom."

"Do you blame me?" I ask, voice trembling, as I sit just as still as he is, afraid that if I move, I'll awaken The Beast inside of him.

He sighs in defeat and shakes his head. "Of course not. I know I lost whatever trust you had in me the moment I laid my hands on you.

I regret it more than you can ever know, but I can't take it back. I can only promise that it will never happen again. I will never hurt you, Bella. I will never take your blood without your consent. I would rather die."

"Can you? Die, I mean."

"Yes, of course I can. Fire can kill me. So will a beheading or and stabbing of the heart with pure silver. If I don't feed for long enough, I can die that way as well, but I will become something I never want to be long before that happens. The Beast won't allow me to starve myself. I can control the hunger just fine, I can go days without needing blood, but I've never tried to control it at desperate levels. I don't want to have to try."

"What about the sun?" I ask, remembering stories I've read about vampires.

"The sun weakens me and hurts my skin if I'm exposed to it directly, but it won't actually kill me. It's just...excruciatingly painful."

"So, you've...," I swallow, my fear pounding in my throat, making it hard to speak, "you've killed people."

"Yes. But not in a very, very long time."

"What about the people that have gone missing from New Haven? That was you?"

"Once upon a time, I was a...hunter. I used to wait for people to venture out into the woods so that I could feed. But again, that's not who I am anymore. That's not who I want to be."

"How have you stayed...fed all this time if you're not hunting?"

"People like Louie." He nods to the old man asleep on the sofa next to us. "Louie sought me out. He wanted me to kill him, and I refused. Instead, he stayed here with me and became my friend. It was his choice. I didn't make him stay."

"But you *feed* on him."

"Yes."

"Oh my God." I push the palms of my hands into my eyes,

trying to wipe away the images flashing through my mind. "This is crazy. This is all crazy! Or worse, *I'm* going crazy. I've hit my head and I'm going crazy."

"You're not crazy, Bella. You're beautiful and perfect, and I'm so glad our paths crossed. I never wanted to bring you here, to subject you to this life, to *me*. I know what I am, and I don't blame you for fearing me or wanting to run and put as much distance between us as you can. But you're here. For whatever reason, I found you, and against my better judgement I brought you here. I never intended to speak with you much less *feel* anything for you, but I do. I think you feel it too, and despite the fact that I shouldn't, I desperately want you to stay here...with me."

"Because you need me!" I shout, and then immediately look to Louie, making sure I didn't wake him. I lower my voice. "You need to *feed* on me," I spit out in disgust. "Now that Louie is hurt and may not make it. That's the only reason why you want me here!"

He sighs heavily. "I know it looks that way but trust me, it's not. I have enough blood saved up to last me a very, very long time. I don't need to feed on you. And if it ever comes down to that, there will always be someone else, other options. There always is. I haven't hunted or taken blood from an unwilling person in centuries. I want you here because, for the first time in way too long, I don't feel alone."

I hold his pleading gaze. He looks and sounds so genuine. He hasn't tried to hurt me or feed on me. He hasn't done anything to make me feel unsafe except for the one time when I went into *his* bedroom and interfered in whatever he was doing. I can't lie and say I haven't felt exactly what he just explained. I feel seen, truly seen, for the first time in my life.

"What happened in your bedroom?" I ask, needing to know the truth. "Why did you respond like that? Why did you attack me?"

Another heavy breath. "I was feeding...," he hesitates, and

looks way, jaw tense before finding my eyes again. "I was feeding on a rat, and I didn't want you to see me like that. You caught me completely off guard and then I smelled all the blood on you. It triggered my defenses and I panicked. I'm sorrier than you'll ever know. I never wanted you to see that. I never wanted to hurt you."

The image of him feeding on a rat churns my stomach. "Why were you feeding on a rat when you have Louie?"

"Louie's body has slowly been getting weaker and weaker as he's aged. I don't want to take as much from him, so I've been feeding on animals here and there, to supplement when I need. I know how it sounds but I'm not a monster."

"I...." I don't know what to think much less what to say.

He's a vampire. What else is real that I never knew existed? It's like my entire life has been a lie. I've been more than sheltered, I've been...*oblivious*. And so have the people of New Haven. Everything suddenly feels so small and insignificant. Lucille, Gabriel, his friend Bradley, none of them matter in the grand scheme of things. Vampires are fucking real! And even worse, I've been crushing on and fantasizing about one. Louie's voice echoes in my mind.

Stay here, with Alex. He's going to need you now more than ever. Even if he doesn't want to ask, or to even admit it, he needs you, Bella.

"I...umm, I just need some time to think about...all of this."

"Ok." He nods his head and gives me a weak smile.

I can see the sadness and fear of rejection written all over his features. I don't like seeing him like this, but I can't tell him what I don't feel. I'm not going to lie to him and tell him everything he's revealed is fine and that I don't care because I *do* care...a lot!

"I'd like to show you something if you'd let me. I think it's something you'd really enjoy and might help take your mind off things any time you need a distraction."

"What is it?" I ask, skeptically.

"A special place. One I don't often share but would like to share with you."

"Ok," I whisper.

He gets up slowly and starts walking out of the sitting room. I glance over at Louie, and he sees my hesitation.

"He's going to be out for a long time. There's nothing more we can do for him."

I nod because I know he's right. He grabs one of the lanterns from the side table next to the sofa and leads me down the hallway. We ascend the stairs that lead to our bedrooms, and he turns right at the top, walking towards the South Wing. I hesitate at the top of the stairs, the memory of what happened last time I was here sharp and vivid in my mind, and now I know the truth about him. *He's a vampire and you're following him into the dark unknown, Bella!* I can't help the panic that grips me.

Alex turns to face me, and my heart breaks a little. He looks absolutely devastated. "I'm not going to hurt you," he repeats, for the millionth time.

And the logical part of my brain knows he's not going to hurt me. If he was, he wouldn't need to take me anywhere to do it. He can hurt me anywhere, and he can easily overpower me if he wanted to, but he doesn't want to. He wants me to trust him. Once again, Louie's voice echoes in my mind.

Trust me. And trust your gut.

My gut is telling me that I'm safe here, that I've always been safe here. So, I nod, and continue following him down the dark hallway.

We come to a stop between the two rooms I discovered earlier, and Alex reaches out and pushes on a section of the wall. A secret door swings inward, revealing a set of narrow steps leading up into more darkness.

He begins to climb, and I have little choice but to follow him or stay here. I follow him. The stairs are steep, and I trail my palm along the wall to help keep my balance, but then my foot lands awkwardly on one of the steps. My hurt ankle screams in protest as I try to catch my weight on it, and it buckles underneath me. I let out a cry of pain and panic as I start to fall backwards. Alex is suddenly there, his strong arm wrapping around my waist, pulling me into his firm chest, and saving me from a fall that would surely have killed me. Ok, maybe not *killed* me.

I'm breathless and breathing hard, my heart pounding in my ears, and I'm not sure if it's because I almost just biffed it, if I'm scared that I'm this close to him, or if it's because I'm excited to be this close to him. I know I should be scared of him, but when he keeps saving me like this and looks at me like this…it's hard to see him as anything dangerous.

"You ok?" he asks quietly, his voice sounding even more intimate in the dark, private stairwell, as it whispers across my skin.

"Yeah." My voice is low and breathy.

I hope he thinks it's from the panic of almost falling and not because my palm is flat against his rock-hard stomach. I can feel the hard planes of his abs beneath my hand, and I have the strongest urge to slide my hand under his shirt and trace every muscle with my fingertips.

He slowly releases me, making sure I'm steady on my feet before he lets go. Honestly, I wouldn't be steady on solid ground with him this close to me, and I can smell his clean skin and the spicy scent of cinnamon on his breath.

"Here. Take my hand," he offers. "We're almost there."

I slide my hand into his and immediately feel better when his large hand gently wraps around mine. The warmth of this one simple touch seems to seep into my body and ignite a fire inside of me. I don't know why he affects me this way but it's damn near impossible to fight. I want to be cautious and not the naïve girl I was with Gabriel but this thing with Alex feels entirely different. I can't ignore it and I can't run from it. *Do you even want to?*

I don't have time to answer my own question because all thoughts are wiped out of my head as we reach the landing and Alex hits several light switches.

Books.

Rows and rows and shelf after shelf of books are laid out in front of me. I step further into the room and slowly spin, looking at every inch of books surrounding me. I tilt my head up and the shelves seem to go on forever and ever, climbing up the tower.

"Oh, Alex," I whisper in awe.

"Do you like it?"

"Do I like it?" I mock. "I love it!" I exclaim, a cheesy smile on my face.

When I finally bring my eyes back to him, he has his hands pushed into his pockets and his chin dipped down, a shy smile on his lips. "I'm glad you do. That smile on your face is everything to me right now. I was afraid I'd never see it again."

It's my turn to duck my head shyly before returning my gaze to the room around me, trying to hide my damn blushing cheeks once again. "I think I've died and gone to Heaven! I can't believe you have all of this."

"It's yours. Whenever you want."

I turn back to meet his intense silver gaze. "Do you mean that?"

"With all my heart."

"I don't want to intrude on your space. You said you don't share this with people, and I don't—"

"You're not just people to me, Bella. I want you here. I want you in my space. I want you everywhere. I. Want. You."

I think my heart drops into my vagina because it's pulsing like it has its own heartbeat, at not only his words but the way he said them. The way he's looking at me with that heated desire again. All traces of the shy, insecure Alex from just a moment ago are gone. The Alex that stands in front of me now is a man. A sexy man that knows exactly what he wants.

Me.

And God above, forgive me for my sins, but I want him, too. I want this man despite everything he's told me.

He's a vampire.

A killer.

A beast.

And I want him like I've never wanted a goddamned thing in my life. So, what does that make me?

ALEX

In Chains by Shaman's Harvest

I left her in the library. She was worried about leaving Louie alone even though I told her he would be fast asleep for hours, but she didn't care. She demanded that one of us be with him at all times.

"If you were in his position, would you want to be left alone?" she had asked. "It's about knowing someone is there with you. He may not be awake but that doesn't mean he's not aware. He'll know if we're there or not," she insisted.

And how can I deny her when her request is so logical. If I was in Lumineux's position, of course I'd want someone with me. I'd want *her* with me. Hell, who am I kidding? Even if her request was outlandish and made zero sense, I still wouldn't deny her. I'll give her everything she wants and needs and more. I'd cut out my own dead heart and give it to her if I thought she'd want it.

Speaking of my heart, her concern for Louie does weird things to it. It makes it swell and feel like it's being crushed all at the same time. She's exactly the type of person I want in my life. She's stunning to look at but she's even more beautiful to be around. She's calm and soothing, funny, and awkwardly adorable, and when she was in my lap, seconds away from putting those tempting lips on mine, looking at me with heated blue flames, she was the sexiest woman alive.

And my cock thought so, too. I could feel the warmth between her legs as she straddled my lap, and I just couldn't keep him in check. Just imagining sliding into her warmth sends a shiver down my spine and makes my balls ache. Jesus, I've never been this wound-up and desperate before. *It's because you haven't had sex in ages*, my rational brain reminds me. But my heart says something entirely different. Either way, I want her. No, I *need* her. Fuck, I hope she chooses to stay.

I've done all I can for the moment. I've left her to her thoughts, and I have no doubt she's going to make her decision soon, if she hasn't already.

You could make her stay, a vicious little voice echoes in the back of my mind. I ignore it and push it back into the far reaches of my mind. I would never do that to her. I would never be able to live with myself if I held her here against her will. I want her to choose to stay here, especially now that she knows the truth. I want her to *choose me*.

I sit on the couch with Louie instead of in the chair. I gently lift up his feet and slide beneath them, setting them back on my lap. I let my head fall back and close my eyes, releasing a frustrated, pent-up breath.

"I really fucked up this time, Lumineux. I could really use you now, you know. Your advice and wisdom."

I open my eyes and look into the old man's face. The reality of how old he is kicking me in the gut. It's like he aged overnight. I know that's not true, but it was harder to see when he was always so full of life. Even though he really didn't have much to live for day to day, you'd never be able to tell with how kind and upbeat he always was. He's one of the few genuinely good ones.

Like Bella.

"I sure could use your connection with Bella. She trusts you, and for some god-awful reason that I can't fathom, she actually *likes* you," I tease, hoping that somewhere in there, he can hear me. "But nooooo, you had to go and knock yourself silly, leaving me to clean up my own mess." The bedroom incident plays back in my mind on repeat. "And boy what a mess I've made, my friend. If there's any chance of cleaning this one up, it's slim."

I look back over at Louie's face, peaceful in his drug-induced sleep, and I can't help but be grateful for one thing. "I'm glad you didn't have to see me like that," I whisper. "You would have been so disappointed. You would have been ashamed of me. Like I am."

A gentle snore is the only response I get.

I scoot down lower, getting more comfortable as I sit in silence with my dear friend, listening to his shallow but steady breaths, evidence he's still with me. And I cling to that sound. I hold on to it as tightly as I can. No matter how many deaths I've seen, no matter how many friends I've had to let go, it never gets easier.

I'm not sure how my heart beats in my chest, considering I'm technically dead, but it does. And even worse, it still feels pain. *I still feel pain.* I can feel the noose snaking around it, slowly tightening, squeezing one more life out of it. It feels as though all of those that have crossed my path are somehow tied to my own bleeding heart, and when they die, I die a little more inside, too. Honestly, I don't know how many more pieces I have left to give.

I feel like I'm at my wits end. A breaking point. I don't want to do this anymore. I can't go on enduring all of these losses and being the only one to go on living, again and again, for fucking eternity. My only tie to hope is currently in my library, and that rope is more like a thin thread being pulled tightly, ready to break at any second. Even if it doesn't break, if that thread somehow manages to reinforce itself, it's still only temporary. It can build up to an unbreakable thread only to slowly unravel due to time.

She will age.

She will die.

I will not.

The thought of being with Bella overrides my common sense. I shouldn't want to subject myself to the kind of torture she will surely bring. I can barely withstand the pieces being chipped off my heart now. What happens when she takes the whole goddamned thing with her? What will happen to me then? What will I become?

I shudder at the image of a beast, a truly heartless beast, terrorizing the world. Because without a heart, that's all I'll be. Stripped down to the very core of being undead. So why go down this road? Why take the chance when I know the only outcome?

Maybe I shouldn't. Maybe I should just let her leave and save whatever sanity I have left. Save whatever scraps of my heart still remain. She deserves more anyway.

"Well, old man, at least I don't have to hear you tell me what I need right now. There's a silver lining."

What I need is for Bella to stay, like Lumineux said, to continue to feed The Beast. But if she stays, I won't be able to stop myself from falling. I've already climbed the fucking mountain. I'm standing on the cliff, teetering on the edge, peering over to see my certain destruction down below. But there's no denying one thing, the free fall will be fucking thrilling while it lasts.

All good things come to an end.

Bella

I'm taken aback and practically speechless by the sight in front of me. I can't believe all of this is here, in this castle. I can't believe this is all Alex's. It's such a shame that something so magnificent isn't seen or appreciated by others. Although, if it was mine, I can't say I'd be any more generous with it. I love my books and get quite possessive and protective over them, so I don't fault him for keeping this place private and safe. I don't blame him for not wanting to share it. But he did. He shared it with *me*.

It's yours. Whenever you want.

His words have nestled their way inside my heart, hunkering down and getting cozy. Not that my damn heart needs another reason to like him. I know what this place means to him because I know exactly what it would mean to me if it were mine. He may as well have dropped down on a knee and proposed, that's how big this gesture is. And I'm excited and terrified at the same time. I know I should leave. I should go back home and save myself while I have the chance because what on earth is going to happen to me if I stay?

What if he loses control of The Beast and hurts me, or worse, kills me. I shake my head and roll my eyes at myself. *You don't really believe that*. Louie has been here for fifty-five years and has been just fine. There's no proof or sign of The Beast having ever inflicted pain on Louie. And I don't think he'd lie about it if it had happened. My mind keeps racing, going round and round in pointless fucking circles, trying to decide what's right and what's wrong. What I should do versus what I want to do. Because right now, what I want is to stay right here. I could live in this room for the rest of my life and be a completely content shut-in.

Once again, I push away the challenging thoughts, the questions I don't have answers to, and take in my surroundings. Now, seeing this and the way it's so obviously cared for, all my doubts about Alex being a genuine reader are squashed. No one collects this number of books just because. And as my fingertips happily dance across the shelves, touching and exploring titles, I'm shocked to see so many I know. They're not just old, dusty tomes lining these shelves.

There's fantasy, romance, thrillers, sci-fi, mysteries, romcoms, horror, even non-fiction books, everything a bookstore or library could possibly have, Alex has it. And I see authors like Hemingway, Austen, Shakespeare, Poe, and Dickens, but I also see new-age authors as well. Like Stephen King, J.K. Rowling, Riley Sager, Christina Lauren, Colleen Hoover, Kerri Maniscalco, SJM, and even one of my personal favorites, Laurell K. Hamilton. Not to mention all the thousands upon thousands of names I don't know but am eager to learn.

I seriously have died and gone to Heaven. Either that or the first book I chose to pick up here, *Alice in Wonderland*, has significant meaning and is a clue that, just like Alice, I've fallen down the rabbit hole and am essentially *tripping*. If a hookah smoking caterpillar turns up and starts speaking to me in riddles, asking me who I am, I don't think I'd be surprised. I mean, vampires are real for fucks sake, why not talking caterpillars?

A break in the shelves finally manages to shake me from my

trance. Another enormous fireplace takes up space along the wall. It's so big that I could easily stand up inside of it. This castle, Alex, Louie, and now this library, are all proof that magic does in fact exist. I may not have fallen down a rabbit hole to get here but there's no denying I'm in another world.

I finally turn around to face the room and am shocked to see the door we came through is no more than a small black hole on the other side. This room is bigger than it looks. Or maybe I was just too distracted by all the books to really notice. But now I notice the large, gleaming desk in front of me. Alex's desk. Even in this big 'ole room, this desk feels huge and intimidating. Maybe it's because of what Louie told me.

...there are some journals. He keeps them in his desk in the library...

My heart immediately starts to race, and I glance at the open doorway across the room, certain that Alex will be there, watching me, waiting to catch me as if he knows what I'm about to do. As if he can hear the little voice in the back of my mind whisper yelling, *read them!* As if he can hear my nervous heart slamming in my chest all the way in the sitting room. Afterall, he is a vampire and said as much. But from how far away can he really hear my heart beating? And being a vampire doesn't mean he can read my mind. I laugh nervously, the sound breaking the silence of the serene space. *Can he read my mind?* Oh God, that would be *so* embarrassing if he can. Like... level dead, mortifyingly embarrassing. That's a question to move to the top of my list.

"Alright Bella, focus!" I try to calm my racing heart and thoughts.

Alex isn't here, he's with Louie. Nor is he waiting just beyond the door, ready to pounce on me the second I do something wrong. And why is an image of him pouncing on me, naked, suddenly taking over? I shake my head to clear that delicious image and hurry over to the desk. I slowly slide the heavy chair back. It's so big and polished that it looks more like a throne than a desk chair. I manage to pull it out enough that I can squeeze between it and the desk and slide onto the plush leather seat.

I'm sitting where he, *and only he*, sits. The thought makes my heart soar in my chest and the butterflies start to wake up inside of my stomach. This feels oddly intimate, and I sink further into the chair, letting my body feel what he feels. His scent invades my senses. He smells like…crisp evening mountain air with that familiar scent of cinnamon that always lingers. He smells like fall. He smells fresh and clean but also warm and comforting.

It's everything he is.

When I'm with him, all I feel is warmth…ok, I always feel dangerously hot when I'm around him, like I'm a volcano and I'm about to burst out of my own skin, but in a thrilling and exciting way. Ok, I suppose a volcano is also extremely destructive, too. But he's always made me feel so comfortable, the bedroom incident not counting. Why do I keep pushing that away as if it's not a big deal when it should be the biggest deal of all? Especially after Gabriel showed me his true colors and I tried to give him the benefit of the doubt. He told me it would never happen again, just like Alex is telling me it will never happen again, but it did happen again. And, it would have continued happening. Am I wrong to want to believe that when Alex says it won't happen again, it won't?

Yes. It is wrong. I can't be ignorant and naïve and just push the truth aside, nod and smile and say ok. I need to be stronger than that. I need to be smarter than that. I refuse to let myself run away from one beast only to end up in the hands of another. With my new resolve, no matter how shaky, I reach for the bottom drawer. The smell of leather fills the air as I slide it open. Two neat rows of leather-bound journals fill the space, their worn and cracked spines lined up perfectly. I let my fingertips gently skate over them, but I hesitate to actually pick one up.

This is wrong. These journals belong to Alex, and unlike this library, I'm sure they're not on the list of items he's willing to share. These are his private journals, filled with his most intimate thoughts and feelings. I can't think of anything that would be more disrespectful and intrusive than reading these journals behind his back. So, why would Louie encourage me to read them? Has he read them? Is that why he chose to stay here with Alex, even knowing what he is? Is the key to knowing Alex at his core in these journals?

And because I'm not perfect, because I am only human and curiosity is a nasty little demon, I choose one of the journals from the back row and slide it free. Just like the naughty, curious cat, I can't seem to help myself. I just hope that, unlike the cat, I don't get killed.

I gently lay the journal on top of the desk and trace the sweeping, elegant letters of Alexander Knightwell's name engraved on the front. I dart one last look across the room, towards the doorway, take a deep breath, and then flip open the cover.

I'm immediately met with a sketch of a beautiful woman. The piece of parchment it's drawn on seems old and delicate. I don't dare try to pick it up, but I admire it where it sits. The woman looks to be my age, maybe a little bit older. It's just a sketch, not a full-blown portrait, but there's no denying her beauty and her grace. I don't know what color her skin was, or her hair and eyes, but there's no denying the light coming from within her. Her eyes are soft and warm but determined, sharp. Her face is the same, as if she's both sides of a knife; dull and safe yet sharp and deadly. Whoever the artist was, he was incredibly talented to be able to capture her authenticity with a few brushes of charcoal on parchment.

I wonder who she was? Or who she is? Is she like Alex? Is she a vampire and still alive? Or is this someone he's lost? And who is she to him? A mother? A sister? A lover? That last thought cuts like the sharp end of the knife into my gut. Unlike with Gabriel and Lucille, this cut, even though imaginary, fucking hurts. What in the actual hell? Is this jealousy? If it is, I don't want to ever feel it again.

I quickly but gently flip the page and hide the shrewd and knowing eyes of the woman in the sketch. I'm met with a beautiful flowing script deftly sprawled across the page with precision. There's not one error or smudge of ink marring the page. It takes me a few minutes to process the information I'm seeing and to let it sink in.

"Holy shit," I say, in awe.

If I didn't believe him before about being a vampire, I don't know how else to explain what I'm seeing. Before I can talk myself out of it, I start to read.

Journal Entry - Year 1622

My father insists that I attend these ceremonies, even though I have little interest in running the Kingdom and have told him so on more than one occasion. As the middle son, I am not next in line to inherit the throne and that suits me just fine, but Father demands that we all learn how to rule in case it comes to it. Considering my father has fought long and hard for the peace we have had for the last decade, I do not see why. Henry will continue the peaceful rule after my father, and I see no need for my presence here, listening to the troubles and requests of the people. Not that I do not care about them, because I do, but I am in no position to do anything either way. The King will make his decisions and his decisions are final. And he is a good man, my father. He is fair and honorable and cares about his Kingdom. It's why he has maintained peace for so long. There really is no need for me to be here, but on this day, one of stifling heat, causing everyone to be sweaty, cranky, and utterly miserable, I am suddenly sitting up straighter in my seat, thankful to be exactly where I am.

I do not think I have ever seen anyone or anything more beautiful than the girl walking towards us. Walking towards me. She is a commoner, her simple dress dirty and torn and looks to be too big for her, as if it was handed down from someone else. Still, she holds herself with the highest level of dignity, befitting a Lady of Station. Her shoulders are pulled back, head held high, and the prettiest and brightest golden hair I have ever seen flows in waves down her back.

She kneels before us, before the King, and I want to run down the steps and lift her back to her feet. No one of her beauty and magnitude should ever kneel to anyone, but like an obedient Prince, I am riveted to my seat, left only to stare at her and give her all my attention.

She has concerns about people dying. Commoners, of course. She says they are killed but there is no blood, even though some of the bodies are torn apart, as if an animal has attacked them. She says more and more people are going missing or showing up, dead, in alleys. She wants to know what we are going to do to find this killer, or killers, and how we are going to keep the people safe.

I do not hear a word my father says because all I can think about is how can I keep **her** safe? How can I speak to her? How can I get to know her? How, how, how? And then she stands, and it is as if she can sense my desperate eyes on her, because before she turns to walk away, she glances at me. Just the briefest second where our eyes meet, but in that second, I swear I have been pierced straight through by her striking green eyes. But then they are gone. Too quickly, they are gone. Green and gold is all I can see long after she has left the room.

The rest of the ceremony and meetings drag on and on in a never-ending and tediously dull bore. My leg is bouncing, anxious to push out of this seat and run in the direction she went. I need to find her. But how will I ever succeed when I'm stuck here as she gets farther and farther away from me.

The second my father dismisses us, I am tearing out of the throne room like a wild stallion, behaving in no way like the Prince I am. And for once, I do not care how I look, racing through the castle halls, eyes darting this way and that way like a raving lunatic. I charge outside and shield my eyes from the burning sun. I am doubting myself, the ability that I will be able to find her now, after so much time has passed. She is probably beyond the castle walls, back in the lower city, back on those deadly streets.

Then a glimpse of gold catches my eye before disappearing around the side of the castle. I run down the steps, bumping into people, and yelling my apologies behind me as I continue my chase. I find her walking the quiet paths in the garden. As a commoner, she should not be here, strolling through the Queen's personal garden as if it were her own. The fact that there was no guard at the entrance is a concern, but I will address that later. For now, I am captivated at how peaceful she looks as she stops to smell some purple flowers that I cannot name. Then, she gently reaches up and plucks one free.

"I could have you arrested for that," I say calmly, as I approach her.

I expect her to gasp in surprise and cower in fear at being caught, but she ignores me, keeping her attention on the flower in her hand. She twists it back and forth, examining every angle before she lifts it to her nose, closes her eyes, and inhales.

"Irises have been selfishly claimed by royalty and deemed fit for only those with royal blood, but did you know they actually represent wisdom and respect? Where, do you think, is the wisdom and resect with claiming ownership of a flower and punishing anyone with common blood who dares grow them?"

She finally levels me with her beautiful green eyes, but their earlier softness has vanished. I see all the resentment towards my family, towards me, flashing daringly in them. Still, I am left utterly entranced. Not only by her beauty but by her bravery.

"Not only have you trespassed into the Queen's Garden, but you have stolen from her and insulted her, and me for that matter, all in a matter of minutes. That goes from simply having you arrested to hanging you in the square for all to see. Is a flower worth your life?"

"It is not about the flower, and if you believe it is,

you are just as spoiled and entitled as I imagined."

"What is your name?"

"What does it matter?" She tips her chin in defiance. "Commoners who hang are always nameless."

My God. The fire in her soul is scorching and I cannot help but hold my hand to the flame to see if it will burn me. I approach her slowly but with confidence. I take the flower out of her hands, brush her hair behind her ear, and tuck the flower into her golden locks.

"Because I wish to know the name of the woman who puts the beauty of this so-called royal flower to shame. Because I wish to know everything there is to know about you, but I'll gladly start with a name."

Her stare slowly turns from one of disgust and uncertainty to one of curiosity. I make it my mission to gain her trust and change that look to one of admiration, maybe even love. Though I may be getting ahead of myself. A name first. The rest later.

"Selah." She finally gives in.

"Selah," I repeat. Her name is music to my ears. "I am Alexander Knightwell. Not only am I not going to have you arrested or hanged, I am going to ensure you get safely out of the castle walls **with** your royal flower."

"I would rather you ensure the safety of my people, of **your** people," she demands.

"I promise that I will look into the issues you

brought forth personally, but I will need an assistant. Someone who knows more about the streets and the commoners than I do. So, you see, I cannot have you getting caught now, can I?"

A small smile tugs at the corner of her lips. "I suppose not."

"What do you say, Selah? Partners?" Although improper, I reach my hand out to shake hers, eager to solidify our partnership that will allow me to get to know her and to help the people of the Kingdom. Both tasks I genuinely want to see to, but I admit, one has a bit more priority than the other.

Not wanting to waste any time, I agree to meet her outside the castle walls at midnight. If you have been a prisoner your entire life, even one of Status and Royalty, you learn how to slip your bonds undetected. I can get out of the main city without notice easily, though I do not do it often.

Wrapped in a dark cloak, with the light of the moon to guide me, I meet Selah at a well-known pub close to the castle walls. Even in the moonlight, there is no hiding the shine of her hair or the confidence with which she holds herself.

"I honestly did not think you would come," she admits, as I approach.

"What good is a man if you cannot trust his word?"

There it is again, that curiosity, as if I keep surprising her. I'm happy to continue proving her wrong when it comes to how she thinks of me. Yes, I am a Prince. Yes, I have grown up without the struggles most people face. Yes, I have grown up with luxury and security, along with two parents that love me fiercely. It does not mean I believe myself and my life to be of more value or more important than any other.

"Come. We should go farther into the city where it is less likely for you to be recognized. That is where the killings usually take place."

"And what is your plan once we are there?"

She shrugs. "I do not know. Hide and watch. Be on alert for anything or anyone that looks suspicious."

"And if we do come across someone that looks suspicious?"

"Are you scared, Prince?"

I snort. "Hardly. I train daily in the use of every type of sword, knife, and weapon there is. I did not come unprepared. I just want to know what you think is going to happen?"

"Well, if we are lucky, we catch the bastard that has been killing our people. If we are **really** lucky, you'll kill the bastard."

I cannot help the laughter that bubbles out of my throat. She stops walking to place her hands on her hips and glares at me with her own shrewd weapons.

"You think this is funny?"

I stifle my laughter and shake my head. "No." Once again, I close the distance between us, not able to help myself from wanting to be in her space, no matter how deadly it may be. I stare down at her from inches away. She holds her ground, but her breathing comes in shorter pants, revealing her nerves. "You caught me off guard, is all. You continue to surprise me. You do not treat me like a Prince, you treat me like a **person,** and I am in awe of your bravery and your honesty. That mouth of yours is quite vicious and I find it rather refreshing, and quite...," I reach out to touch her cheek and trace my thumb gently over her lips, "delightful."

We stare at each other for several long, heated seconds before she clears her throat and steps away, breaking the spell.

"Yes, well, Prince or not, you still bleed like the rest of us and will one day meet your end in the ground. Other than circumstances we are born into, we are not any different in the end."

We end up sitting on a bench in a poor and rundown part of the city. This is where the bodies have been found. Whether they were hunted here or just dumped here remains to be seen. As the minutes tick by, I lose sight of why we are even sitting out here, in the quiet hours before dawn. All that I see is Selah. All that I hear is Selah. She is hesitant to open up to me, but as we get more comfortable with each other, her defenses start to lower, and her soul really starts to shine. Not that it did not before but when she is truly passionate about something she lights up brighter than the moon itself, brighter than the brightest star, and stronger than the hottest sun.

She is beautiful.

"Did you hear that?" she asks in a hushed whisper, as her eyes dart to the alleyway across the street.

Before I can respond, she races across the street, headed straight for the dark alley and whatever monster may be lurking inside.

"Selah!" I yell, as I chase after her. "Wait!"

A scream echoes through the empty, quiet streets before it abruptly cuts off. My heart sinks in my chest as I approach the alley, knowing I am too late, knowing exactly what I am going to find. I charge inside, heedless of the danger I know is lurking in the shadows. I collapse at Selah's side, dragging her body into my lap and ignoring whatever else is in the alley with us. Her golden hair is sprawled across her face, sticky and wet with blood. I move the strands aside and those bright green eyes are wide with fear as they stare at me. She tries to speak, but her throat has been ripped out and all she can do is gurgle as blood spews from her mouth and gaping neck.

I continue to brush her hair back, away from her face, rocking her in my arms. It takes a couple of tries to find my voice, but I finally manage to whisper words that I hope will bring her comfort in her last moments.

"I am here. I have you and I am not going to let you go. Shh, do not try and speak. I am here, Selah, I am here. I promise, you will never be forgotten as long as I live. You will never be nameless."

Tears run down the side of her head as she continues to choke on blood. I continue to rock her long after the struggle has left her body and only silence and darkness remain.

"I know you are still here," I say, without looking away from Selah's dead eyes. Eyes that are going to haunt me for the rest of my days.

Not a single sound is made as a well-dressed man walks out of the shadows, Selah's blood coating his mouth and chin. His eyes shine like that of a cat's in the dark, reflecting the dim light.

"You are no commoner." His voice is as calm and smooth as his steps. "So, what might you be doing in this despicable part of the city, in the middle of the night, with her?"

"Looking for you," I seethe.

He spreads his arms wide and chuckles. "Well, you

have found me."

I gently place Selah's body on the ground and stand, facing her killer. The killer that has been terrorizing the city, **my city.**

"Yes, I have, and now, I'm going to kill you." I draw the knife from the belt at my waist, gripping the handle tightly and welcoming its rough comfort in my palm.

The killer grins, his straight white teeth still stained with her blood. "They are so very rarely brave, you know. Even when they claim to be, they always cry, and plead, and **scream.**"

"You will get none of that from me, only the tip of my blade piercing your heart."

"I can see you believe that. I do not taste fear. No, you truly are a brave one. You would make a wonderful vampire."

"What?" I ask, confused. "What is a vampire?"

"Allow me to show you."

Before I can even blink, the man is gone, disappeared as if he had never been there, never been real, just a figment of my imagination. However, Selah's body is still dead at my feet, and then a strong grip is on my wrist, immobilizing it, and my head is wrenched to the side. I grit my teeth against the sudden shock of pain radiating through my neck before it dissipates, and I melt.

That is what it feels like.

It feels like my bones turn to liquid inside of my body and I am no longer standing in the dark and dirty alley.

I am floating into the night sky with the taste of copper on my tongue.

Bella

I close the journal and fall back against the chair, my mind reeling. He's a prince, royalty, or at least he used to be, and this is indeed *his* castle. This is where he grew up and where he's spent, what, four-hundred fucking years? My mind can't even begin to process that information. He looks to be only a few years older than me, maybe twenty-seven or twenty-eight, but he's not. Not even close.

He's a vampire.

And he didn't have a choice.

My heart aches for him and his story. I open the journal again and stare at the sketch. There's no doubt in my mind that this is Selah, the woman that caught his eye. The woman that he wanted to get to know. The woman that he wanted to love, even though she was a commoner, and he probably wouldn't have been allowed to be with her. He never got the chance to try and worse, she was killed and died in his arms. I can't imagine what that must have been like for him. And then to have his own life taken and turned into something else entirely, a beast, without his consent or knowledge of what he'd become.

"Oh, Alex," I whisper into the quiet of the library, my heart breaking a little inside my chest for the beautiful man I barely know.

I desperately want to continue reading the journals, but I also need time to process the information and want to check on Louie. I gently close the journal again, hiding away Selah's picture once more, and slide it journal back into its place alongside the others, closing the drawer.

I slide out of the chair and push it back into place and hurry across the room. I pick up the lantern that's still sitting next to the doorway, and then turn to look back at the room behind me. The desk is calling to me. I can almost feel the allure of the journals, of Alex's life's story, pulling me back. Before I can change my mind, I hit the switches, concealing the library in darkness, then slowly descend the steep steps, heading back to the sitting room.

Alex is still here when I arrive, sitting at the end of the couch with Louie's legs in his lap. He looks like he may be asleep but at the sound of my footsteps, his head raises off the back of the sofa and those intense silver eyes open and watch me approach.

He doesn't say a word as I take the chair opposite to him, the one he usually sits in. I tell myself it's so we can talk more easily, without being so far away, but it's really because I want to be close to him. He's like my Selah. Every time he's in the room, I can't help but be pulled into his orbit, no matter how deadly it may be.

His eyes stay glued to me, and I can't help but feel like he knows *exactly* what I was doing in the library. He knows that I know about Selah. He knows I've been prying but he doesn't seem to be upset. In fact, he looks almost…cautious. Maybe even nervous? Or maybe it's my own nerves from being a nosey piece of shit that I'm feeling. Either way, I need to deflect.

"How's he doing?" I finally break the silence.

He lets out a defeated sigh and looks down at Louie. "Honestly, he's barely hanging on. His pulse is weak, and his breathing is labored. I don't think he's going to pull through."

"He doesn't want to pull through," I whisper, sadly.

"I know," he says, just as sadly, as he continues to watch Louie sleep.

"I can't imagine how you must be feeling. I've only known Louie for a second and I already love him and don't want to let him go, but he deserves to finally have his happy ending. I think he needs to hear you say it."

He just nods his head, his Adam's apple bobbing roughly in his throat, betraying his emotion. Once again, my heart is breaking for this man I barely know.

How many people has he outlived? How many people has he cared for, *loved*, and had to watch die in his arms? Selah must have been the first, but I can't even imagine how many more there's been over a span of four hundred years. How does he handle it? I guess he doesn't have a choice.

Jesus, it's so cruel.

I can feel my own emotion starting to swell inside of me and have to fight to keep it from spilling over. There will be plenty of tears when Louie passes, I don't need to add any more before that.

Alex finally turns to look at me. "Thank you."

His words catch me off guard. "For what?"

"For being here. For befriending Lumineux the way you did. I don't think I've ever seen him as happy as he's been this past week, with you here. Thank you for giving him that. Thank you for being...you."

Once again, his molten gaze sinks into my skin and into my very soul, as if he can see the rawest and truest parts of me. I feel so incredibly emotionally naked and exposed but somehow it doesn't make me uncomfortable. Alex has only ever made me feel...real. He's made me feel like I'm a person in this world and not just a passing insignificance.

"Your eyes...," I say, as I continue to fall into their depths, "have they always been this color? Or did they change when you became a vampire?"

"They've always been this color. Becoming a vampire didn't change anything about my appearance other than the lighter skin, since I'm unable to be in sunlight." A small smile pulls at one corner of his mouth. "Why? Do you like them?"

"Yes." My voice has gone all breathy with the way he's looking at me and with that teasing smile making an appearance on his beautiful lips. I clear my throat and blink, trying to break whatever spell he cast on me. "I've never seen eyes the color of yours before, unlike my common ones."

"There's nothing common about you, Bella."

I feel myself flush under his unwavering attention. His words stir up the journal entry I read. Selah was a commoner, but he didn't see anything common about her either. Another pang of something unpleasant flutters inside my chest. I want to be more to him than that. I want to be more to him than Selah was. I want to be special. I don't want to feel as though I'm being compared to her. And I know it's silly. It's not like his history with Selah was recent, it was several lifetimes ago. I doubt he's thinking about her right now the way I am. According to his journal, he only knew her for a day, but I can't help my thoughts from going there. These feelings are so strange and foreign. I don't recognize them. I don't recognize myself.

"Do you have power over me?" I blurt out.

He laughs nervously. "What?"

"As a vampire, do you have power over me? I've read about them in books, and you said that everything comes from truth. Well, the vampires I've read about have controlling powers over people. So, is that what this is? Are you manipulating me?"

His face loses all humor, becoming deadly serious. "If I wanted to, I could control you, yes. I could make you do anything I want but I could never manipulate your feelings. It's a very physical type of control. One I would never use on you like that, *ever*."

"Would I even know if you did?"

"Yes. Like I said, I could make you do things physically controlling your body, but inside you would know it was forced. Your mind is always your own, even under the influence of a vampire. That's what makes it so cruel. It's like you're trapped inside of yourself with no control. It's a power I use sparingly and superficially."

I contemplate his words. I know he's being truthful; he has no reason to lie to me, but a part of me needs to know for myself. I need to know what it feels like to be under his control. I need to know that all the feelings swirling inside of me are real. What that means for me if they are is a whole other topic, but I need to know.

"Can you make me do something? Not anything embarrassing or bad," I add, quickly. "Just something simple, so that I know what it feels like."

"Bella, I—"

"Please. I need to know."

He sighs reluctantly. "Alright. Look into my eyes."

I do, falling easily into their depths. The silver bleeds into his pupils until his eyes are nothing but molten silver. I feel a tingle dance across my skin, and it feels oddly like I'm falling. No, not falling, just...floating.

"Stand up," he demands.

And I do. I don't even have to think about the command, I just immediately get to my feet. I'm shocked. It's not that I wanted to stand or didn't want to stand, I just...did.

"This time I want you to try to fight it. I want you to feel the resistance and know what it feels like to be under my control. I don't ever want you to have to question it again." I nod. "Sit down."

I immediately move to sit, but this time I try to fight it. It's no use. My body is moving on its own accord, heedless to my mind screaming, *don't sit down!* I'm thinking my own thoughts, but I have no control. Still staring into his eyes, I watch as the silver fades and his eyes return to normal, if that's what you can call them.

"Holy shit!" I exhale as the tingling sensation leaves my skin and I'm once again back in control. "That was unnerving and a bit...terrifying," I admit.

He nods. "Yes, it can be. I've seen vampires make people do things that will haunt me for eternity. You think people can be cruel; it's nothing compared to an evil vampire."

"I can imagine." I shudder at the thought of all the things a vampire could force a human to do. I want all those thoughts and images out of my head, so I change the subject. "So, does that mean you can't read my mind?"

The amusement slowly starts to return to his eyes as he looks at me, but it's my turn to be dead serious. He shakes his head. "No, I can't read your mind. No matter how desperately I wish that I could."

"Oh, thank God," I laugh nervously. If he only knew all the crazy, jumbled shit running through my head, I think he might be arrogantly satisfied and quite possibly repulsed all at the same time.

He cocks his eyebrow as he narrows his eyes. "Care to enlighten me about what I'd learn if I could read your mind?"

I shake my head rapidly and purse my lips together, murmuring, "Uh-uh."

He unleashes his lips and that body melting smile makes my entire body feel like pudding. Like delicious, chocolate pudding that I wish he'd scoop up and try. *Jesus, Bella!*

"Pretty certain I'd *love* to know whatever thought just popped into that beautiful head of yours."

I hide my embarrassed face in my hands. "Oh God," I mumble into my palms. I am such an inexperienced idiot. I'm way out of my depth with Alex.

"Bella."

I jump when his voice comes from right in front of me. I drop my hands and I'm met with sparkling silver eyes looking into mine from way too close yet not nearly close enough. He's kneeling in front of my chair, a hands on each armrest, caging me in with his body. His proximity makes my heart race and my knees weak. I'm so thankful I'm not standing.

Again, pudding.

"Bella, I don't ever want you to forget that I *am* dangerous. I am The Beast that many people fear, but you don't have to be one of them. You don't need to fear me. I will never try to control you. I will never hurt you. I know I already failed once, and I'm not expecting you to believe me, but I swear, I will—"

"I know."

He's silent for a few seconds before he continues. "You do?"

I nod. Maybe I'm being ignorant. Maybe I'm letting my feelings muddle my common sense, but I know in my heart, in my soul, that he's never going to let what happened in his bedroom happen again.

My eyes catch on his Adam's apple as it dips in his throat again. I want to wrap my lips around it and taste his skin. I want to explore every inch of him and find out what other simple things this man makes ridiculously sexy. My eyes move to his lips and my own lips part, aching to touch his. Automatically, my tongue brushes my bottom lip and his jaw clenches tightly.

"Fuck," he mumbles as he stands, pushing himself further away from me. He runs his hand through his hair and then grips the back of his neck before he lets his hand fall to his side. "I need to get some sleep. Will you stay here with Lumineux for a while? I'll return in a couple of hours and then you can get some sleep. Unless you want to sleep first?"

"I'll stay." My voice is small, sad. I don't want him to go, and I hate that he feels like he has to. I know he's not tired and he's only using it as an excuse to get away for me.

He nods his head but doesn't look at me. "Thank you. Goodnight, Bella."

He turns to leave, and before I can even think about what I'm doing, I'm jumping to my feet and reaching for him. "Alex, wait." I grab his wrist, halting his retreat.

He turns to face me, and I'm not prepared for the pain I see in his eyes. I don't know if it's pain from the regret and guilt he feels from what happened between us, or pain from walking away from me when he doesn't want to any more than I want him to. Whatever it is, I hate it. I want the confident, flirty Alex from the kitchen, the Alex from before everything else happened.

He glances down to where I'm holding his wrist in a death grip, as if I hold it hard enough, he'll be forced to stay. I immediately let go. "Sorry," I mumble. "I didn't mean to just grab you like that. It's just that, well, you were walking away, and I didn't want you to leave, and I wasn't really thinking, I just…," I trail off, realizing I'm rambling again. "I didn't mean to hurt you."

"It's cute that you think you can hurt me. What do you need?"

"It's just that…well, in the kitchen, before all of this happened, I thought…." I lift a shoulder and immediately feel insecure and a little needy. I start to tangle my fingers together in a mess of anxiety and second-guessing.

"You thought what?"

I hang my head, not able to meet his intense gaze as my cheeks heat. "I thought you wanted to kiss me."

"I do want to kiss you."

My eyes shoot up to meet his. There's still pain in them, but his words have lifted a huge weight off my chest. I'm relieved that I didn't imagine what happened between us, and that even though everything has changed since then, he still feels the same way. I'm relieved but also extremely confused.

"Then...why haven't you?"

"I'm not going to do anything to lose your trust again. I won't cross any lines and give you any more reason than you already have to leave this place and never come back. I won't touch you, in any way, unless it's to protect you, without your permission."

"You have my permission," I whisper, barely able to talk through the pounding of my heart in my chest.

Staring up into his handsome face, I watch as the pained look leaves his eyes only to be replaced by heat. His eyes burn like lava, matching the heat boiling inside me. He closes the small distance between us, and I feel dizzy. My body sways and his arm catches me around the waist, pulling my body flush with his. Shit, he hasn't even kissed me yet and I can barely stand on my own two feet. His other hand cradles my face, his fingers slipping into the hair at the back of my neck as he slowly lowers his face to mine. My eyes flutter closed and a second later, his lips are on mine.

It's soft and gentle and warm. I feel a slight quiver of lips but I can't tell if they're my lips shaking or his. My lips part, wanting more, an unspoken invitation to let him in, and he doesn't hesitate. He deepens the kiss with an agonizing slow sweep of his tongue against mine as he holds me tighter. I swear an entire flock of birds take flight in my chest and it feels like they take me into the sky with them. His large hand splays across my lower back, gently digging his fingers into my skin as he grips my neck tighter, but never once changing the slow, sexy way he's kissing me. My hands slide up his chest and around his neck until my fingers sink into the thick strands of his hair. The desperation in his touch is such a contrast to the deliciously unhurried way he's kissing me.

It's maddening and thrilling.

It's everything I've ever wanted and not nearly enough.

He's intoxicating.

He's filling up every empty and lonely inch inside of me with each deep and gentle slide of his tongue against mine. He pulls my bottom lip between his teeth and gently bites down. I think I faint, or at least blackout. I hear myself moan into his mouth as his tongue slides back inside mine for another painfully perfect kiss.

He slowly pulls away and I feel myself fall back onto my heels. I hadn't even realized I was on my tiptoes until now. I open my eyes to find his staring at me.

"Right now, I wish I was a little bit evil, because I really want to make you come back to my room with me."

"You don't need to make me. I want to." *Jesus Bella, could you be any more fucking thirsty?*

He closes his eyes and groans, then shakes his head and slowly releases me. "No. I want you to process this. Us. I don't want you to jump into something that you'll regret later."

"I won't! I—"

"Please Bella, don't make this harder for me than it already is. I don't want you to think that I don't want to." He takes my hand and presses it to the front of his jeans. I gasp at the hardness under my palm. "Because I *really* want to." He releases my hand and takes a step away from me. "But I need you to be certain that you want to, too, and that you're not just caught up in a moment. You need to know that I can't give you a normal life. I can never give you a…a family. And I need you to know that if we cross this line, I won't want to stop. I want more than that with you. You know what I am. You know what I'll desire."

"My blood."

"With you, Bella…everything. I want fucking everything. I want you here with me, and if you don't want to stay, if you can't give me everything, don't make me cross that line only to have it taken away from me."

A little bit of that pain seeps back into his eyes and I hate it. I never want to see this look on his face ever again. I know in my heart that this is *what* I want, that he's *who* I want, but he's right. Am I willing to let him drink my blood? Jesus, that thought is wild and unnerving. I need to know for certain and I need to know everything.

"Ok," I whisper.

"Ok." He gives me a small, sad smile that does nothing but make my heart ache further. "Goodnight."

"Goodnight, Alex."

I stay rooted to the spot as I watch him walk out of the room. I stay there long after he's left. My fingertips touch my lips and I close my eyes as I play back every little detail of that kiss a hundred times, the faint taste of cinnamon lingering on my tongue. Fucking hell, I've never been kissed like that before.

So deliberately.

So selflessly.

Even when I thought Gabriel was kissing me passionately, I was so wrong. He was always kissing me for *his* pleasure, never mine, but I never had anything to compare it to. Well, fuck me. Now I do, and it doesn't even come close.

And it hurts. God, it hurts so good. What does that mean? I've never had a kiss blissfully crush my heart in the most devastatingly wonderful way before. But that kiss has thoroughly sunk its claws into me and I don't think I'll ever escape.

I don't want to ever escape.

ALEX

Walking away feels like a fate worse than living an eternity as The Beast. I didn't think anything could ever be worse, but this...this is far fucking worse. Denying yourself what you want at your very core is maddening.

Wanting her is maddening.

Needing her is maddening.

I haven't felt like this since I was human. If I'm being honest, I thought these types of emotions and feelings died the night I died. *The night she died*. I never got the chance to explore the feelings I had for Selah and I haven't felt them with anyone else since. Not in all my hundreds of years on this godforsaken earth. I've felt power and lust. I've felt hunger, of course, even anger and rage, but I've never felt this.

The intense and griping desire for someone else. The desire to know everything about them. And my desire to know Bella is overwhelming. I want to know every single thought that runs through her mind, no matter how ridiculous or silly. I want to know about her life, her childhood, her experiences, and everything that's made her the incredibly kind and sweet woman she is today. I want to know her wildest dreams. I want to know her darkest fears. And I want to be there with her every step of the way as she lives through all of them. I want her experiences to be my experiences, *our* experiences.

I want to laugh with her. I want to cry with her. I want to *live* with her. And good God I want to drown in her. If there is such a thing as a Holy Grail, I'm certain I just found it. I've never tasted anything so damn lifechanging before in life or death. I would have been content to stand there and kiss her for hours. And if just a small taste, just a kiss, can so thoroughly entrance me, what the fuck is going to happen when I slide inside of her? What will I become once I've tasted her blood? Because she *will* let me taste her eventually, and I am who I am, so I won't be able to say no. I don't want to say no.

Fuck. I'm wound so tight I need a damn release. I can still feel her lips on mine as if our kiss has been branded on them, branded into my damn mind. I still feel her body melting into mine, and when she moaned into my mouth...I almost lost all fucking control. I wanted to grab her ass, lift her up, and take her right there against the wall, without giving a single fuck that Lumineux was unconscious mere feet away.

I yank my shirt off over my head, toss it aside and quickly unbutton my jeans, releasing the restraint on my aching cock. I can still feel the heat of her hand from where she gripped me through my jeans. I want so badly to feel her palm on my skin, to see how much of my dick her small hand can cover as she jacks me off.

I step into the shower, turn on the overhead waterfall showerhead, and let the ice-cold water pelt my burning skin. A shiver races through my body but cold water does nothing to dampen the blazing inferno inside of me or weaken my hard-on. I use the same type of soap that I gave her to use, lather it in my hands, and am immediately drowning in her scent, but it's only just the surface. Her scent is so much stronger and sweeter than the soap that cleans her skin. It's not enough. I want more. I *need* more.

I grab my cock and start to slide my slick hands back and forth, focusing on the sensitive head. I stroke myself slowly, remembering the slow dance of her tongue against mine. I imagine what it would feel like sliding up the length of me before swirling around the tip and then enveloping me in her warm, sweet mouth.

I imagine it but I don't know if I would be able to handle it. My hand has been my only companion for as long as I can remember and I fucking hate it. With her in my castle, within my reach, I fucking hate it. I've refused to let women close to me, even to feed, for the fear of exactly what's happening now. I'm watching it happen, like watching a car crash in slow motion, but I'm powerless to stop it.

The last ten minutes play like a movie reel in my mind. Her big blue eyes staring up at me, vulnerable and full of hope, with the slightest hint of fear. I could practically feel the bass of her rapid heartbeat as it pounded wildly against her ribs.

You have my permission.

Those four simple words almost unleashed The Beast. Perhaps if the bedroom incident hadn't happened, I may have gone further. I wanted to go further. I close my eyes and brace myself against the tiled shower wall. My skin is numb due to the cold water that's been cascading down my body as my mind remains with her. The memory of my fingertips digging into her soft flesh makes me grip my cock tighter as I continue an agonizingly slow speed. I can feel the orgasm building and I want to draw it out for as long as I can. I want this feeling associated with the memory of her for as long as I can have it.

But it's no use. I'm too fucking turned on and too damn deprived to drag this out. I increase my speed and feel my dick hardening further under my touch as the orgasm finally crests and I shoot my cum down the drain.

"Fuck," I grunt, as I lay my forehead against my arm, frustrated beyond belief.

This won't do. This false pleasure and underwhelming release just won't fucking do. I'm still wound tighter than a coiled spring and if something doesn't happen soon, if I don't get to explore every pleasure with her soon, I'm going to fucking snap. And when a coiled spring breaks and snaps free, it's bound to hurt whoever stands too close. I don't want that to happen but at the end of the day, I'm just a man. I'm not invincible. I'm not made of stone.

In all of my hundreds of years, I have never once been weak, but Bella makes me weak. My walls, my willpower, my damn good sense...it falls apart because of her.

But for the first time, I also don't feel so infinitely alone. Yes, I've had companions but it's not the same as this. She sees me as much as I see her. And I know she feels what I'm feeling, too. Our souls know each other. I don't understand why I see the same infinite loneliness in her though. She should never feel alone in this world, and I want to be the one to make her whole. Or maybe I'm just fucking projecting.

I finish washing and then quickly towel dry before climbing into my ridiculously big bed...alone. The silk sheets are cold, and I wish she was here to warm them with me, her body lying next to mine. Just as much as I want every ounce of pleasure with her, I want what comes after just as much, if not more. Sex is not intimacy. Sex is delicious and fun and satisfying. I want sex with Bella with every fiber of my being, but it's not intimacy. The kiss we shared, that's intimacy. Talking to her for hours, that's intimacy. Feeling her fall asleep in my arms and waking up with her beside me, her beautiful copper hair splayed across my chest as I gently stroke her naked back...yeah, I want that.

And that is exactly what's going to destroy me.

Bella

HAZE BY SUNSLEEP

My neck aches. I groan as I sit up and open my eyes. I'm in the sitting room where Louie is still asleep on the couch, the gentle rise and fall of his chest letting me know that he's still breathing. I sigh in relief. He's been unconscious for a long time and I'm starting to worry he may never wake up. What if Alex doesn't get to say goodbye to him? Did they talk at all when he was dressing his wound? I hope that Louie wakes up, just one more time at least, to say his goodbyes otherwise…there's no closure. Closure isn't always possible, it's a blessing, and I hope Alex gets this blessing.

I unfold my legs from underneath me and groan again. Chairs are not meant for sleeping in. I had no intention of sleeping but I guess my body had other ideas. I don't remember having a blanket though. Alex. A smile pulls at my lips at the thought of him coming down and covering me. I wonder where he is. I don't think he'd want to leave Louie unattended. I was supposed to be watching him but failed miserable at my post.

"Sleeping Beauty has awoken." His voice slides over me and into me, warming me up like the most delicious sip of hot cocoa on a snowy day. "Shame, I was hoping I'd have to come to your rescue and kiss you awake."

"I can pretend to be asleep," I eagerly tease.

His chuckle is sexy and deep, and I feel my attraction lighting up my veins. He walks to the table and sets down a silver serving tray, the smell of coffee and eggs comforting me further. I love tea but there's nothing better than enjoying a hot cup of coffee and breakfast when you wake up.

He leaves the tray and walks over to my chair. I instantly lose all interest in coffee as he braces himself on the armrests and leans his large body over me. His clean scent invades my senses, waking my body up more thoroughly than any cup of caffeine ever could.

His eyes land on mine and he's all business again. "Do you have to be asleep in order for me to kiss you?"

I shake my head, but I've lost all my words. My eyes drop to his beautiful lips, portraying exactly what I want him to do. He leans in slowly and softly captures my lips. Once again, his kiss is unhurried and I savor every second of the gentle press of his lips on mine. Then his mouth opens, and I follow his lead, letting his tongue glide against mine before I get the full feel of his lips again. And again. And again.

His hands remain on the armrests and mine in my lap. Only our mouths touch and for some reason that just makes it more intense, but I can feel the heat of his body surrounding me. I can almost feel the heavy weight of him settling between my legs. A low groan escapes my lips and I reach for him. Before I can drag him into the chair with me and see how we can twist ourselves into a suitable position, he pulls away.

"Jesus, Bella."

"I know," I say breathlessly. "I feel it, too."

He nods his head, his eyes roaming over me, hungry for more but he steps away. I'm thankful he has the willpower I don't but curse him for it in the same breath. I don't want to stop. I don't ever want to stop whatever this feeling he gives me is. But his words from the day before come back to me. I need to make sure I can give him everything. That's the deal. All or nothing, and the way this man kisses me...isn't nothing.

He clears his throat. "I brought you coffee, and I'm no Lumineux in the kitchen, but he did teach me a thing or two. I hope you like omelets."

"I do. Breakfast is my favorite meal. I'm assuming you don't actually eat...*food*."

"You would assume correctly."

"That's why Louie said he hadn't had anyone to cook for. Makes sense now." I cautiously get out of the chair, testing my legs for strength, surprised to find them holding me steady.

"I can bring everything to you."

"Not necessary." I walk to the table and kneel down next to it, grabbing the coffee and cream. "I've never been one for anything very formal. I can eat right here," I say, as I get comfortable on the floor.

A beautiful smile spreads across his handsome face, lighting up his eyes as he watches me. "Another thing I like about you." He lowers his large body gracefully to the floor to sit next to me.

"What?" I laugh softly. "That I'm not high maintenance?"

"You're just happy and grateful. You haven't asked for anything since being here, you've made no demands, and you haven't once complained about a single thing."

"What's there to complain about? This place is beautiful and peaceful. I love that I can be myself here and don't have to worry about...well, anything. I guess I am kind of taking advantage of you, huh?"

"Not even close, trust me." He reaches for me, his fingers tenderly tucking strands of hair behind my ear before lightly tracing my jaw. "Your presence here has been lifechanging."

He pulls his hand back and I want to crawl after it. I want to chase that touch and let his fingertips explore the rest of my body, but

I don't. I guess I do have some willpower after all.

"Well, thank you again for finding me, for saving me, and for letting me stay here. I'm not ready to go back yet."

"Will you eventually go back?" he asks, no emotion in his voice, which shows me more than anything else exactly how much he actually cares.

"I have to," I whisper, as I busy myself with stirring cream into my coffee.

The truth pains me to speak because I know it's not what he wants to hear. Hell, it's not what I want to hear either. Just the thought of going back to my life in New Haven, of leaving *him*, makes my heart ache and my stomach knot uneasily.

"It's not that I *want* to, but my mom is there, and she needs me. She doesn't have anyone else."

I guess that answer solidifies his decision to *not* cross the line with me. Reality sidles up and sucker punches me in the gut. This situation isn't permanent. This isn't my saving grace. I have a life and responsibilities. Oh fuck, why are my eyes watering? Why does the thought of leaving this castle, leaving Alex, feel like someone is reaching inside of me and squeezing my throat closed. The thought of going back to my old life is painfully suffocating. I feel like I've finally found peace, finally found my place in the world, but my life has never been about me. My life has never been about what I want. It's always been about us; me and my mom. Everything I've ever done has been with her in mind.

"Hey, hey, Bella, it's ok. I understand. I didn't mean to upset you."

I shake my head, wishing he could read my mind right now. "No, it's not you. I mean, it is but it's not." My voice comes out thick with emotion, adding to the overwhelming pain I feel radiating in my chest.

I feel his warm hand on my face as he wipes away tears from my cheek. I close my eyes and lean into it for a brief second. If I stay here, I'm going to end up crying in his lap like I did the other day. Jesus, I'm a mess. I don't want him dealing with that again.

I slowly get to my feet and look down at him. That haunting pain is back in his eyes and I'm responsible for putting it there. I always put it there. This time, I see worry reflected in them, too. I hate it. "Would you mind if I spent some time in the library?"

"You don't have to ask. I meant it when I said it's yours, whenever you want."

I swallow down the ball of emotion clogging up my throat. "Thank you, Alex. For everything." I turn to leave but his voice stops me.

"Bella." He grabs the plate and the mug. "Take breakfast and coffee with you. You need to eat."

And there they go again, the tears. Even as he's hurting, he makes sure to take care of me, to do what's best for *me*. I don't know how to handle his kindness. I want to wrap it around me like a cozy blanket, snuggle into it, and never let it go. But I can't. I can't cross that line if I'm not sure about my future. That's the *only* thing he's asked of me, to be certain, and I'm just...not.

I nod and take the offered plate and mug and then practically run out of the room. I take a detour into my room before heading up to the library. One, I need a lantern and I have an extra one in my room and two, I need to take a few minutes to eat. My stomach doesn't feel like accepting food, but I do need to eat a little bit if I don't want to wither away. This whole mess and Louie getting hurt has really thrown off my appetite and general self- care which I know isn't healthy.

I manage to eat most of the omelet and finish all the coffee. Grabbing the lantern, I don't waste another minute as I hurry down the hall and then up the stairs to the library. My goal for coming here was completely selfish. I plan to read Alex's journals. I'm only delaying the inevitable. I'll find out the truth about his past, about who he really is, and I'll either run like hell back to New Haven, or my feelings for him will be solidified. Either way, I *need* to know. Because I'm seconds away from crossing that line and reaching the point of no return.

Journal Entry - Year 1623

Today is the one-year anniversary of my death. Or, as my Maker likes to remind me, my true beginning. He thinks if he says it enough, I will eventually believe him. I will not. Nothing good has come from what he did to me. Nothing good has come from the life he took from me. Everything has gone to hell.

My life.

This world.

Vampire. That is what I have been turned into. We are widely known now. They...we, no longer lurk in dark alleyways and kill in secret. No, they...we, kill out in the open for all to see now. And why would they...we not? Humans are not strong enough to stop us. Werewolves are, but they are too busy trying to grow their packs, to get bigger, stronger, just as we are. It is a war out here and I do not think it has even really begun. I shudder at what is to come.

Humans have no chance of surviving. Not now, and certainly not once we start to fight for power and dominance over the other preternatural creatures. Animals. That is all we are now. Barely better than the wild wolf or bear. I think even a wild animal can control their hunger better than a new vampire can.

Better than I could.

The memory of that night and what immediately followed still haunts me. Not only in my dreams but when I'm wide awake, too. The blood on my hands may have long since been cleaned, the bodies buried in the ground to rot leaving no evidence behind, but the truth will forever taint my soul. The truth will forever follow me. No matter how far I try to run, the truth is always there, waiting for me.

Haunting me.

Terrorizing me.

Reminding me that I am nothing more than a beast.

So, it is only fitting that I come home on the anniversary of my death, to finally face what I have done, what I have tried so hard to outrun but have been unable.

I killed my family.

Even the memory of Selah's death is insignificant to the memory of my family being torn apart...by my hands. I was completely aware of what I was doing, and I was powerless to control it. I was powerless to control my hunger and I was alone. The one who Made me allowed me to run off after he changed me. He let me go knowing full well what I would do. What I would become.

He only came to me when I was terrified and cowering in a dark corner of a room, sunlight flooding in. He delighted in seeing the slaughter. He tried to get me to see the beauty of it; that I would no longer be tied to these weak humans. He thought it would help to set myself free. He was wrong and swiftly left me trapped in the dark corner, where I was forced to look upon the mutilated corpses of my family. Whatever was left of me died in that room as I was forced to face what I had done.

Alone.

Once the sun went down, I ran. I ran and did not stop running until I had control of The Beast inside me. I still do not have complete control, but it is better than it was, and I work towards controlling it every day. I have met others along the way, others like me and others like my Maker. Unfortunately, there are more like him than there are like me. There are more who enjoy the power and who relish in the hunger...in the blood.

It is easy to do. It consumes you. It sustains you. But just like anything else, you can either be a victim to its control or you can learn to control it. I am working on learning to control it because I refuse to be like the others. I refuse to succumb to The Beast. I know I am no longer human. I am no longer anything close to human, but I do not have to be The Beast either. I can be something in between.

I am going to start being that something now, here, in my home. I am going to attempt to regain control of this place and make it a better place than what it has become in my absence. It will not be easy. As vampires go, I am extremely young and extremely weak, but that will not stop me from trying to make this place better. I do not care how long it takes. After all, I have all the time in the world. Unless they wish to kill me, truly kill me, in which case I would not fight too hard.

I am not entirely sure where to start. There is no more Rule. There is no more King or Kingdom. There is just vampire and human.

And now, there is me.

Journal Entry - Year 1722

A hundred years have gone by but I haven't aged a day. Not physically, at least. I guess that's a perk of being undead if there is one. I've always known I was physically appealing, now, I don't have to worry about ever growing old and losing that appeal. That aspect of being a vampire suits me just fine.

I've accomplished a lot in a century. Then again, who wouldn't be able to without the strains of humanity weakening them? I'm not human. No, I've only grown stronger in the past one hundred years on this earth. I've grown into such a formidable power that I now own this territory. I've regained ownership and, if vampires had King status, I'd be one.

I've become what the vampires call, Mèt Nan San, which translates to, Master of Blood. Basically, I'm at the height of my power. More powerful than most as I am able to sire new vampires. This power is the most coveted amongst our kind. I initially refused to sire any more monsters. The world has plenty without me adding to the masses. Not only that, I didn't want to make anyone into what I was made into, what I've become. But then…life got lonely.

One hundred years is a long time to be alone.

Once I became my own Master, it severed the tie I

had to my Maker. Another perk, as I never wanted to be connected to him. I never wanted to feel any type of bond with him because he is a truly evil being. As a sire, I didn't have a choice. Now, I do. And now I understand the thrilling power of having my own sires. It adds to your powerbase. It fuels you in ways blood can't. It's more of an...essence. I don't know how to explain it, but it is a heady surge of power and, now that I've had a taste, it's hard for me to control the urge to make more. To take innocent lives.

Except when it comes to her.

Katherine.

She first approached me several years ago at one of my lavish balls. She was bold and fearless and unapologetic in her pursuits of what she wanted. Me. I was intrigued by her sheer confidence, her unspoken challenge daring me to ignore her. Not to mention she wasn't hard to look upon. I wasn't...enamored, but then no one had caught my eye in such a way since Selah.

Katherine became a steady companion. I enjoyed having her around because she didn't fold and quake before me. She believed herself to be better than most and with that belief she expected to be chosen. She expected to be turned so she could truly be better than a mere mortal.

I suppose that's why she sought me out in the first place. Her ambitions have always been at the forefront, giving her that reckless fearlessness. In fact, I'm not sure she ever truly loved me, although she swore upon it. It was a moot point because I didn't love her in return. Therefore, I didn't care about her feelings, however driven they may have been.

She wasn't a good person at her core. I knew this instantly about her. I should have just killed her and rid Earth of her wickedness, but I was too busy playing with my food. I was too much like she was, arrogant. I was immensely powerful and felt untouchable. I have never been more wrong in my entire life.

Katherine all but destroyed me.

I refused to turn her into a vampire. I told her I didn't love her. I used my power to make her leave my side. I was cruel and unfeeling in my rejection of her. It cost me everything.

As she was forced by my own words to leave my city and never return, she cursed me. Katherine was a Master in her own world, one of Voodoo. Something I never believed in until the day I saw its power unleashed upon me and mine. She claimed I was incapable of loving anyone but myself and that I didn't deserve the love of those I created. She took all of my sires from me, took the undead life right from their bodies, and cursed me from ever making another.

I laughed in her face at her nonsense. I refused to

believe such witchcraft existed. Why? When I myself am a product of something unnatural, I don't know. I don't know why I doubted, but I did, until it was proven again and again. I am unable to sire another vampire.

I've searched for Katherine but she either doesn't want to be found or she no longer walks this earth. Even with my power, I cannot find her. I don't know if the curse will die with her or remain. I don't know how long this curse will last, or if it can ever be broken, but I will continue to try. I will continue to try until I'm truly dead and can try no longer. What other choice do I have?

I don't want to be alone for eternity.

Perhaps she did love me because love, and unrequited love, makes people do cruel and evil things. Or, perhaps it was just the fact that she was denied the one thing she wanted most.

I guess I'll never know.

Journal Entry - Year 1822

Another century gone. It's been two hundred years since I died and one hundred years since I was cursed. I should be relishing in my power. My territory should be thriving. I should have a family of sires surrounding me.

I have none of it.

I still have my power. Once a Master, no one and nothing can take that away from you except true death. But all the power in the world cannot break this damn curse. And I curse her in turn every day for it. I curse her name every time my attempt at siring a vampire only ends in their true death.

I've lost everyone from two lifetimes now. I've outlived humans, animals, and hell, other preternatural creatures of the night. I've lost everyone. And I can't handle any more losses. Not like this. My sanity will not survive.

I refuse to allow anyone else to ever get close to me again. I've closed down the castle, shut everyone out. I will unleash the hunger. I will hunt to feed, and I will not allow anyone inside. Not inside the castle. Not inside my heart.

I'm embracing the darkness.

I'm embracing The Beast.

It's the only way I'll continue to survive.

Journal Entry - Year 1900

I've become nothing more than a monster. I'm the monster in the dark that people fear. I'm the threat that parents use to scare their children. I'm not the monster under your bed but I am the monster in the shadows.

I don't remotely feel human anymore. The Beast has no humanity. The Beast knows only one thing.

Hunger.

But even The Beast is tired of this game. Or maybe I'm just stronger than I want to believe. Maybe my humanity hasn't left me completely yet, despite how much I've tried to bury it, despite everything I've done.

Maybe that's why I made the deal with Cogslow.

His daughter, only seven years of age, ran into the woods, into MY woods, and got lost. The Beast found her. It was in this moment that I started to push through the hunger and take back control I'd given to the monster inside me. Because though I hunt rapaciously and without mercy, even The Beast could not take the life of an innocent child.

Cogslow didn't know this though. He was certain I would kill him and his little girl. When he found us, I was crouched down over the unconscious child, debating what to do, terrified to touch her for fear of hurting her further. I had not laid a gentle hand on anything living in close to a century, but I knew I would not let myself harm the child.

In fear of her life, her father bargained his instead. He begged for me to take his life and let his little girl go. In that moment, I knew I was done with hunting like an animal. I made a deal with Cogslow, that he must come back to my castle and be my source of blood until the day he died. That was my offer, and he took it without hesitation.

It took years to adapt to being somewhat human again. Ever so slowly, I came back to myself. I came back to the Alexander Knightwell from before this all started. By the time I did, Cogslow had spent twenty years in my castle, doing things here and there to update it and keep himself busy. I tried to set him free, the guilt of taking him from his daughter, from his life, eating at me in a way the blood hunger never did. He refused to go back stating it would only open old wounds and cause more hurt when he died and his family lost him a second time. He said it was better they thought he was dead and had learned to move on without him.

He taught me many things about the inventions and conveniences the world had adapted in my time hidden away as The Beast. I worked by his side to install electricity into parts of the castle, learning and absorbing as much as I could from him about the outside world. We become close in the end. I don't believe he ever forgave me, how could he? But he did befriend me, and we lived out the rest of his days in peaceful companionship.

Selfishly, I did try to sire him before the end. He only died in my arms, confirming that the curse set on me is still in place. Confirming that I am doomed to forever be alone in this world.

Journal Entry - Year 1968

The legend of The Beast has served me well. It's kept most people away from my castle, away from me, which suits me just fine. But occasionally, I get those that seek me out directly.

Lumineux is the third.

He has a sad story, no doubt. I feel for him deeply because I understand exactly what he feels. The emptiness of being alone and losing everyone you love is not one that will ever go away. Still, I can't give him what he desires.

I refuse to take his life.

I will not take another life as long as I live if I can help it. My days of being that version of myself, being The Beast, are over. It was never who I am, and I let myself lose sight of that. I let the cruelty of this world infiltrate my heart, my soul, until I was just as cruel. But the world is also beautiful and full of life and love. It's often harder to see, harder to hold onto, but it's there if you take the time to look for it. I can't say I'm taking any time to look for it, but I no longer want to belong in the darkness of cruelty. So, whatever that looks like, that's where I am.

And even though Lumineux is surrounded by the same darkness, he hasn't let it infiltrate his heart. He's a beacon of light and hope and I hope that he chooses to stay. Because I need his light. In fact, I'm starting to crave it *more and more...*

...Her cries ripped through my heart instantly. Without ever laying eyes on her, she gutted me, deeply.

*She's beautiful. She's hurt and scared but God, she's beautiful. I shouldn't have brought her here but how could I let her go? I haven't felt this way since...well, I haven't ever felt...**this**. The more I watch her, the more I listen to her, the more I fall for her.*

Bella.

Bella.

My beautiful, Bella.

Bella

I close the journal and sit back, stunned at what I've read. The last journal sits on the desk in front of me and I notice a gap, as if something has been wedged between them. I reach for the breach in the pages and slowly pull it open. My hands seem to move in slow motion as I gather up the parchment inside.

It's me.

Hand sketches, like that of Selah's, but of me. Me laying on the sofa, my hair a mess of leaves and twigs and dirt. He left out the bruises and scrapes from my face, leaving me looking peaceful in my sleep. Another of me sitting on the bench in the garden, an open book in my lap but my eyes are on the sky, a faraway look in them. The last one looks like it's from his view of me from inches away. My eyes are heavy-lidded and my lips are parted. *Oh geez, Bella, could you look any more twitterpated?*

Alex doesn't need to read my mind; my thoughts are written clear as day on my face. I lay all three sketches side by side. I've never seen myself from this point of view before. As I study each image, I can see how much of my soul he's captured in each one. As if he knew exactly what I was feeling in each moment.

I *was* peaceful in my sleep knowing I was in the castle, safe and out of Gabriel's reach.

I *was* far off in thought, thinking about how I was directly responsible for my own happiness, regardless of aspects of my life.

I *was* completely smitten, taken over by desire right before he kissed me.

It's like he knows me on a deeper level than anyone else ever has, even my mother. And even if he doesn't actually know me in this way, he sees me. God, he sees me how I've never even seen myself. It's beautiful and heartbreaking and I have the overwhelming need to thank him. I need to let him know how grateful I am that he sees me for me. I need to let him know that no one else ever has, and regardless of what ends up happening between us I will always remember him and how he made me feel.

I tuck the sketches back into the journal and return it to its rightful place in the drawer along with the others. A sense of urgency drives me from the library. Something telling me I need to find him. I need to find him right *now*.

I powerwalk toward the sitting room, my ankle still giving me a bit of a twinge as I try to move too quickly. Reaching the doorway to the sitting room, I'm disappointed to find the stunning vampire missing. Louie's body still takes up the space on the sofa, but Alex isn't inside. I hurry towards the back exit to the garden but stop in my tracks as soon as I pull the door open. More snow covers the ground now, quite a bit more. I hadn't even realized it had been snowing. I've been too caught up in what's going on inside the castle to care about the world outside.

There are no footprints in the snow, so I close the door and walk back into the castle. I check the kitchen only to find it dark and empty as well. There's only one other place I can think to look for him since I know he wasn't in the library. His bedroom. My heart starts to speed up a bit as I climb the entryway stairs and move down the hall towards the South Wing. Towards his bedroom where I first saw The

Beast.

As I approach the large black doors, I stop to inspect them. I lift my lantern closer and reach out my fingertips to trace the carvings in the wood. Roses. Beautiful vines of blooming roses carved with the most intricate and delicate details. It's almost as if the thorns will prick my fingers if I'm not careful.

I gather my courage and knock lightly. I know he'll hear me, he'll know I'm out here, as long as he's not...distracted. After all, he said he heard me scream when I fell in the forest. He'll definitely hear me now.

"Alex? Are you in there?" My voice betrays my nerves. The image of those red eyes and bloody fangs flashes in my mind. *That's not him. That's not who he is.* I try to calm myself.

I knock again, harder this time. "Alex?"

Only silence replies. What if he's not even here? What if he went out? He could have easily gone out another door. I take in a deep breath and reach for the handle. I turn it slowly and gently push the heavy door open.

"Alex? Are you in here? Can I come in?" I yell into the dark room. Again, no response except eerie silence.

I push the door open further. "I'm coming in! I don't want to interrupt you if you're...*feeding*. You've been warned!"

My legs barely seem to move, my body is fighting against going any further, the trauma of what it experienced last time taking control. I stop a few steps into the bedroom and take another deep breath and blow it out slowly. I close my eyes and picture Alex in the woods, saving me from the coyotes. Alex in the kitchen when he first smiled at me and brushed the flour off my cheek. Alex from the sitting room when he held me close and kissed me like I was the most precious thing in the entire world.

That's the Alex I know.

That's the Alex I trust.

I get my feet moving further into the darkened bedroom, my lantern lighting my way, providing only glimpses of the massive room. As I pass the bed, cold air touches my skin and I shiver. There must be a window open. I continue on, following the cold breeze until I come to its source. Not a window, a door. A door to a balcony and that's where he stands. Most of him is lost to shadow, but I can tell that he's upset. His back is rigid, and his hands are gripping the balcony railing tightly. It does not look like the comfortable stance of someone enjoying the fresh evening air.

I stop just inside the door, not invading his space. "Alex? Are you ok?"

"I'm fine. You should go." His voice is hollow and just as cold as the winter air surrounding us.

Something stirs inside of me; that sixth sense that seems to pick up on the clues and energy that a conscious mind will never be able to see or feel. Something's wrong and my gut is telling me not to leave him.

"I'm worried about you," I say softly.

I watch as his head falls, and he sighs heavily. "I said I'm fine. I just want to be alone right now."

All the words I read in his journals are fresh in my mind. He's been alone for a long time, too long. I think it's what he knows and what he's used to. Being alone has become his comfort zone, his safe place when he's feeling unsteady, but deep down I know what he craves because I crave the same thing.

"No, you don't." I gently set the lantern down on the floor. It's cold out here and I fight the chill trying to grip my body. It's not about me right now. It's about this beautifully haunted
man standing in front of me and I'll suffer any weather for him.

My steps are cautious. I don't think he'll hurt me, but

unwavering trust hasn't been established between us yet. There's still the smallest chance that The Beast inside of him will lash out, trying to protect him in the only way he's ever known, by pushing people away. He doesn't move a muscle as I stop right behind him. His head is still hung low, body tense. I place my hand on his back, letting him know I'm here and gauging his reaction to my touch. His back tightens even more but he doesn't pull away and he doesn't ask me to leave.

Taking the last step, I close the distance between our bodies and wrap my arms securely around his waist as I lay my cheek against his back and hold him.

"I'm here," is all I can bring myself to say. I don't know exactly what's wrong so I can't provide anything else besides comfort and support, and I'm hoping that's enough. I'm hoping he accepts it…accepts me.

His body slowly starts to relax, and he moves one arm to cradle mine where it's wrapped around him. We stand like this, in comfortable silence for a long time. When he finally speaks, it's a pained whisper that rips open my chest and slices my heart.

"He's gone."

Those two simple words plunge inside of me and sink like an anchor, dragging my heart into dark depths. Louie. Gone. I felt it when it happened. When I was in the library and got the sudden urge to find Alex and be with him. I wonder if it was Louie himself talking to me? I manage to smile through my tears at the thought of him watching over us. He always has, and will, just now in a different way.

"I'm so sorry, Alex. I know you loved him. I did too, but you don't have to face this loss alone. *I'm here*," I repeat, trying to solidify my position. "Whatever you need, I'm here."

He turns, and I have to loosen my hold on him as he moves to face me. The tears in his eyes match my own. It doesn't matter that I only knew Louie for a short time versus how long Alex knew him. We both loved him in our own way and we both feel the pain of his loss. Pain is pain. Some greater than others, but who's to say how anyone feels that pain. It's not a contest, every ounce of pain matters, and this time he doesn't need to face that pain alone.

His hands cup my face as his eyes clear and he stares down at me with sparkling silver stars. He stares at me for a long time, his sad eyes darting back and forth between mine, the pain still raw on his face. I have a second of doubt creep in. Am I doing the right thing? Or should I have left him alone like he asked?

"Whatever I need?" he asks, never taking his intense gaze off me.

"Whatever you need," I repeat.

"I need *you*, Bella. I need you like I need blood to survive." He closes his eyes and leans his forehead against mine and swallows hard. "Please tell me I can have you, all of you."

"I need you, too," I admit. "Alex, look at me." He pulls back and opens his eyes; his jaw is clenched tight, but his hands are still holding my face gently. "I'm yours."

Those two simple words unleash him. He's done hesitating. His lips are on mine and he's devouring me with a furious need I've never felt before. He's kissing me like a wave kisses the shore during a hurricane.

Strong.

Forceful.

Terrifying.

Deadly.

And I'm kissing him back just as hungrily because the thought of not being able to have this man is terrifying. I barely know him. I haven't seen him at his best and I sure as hell haven't seen him at his worst, but the thought of not getting the chance to experience those things and everything else in between feels like it might kill me.

His strong hands leave my face to slide down my sides until they cup my ass and lift me effortlessly into his arms. My legs wrap around his waist, and he walks us back into his bedroom. The balcony door slams and then, seconds later, my back hits his soft mattress.

His deliciously heavy weight falls onto me, and I wrap my legs around him tighter, needing him closer. He pushes his hips into me, rubbing his hard length against my center, and I moan my pleasure into his mouth. I can already feel myself growing wet, needy for him, and we haven't even started yet.

His hand slides under my top and his cold touch makes me hiss and goosebumps erupt across my skin.

He breaks our kiss. "Shit, sorry. My hands must be freezing." He starts to slide his hand out of my shirt and I grip his wrist, halting his movement.

"No." I shake my head. "I mean, yes, they are but please don't stop."

His eyes are lost to the darkness of the room. I can barely make out his features and I desperately want to see them. I want to greedily take in every detail of this man as he reveals himself to me for the first time, inch by inch.

"Actually, does this room happen to have a light in it?"

His low chuckle is sexier than it's ever been as it rumbles through his chest and sinks into me. "Looks like you're the one with mindreading ability because I was just thinking the same thing."

He pushes himself up and I have to unhook my ankles to let him free. He slides off the bed and I lose sight of him. A few seconds later, a flame flickers in the darkness before it's met with another, and another, until the room is glowing in flickering light. Lastly, he lights candles on the nightstands on both sides of the bed.

"I never cared to have electricity installed in here. I can see just fine in the dark, so I hope you don't mind the candles." He sets down the lighter he used to light them and then his full attention is back on me where I'm now flooded in beautiful golden candlelight.

"It's perfect." Now that we've slowed things down, it gives me time to really think about what's happening. This is real. This is happening...with Alex. I'm suddenly extremely nervous, or is that excitement? My heart can't tell the difference as it pounds erratically in my chest and I know he can hear it.

"We don't have to do this." His voice is calm and gentle but his eyes are searing into me hotter than any flame.

"I want to," I assure him.

"What do you want?"

"I umm, I want to see you." My voice betrays me yet again as it shakes in a breathy whisper.

"Ok," he says calmly. He reaches behind him, grabs his shirt, and pulls it off in one smooth motion, tossing it aside.

"Wow," I whisper, in awe. "Wow. Ok, now that is just not fair." My eyes must be popping out of my head as they slowly rake down his solid chest, over ripped abs only to get hopelessly caught in the extremely deep V disappearing into his dark jeans. A beautiful solitary white rose is inked into his right side. "There's no way you're real."

His beautiful laugh sinks deep inside of me, warming up my cold skin and heading straight for my heart. Or maybe it's the V that went straight to my heart, maybe a combination of both, but both equally fucking deadly.

"Bella, I can assure you I'm one hundred percent real." His arrogant smile remains on his face as his fingertips move to undo the button on his jeans, then the zipper is down and he's hooking his fingers into his jeans and underwear, sliding them down his massive thighs. I watch, transfixed, as every inch of skin is revealed and he slowly stands back up, completely naked.

"Holy fuck," I whisper.

I've forgotten how to breathe as I lay here on his bed, soaking up the sight of him. His body is perfect, every inch sculpted in smooth, lean muscle. His dick is hard and hangs heavy before him. I never thought I'd think of a dick as beautiful, but if there is such a thing, this is it.

I move my eyes back up his body, taking in his thick arms and well-defined shoulders before finding those heated eyes again. "You're beautiful. You're perfect."

"I'm far from perfect but I'm glad you think so. Now don't leave me hanging, quite literally. I want to see you, too."

I suddenly feel really shy and completely inadequate compared to the Greek God standing in front of me. Just the thought of letting him see me so openly and freely makes me blush. I drop my gaze, no longer able to meet his heated and expectant stare. I never felt this way with Gabriel. I guess I never really cared what he thought about me, but I care way too much about what Alex will think about me.

"Bella, look at me."

His voice is dangerously low and commanding, and even though I don't feel the tingle of his compulsion on my skin, I have no choice but to comply.

"Come here." He pats the edge of the bed right in front of him. I get my legs under me and crawl slowly over to him. His fingers find my chin and lift my face up until I'm forced to hold his suddenly serious gaze. "I'm not lying when I tell you that you are the most beautiful woman I have ever seen. Not just because of what I can see with my eyes but what I can feel with my heart. There's not one single piece of you that won't satisfy me *immensely*. But if you don't want to do this, we stop it right now. If you're uncomfortable in any way, we stop this right now."

I swallow hard. Damn this man is beyond perfect. How did I

get lucky enough to end up here, in his arms, with those incredible, honest eyes shining like polished platinum down on me?

"I want to," I say, managing to sound steady and certain.

He holds my gaze for a few more seconds before he lets his hand drop. I feel his fingertips slide under the hem of my shirt, his calloused hands scratching gently across my smooth skin eliciting a delicious shudder as he slowly raises my top. I lift my arms, and the shirt comes off slowly before it's discarded somewhere on the floor. He holds my gaze, never once taking his eyes off mine as I reach behind me and release the clasp on my bra. His fingertips find the loosened straps and slide them just as slowly down my arms, letting the bra fall to his feet and still he doesn't take his eyes off mine.

He cups my cheek, and his thumb traces my bottom lip. "You're beautiful." His hand falls down my neck and barely grazes my breast, my nipple immediately peaking under his touch. It has nothing to do with the chill and everything to do with *him*. He continues down my stomach until both of his thumbs are hooked into the waistband of my leggings and panties. He slowly pushes them over my ass and down my hips. Falling back onto the bed, I give him my legs so he can take them the rest of the way off. I end up lying back on my forearms, naked before him, and still his eyes are on mine

Until they're not.

I watch his reaction as his eyes finally drift down my exposed body. They don't linger on anything in particular. They seem to take in every part of me equally, thoroughly, and ardently.

"Like I said…," his eyes finally meet mine again, only this time there's a hint of something more in them. The Beast. But not in a frightening way, in a thrilling and addictive kind of way, "beautiful."

He wraps a large hand around his hard dick and strokes himself as he looks down on me. *Holy shit*. The way he's looking at me and unable to resist touching himself at the sight of me is exhilarating.

It's intoxicating.

It's addicting.

If I was lacking confidence before, his look has me brimming with it now. Releasing his cock, he places a knee on the bed. I push myself back further onto the gigantic bed, giving him plenty of space for his large body. My legs part instinctively, allowing him space as he crawls on top of me. He finds my lips immediately and he's back to kissing me with absolute control. He may be kissing me slowly, his hunger reined in, but it's not one ounce less passionate. His lips leave mine to trail along my jaw and down my neck, following the same path his hand took moments ago.

"I want to feel and taste every inch of you." His voice is deep and sexy against my bare flesh, awakening my nerve endings in a way I didn't know was possible. I can feel every little graze and whisper of breath on my flushed skin.

His tongue traces my collarbone before dipping lower. Holding himself above me, he shifts his weight to one side as his other hand caresses my stomach. His hand slides up my ribs until his thumb finds the underside of my breast, stroking the sensitive skin lightly. Just as his mouth closes over one nipple, his fingers tease the other one. The sensation of his hot mouth in direct contrast with his still cool touch has me arching my back and moaning my pleasure to the ceiling.

His weight lifts off me and his devious mouth moves further down my stomach. Once he passes my bellybutton, with no intentions of stopping, I begin to panic.

"Alex, what are you doing?" I squeeze my legs shut, pausing his descent.

"I told you; I'm going to touch and taste every inch of you."

"Umm…ok but wait."

He stares up at me, patiently waiting for me to continue.

"It's just that I, uh…." My thoughts swirl around in my head like a goddamned tornado. I don't know how to say everything that I need to say. It will most likely ruin this moment before it even gets started. Fuck, why didn't I say all this before? "I uh…well, I was with someone, and I found out he wasn't faithful so…umm, I don't know if…oh God, this is so embarrassing. I don't know if I'm clean." I can feel the heat of the blush burning my cheeks. I can't believe I'm having this conversation with him while his head is between my legs. I'd like the world to swallow me up now.

"I'm a vampire. I can't contract any human illnesses and, even if I could, you don't have one."

"Oh. Ok, well that's nifty. But umm, how do you know?"

"I would be able to smell it in your blood."

"Oh. Ok. Yeah, umm…well…," I clear my throat, "that's good I guess."

"Now will you please loosen your death grip on my head so I can get back to pleasuring you?"

Oh shit, oh shit, oh shit. The blush from earlier only intensifies. I don't know why I never imagined this moment would come, I just…didn't.

"Bella?"

"Mmhmm?"

"Has no one ever tasted you before?"

Oh God. Yup. This is beyond mortifying. My worst fucking nightmare. All I can do is shake my head in shamed defeat.

"Do you trust me enough to let me?" he asks, solemnly.

I don't even hesitate. I nod because I do. I trust him explicitly.

A wicked grin blooms across his face and that beastly look flashes in his eyes again. "Good."

Then his hands are on my knees, easily pushing them away from his face, and before I can register what just happened and the preternatural strength in his hands, his tongue swipes up my center and I fall back to the mattress with a gasp.

"Oh fuck," I mutter.

His tongue is wet and warm, and oh my God, I've never felt anything so fucking good in my entire life. All insecurities and embarrassment are forgotten as the absolute pleasure takes over every other thought and every damn nerve in my body. All I can focus on is the feel of his smooth tongue devouring me. His fingers dig into my legs where he's gripping them, holding them hostage, demanding my attention. Lifting my head, I look down my body to see his silver eyes practically glowing with wicked fire, showing me exactly how much he's enjoying this. More ink on his back catches my eye but I can't make out what it could be from this angle and, honestly, I'm too distracted to care.

I've never been turned on so thoroughly before in my life. Seeing this gorgeous man diving into the most intimate part of me physically, and feeling the soft, firm flick of his tongue against my sensitive clit, has me rolling my eyes back and collapsing onto the bed. I feel a tingle starting from my head all the way down to my toes.

"Oh fuck," I repeat. "What's happening?"

It feels like that hurricane that started with our kiss is now building and building inside of me, low in my belly. I feel it swirling and picking up speed, matching the movements of his devious tongue, as my climax gets closer and closer.

"Holy fuck, Alex. Whatever you're doing, please don't stop."

He growls an approving moan against my core at the same time I feel his fingers slide inside of me. The sensation of him penetrating me while his tongue continues to massage my clit is more than I can handle. I grab ahold of his hair and hang on for dear life as the orgasm slams into me.

Strong.

Forceful.

Terrifying.

Deadly.

It feels like it rips me apart in the most intensely pleasurable way. My back is forced off the bed as I try to escape his relentless tongue but it's no use. His strong hands hold me to his face, and I can feel myself pulsating around his fingers, clenching and releasing as I come. All I can do is spasm and whimper and hold on for dear life as I'm left to helplessly lay here and feel my soul leave my body.

When the shivers and wracks of pleasure finally fade, he moves back up my limp body, his wet lips landing on mine, tongue sliding into my mouth with that delicious hint of cinnamon on his tongue. And now something else.

Me.

Fucking hell. The taste of my arousal on his tongue is heady and I want more of it. As he continues to kiss me back to life, I feel the solid pressure of his erection as he rubs it against my sensitive clit, bringing that tingling sensation back to race across my skin.

He breaks the kiss, nipping at my bottom lip as he pulls away. "Jesus, that was one of the most beautiful things I've ever seen. And the way you taste, the smell of your skin, and your arousal on me...Cod, I want to have you forever." His hot and steely gaze meets mine, and just when I thought I was catching my breath, it's gone again with that look. "I want to be inside of you. I *need* to be inside of you." He pushes his dick harder against me. "Tell me I can have you. Tell me you want this. Tell me you want me."

"I want you, Alex. Fuck, I want you so bad I can't even see straight."

He chuckles and grins down at me, dimple on full display as he teases. "That's from the orgasm. But I *want* you to see me. I want you to look at me as I push inside of you." His fingertips caress my cheek. "Do you see me, Bella?"

"I see you," I say earnestly, because I *do* see him, and I love everything that I see.

He reaches down and grabs his hard dick, rubbing it against my soaked center before positioning himself at my opening. His other hand finds mine and intertwines our fingers, holding my arm above my head, never breaking eye contact with me as his hips start to push forward. I gasp, mouth parting, back arching, legs wrapping around him, and hand griping his tightly as he slowly slides inside of me.

He groans and his eyes flutter closed for a second. "Fuck," he mutters, before lifting his eyes back to mine.

My body is tight around him as he pulls back out and pushes forward again, getting further this time. He pulls out again and when he pushes in a third time, I take all of him. The feel of him filling me up completely and his weight on top of me, consuming not only my body but my heart and my soul too, feels like I'm finally whole. There's so much I want to say but no words seem capable enough to describe this moment and what I feel.

His other hand finds mine and moves to join the one above my head as he starts to thrust his hips in a beautiful and dangerously slow rhythm, exactly like the way he kisses me. I move my hips to match his deliciously slow strokes. His eyes are glued to mine and nothing else outside of *him* exists. This moment is excruciating and maddening, and it feels so fucking good both physically and emotionally. We're in the eye of the hurricane together and we're holding on to each other for survival.

He quickens his pace; his dick pushing harder inside of me, making me moan and beg. "Please don't stop."

"God, you feel so good."

Our words are whispered prayers. Our breaths are ragged and chaotic. I can't tell where he stops, and I begin. I'm swallowing down his pants, his essence, his fucking soul…in exchange for mine. In this moment, I give him everything.

No one else has ever deserved it.

Nothing else has ever felt this real.

"Alex," I whisper against his lips, as once again the pleasure builds to unfathomable limits inside of me until it's too much for me to contain and I break.

I break apart underneath him and only his strong arms holding me keep me from scattering to the ends of the earth. His eyes are my center, my gravity, my safe haven, and I let myself fall completely as the second orgasm takes me. When I can no longer keep my eyes open, his lips are on mine again, suffocating my cries and securing my connection to him even more, taking me higher than I've ever been. He groans into the kiss as he pushes one last time, fingers gripping tightly onto mine, and I feel the pulse of his release inside of me.

I don't know how long we stay this way, both reeling from the pleasure that just flowed through us, but eventually he unlocks our fingers, slides out of me, and falls to the bed beside me. Another small sliver of worry starts to bloom in my chest. *What now? Is that all he wanted from me? Should I leave?* I never had to think about it before because Gabriel was always the one to leave me, immediately after he was done.

I'm about to get up when Alex's hands find me and pull me down next to him. "I hope you weren't thinking about leaving me. You're crazy if you think I'm going to let you go."

"I uh...wasn't sure what you wanted."

"What did I tell you, Bella? With you, I want everything. Fucking everything," he says, as he holds me tight against his body.

Everything.

That should scare the shit out of me. No, what should terrify me is the fact that I *want* to give him everything. The fact that maybe I already have.

Bella

I wake up in a cocoon of warmth and muscle. Unlike anytime I've woken up next to or in Gabriel's arms, I feel nothing but content and comfort. This warmth doesn't suffocate me. This strength doesn't scare me. Quite the opposite actually. Everything about waking up in Alex's arms makes me feel unimaginatively happy.

And safe.

A smile immediately pulls at my lips as last night's events come rushing back. I've never experienced sex so…profoundly before. The way he made sure I felt comfortable and continued to ask my permission before every next step was empowering. For the first time, I felt like I was in complete control. If I didn't want something to happen, it wouldn't. But what I love most about last night is the way he stayed in each and every moment with me. He never went somewhere else in his head, and he never stopped watching and listening to me.

Gah, I was such a fool to fall, even a little, for Gabriel's selfishness. Because now that I know what it feels like to be seen and appreciated, to be taken seriously, and to have my needs and wants put first, I will *never* except anything less. *Such a damn fool, Bella.*

Moving slowly, I turn in Alex's arms. I come face to face with the most handsome man I've ever laid eyes on. His eyes are already on me, shining brightly even in the dim light streaming in through the high windows. I've lost all track of time. I don't know if it's dawn or dusk gracing us with its presence. I find I don't really care. My heart starts to race simply from the proximity to his naked body and the way he's looking at me.

"Hi," I whisper nervously, with a ridiculous cheese-eating grin on my face.

"Hi." He smiles back just as broadly, his dimple on full display.

"I think you use that dimple on purpose; to disarm me."

"Why would I want to do that?" His fingertips brush the hair away from my face before gently drawing random circles on my bare shoulder causing me to shiver in pleasure.

"So you can have your way with me," I tease.

His fingertips stop moving on my skin and his smile fades. "Bella, I would never take advantage of you, just like I would never hurt you. I thought last night that you—"

"I'm teasing, Alex." I can't help but laugh. His words are perfect, and I know he's sincere but he's so serious. I don't want him to think that he needs to walk on eggshells around me anymore. "I know that you respect me, and I know that you would never hurt me or make me do anything I don't want to do. You've shown me that truth again and again. I don't want you to have to keep trying to prove what's already been proven. I want you to feel comfortable around me and not hold yourself back or fight your instincts. If you want to touch me, touch me. If you want to kiss me, kiss me. You have my permission and…I'm not scared of you."

A new smile tugs at his lips. "Ok."

"Ok," I echo.

"God, you're beautiful."

His fingertips find my cheek. It's as if he can't help but touch Me and it makes my heart swell in my chest because I don't want him to ever stop wanting to touch me.

"I don't want to ruin this...but I also don't want to assume. I asked you before to be sure. I asked you not to cross this line with me unless you truly meant to give me everything. To stay here with me. To *be* with me."

"You did."

"And last night?"

"Last night was...." I can feel the heat tinting my cheeks pink at the image of him looking up at me from between my legs, and I bite my lip in an attempt to stop another ridiculous smile.

His fingers gently tug on my bottom lip, freeing it from my teeth. "Use your words, Bella."

"Last night was the best decision I've ever made in my life. It's also the first decision I've ever made that wasn't made with someone else's needs in mind. I said yes because it's what *I* wanted. Last night was the first time I've ever done something selfish. And you know what?"

I'm rewarded with another heart-stopping, panty-dropping smile. *Oh yes, I could get use to this.*

"What?"

"I don't feel even a little bit guilty. In fact, I feel like I finally took a step in the direction of living the life *I* want. And what I want, more than anything else in this world...is you," I whisper, the truth of my words and my admission leaving me feeling breathless and dizzy.

His response is the best response I could have asked for. His lips land on mine in a soft, gentle kiss. When his tongue sweeps into my mouth and dances with mine, my heart explodes in my chest. Just one slow, gentle kiss from this man has me feeling like I just ran a marathon.

I'm terribly frustrated when the kiss ends up being just that, a kiss. Granted, as far as kissing goes, I am *not* complaining. I already know I'll never get tired of kissing him. Ever. But this is all so new, and my body is eager and hungry for more. I got the smallest taste of him last night and now I'm *starving* for more.

"I know how much you love your mother and how much she depends on you. What does this decision mean for your situation?"

I shrug. "My mother will understand. She's only ever wanted me to be happy and live my life. And it's not like I'm leaving her completely. She's not far, and I can still visit her all the time and check in on her. You'll help me through the woods, won't you? You'll keep me safe when I go to visit her?"

"Of course, I will. Whenever and as often as you want. Whatever your heart desires, if it's in my ability to give it to you, is yours."

"I want this. Whatever this feeling is, in here." I place a hand on my chest. "I don't even know how to explain it because it doesn't make any sense." I laugh, suddenly feeling silly trying to describe a foreign feeling. "It's heavy yet light. It's the overwhelming buildup of anxiety as you slowly tick to the top of a rollercoaster and it's the thrill of the freefall afterwards. It's terrifying and exciting but also peaceful and.... and I'm rambling again, and this doesn't make any sense." I hide my embarrassment behind my hand.

He gently grips my wrist and pulls my hand away from my face. "I know exactly what you mean. It makes perfect sense to me. *You* make perfect sense to me."

"I want more of this, too. More of just lying in bed with you. I want to talk about everything and nothing with you. I want to explore every inch of your mind and good Lord, I definitely want to explore every inch of your body." I feel the heat in my cheeks again at my bold admission. I wonder if I'll ever stop being embarrassed around him.

His eyes sparkle with amusement and excitement. "Oh yeah?" He takes my hand and places it on his chest, sliding it slowly down his stomach before releasing it, leaving my hand firmly planted on his abs.

"You also have permission to touch me and thoroughly explore me anytime you'd like. I. Am. Yours."

That beastly look is back in his eyes, a challenge, I think. But there's also yearning in his intense gaze, too. The thought of him wanting me to touch him as much as he wants to touch me is so intoxicating. I can see how this, us, could turn all-consuming if we're not careful. And I'm so tired of being fucking careful.

I want to let my fingertips explore every dip and muscle in his stomach until I find that line that will lead me south. I'm curious to know what I'll find when my hand reaches its destination. Will he be soft? Will my touch start to stir him to life? The thought of feeling him grow hard under my palm makes my core tighten with desire. Better yet, I want to take him soft in my mouth and feel him grow hard as I lick and suck him. Or will I reach down to find him already hard and waiting for me? All options excite me, and I want to experience each of them with him.

"What are you thinking about?" His voice is a strained whisper, pulling me out of my thoughts.

I open my eyes, I hadn't even realized I had shut them, and I'm met with that hot flame in his, the same look from last night. My chest rises and falls with my shallow breaths, and I can feel the growing slickness between my legs at just the thought of doing things with him. He hasn't moved a muscle. We're still laying on our sides next to each other. Our only point of contact is where my hand still sits, unmoving, on his stomach as it rises and falls with his own heavy breathing.

"I umm...," my mouth has gone all watery and I have to swallow in order to keep talking without drooling over him, "I was just wondering if I would find you already hard and excited or if I would have to, umm.... help you out a little."

"I think you already know the answer but why don't you find

out."

I move my hand off his stomach and cradle it against my chest, so it doesn't do *exactly* what he suggested and travel south to find out.

"I don't want you to think that I don't want to because I very much want to. I want to stay in this bed with you for the foreseeable future and never leave, not even to eat."

"But?"

"But...." I know this next part is going to be *the* killer of all mood killers, but it needs to be said. It has to be addressed. "We need to bury Louie."

As soon as the words are out of my mouth, sorrow replaces the heat in his eyes and I see his chest deflate. I hate this look. I hate this situation. I hate that our coming together is tied with such a heavy loss. I hate that we can't just get lost in each other and to hell with everything else. If it wasn't for Louie, I would do that in a heartbeat. I would let the outside world burn to ashes just to keep this look off his face.

"You're right," he finally says. "Let's get dressed and give Lumineux the peaceful rest he deserves."

I nod my head, the thick emotion already starting to fill up my chest, threatening to suffocate me. I watch as he climbs out of bed, giving me his backside as he walks toward the bathroom. I have a few seconds to roam over his body. It goes without saying that his ass is just as sculpted as the rest of him, but I barely notice it. His entire back is covered in ink and I'm staring into the eyes of a deadly animal. A beast. I can't make out exactly what it is before he's lost to the shadows.

As much as I want to call him back and say I'm wrong, that I want to explore him after all, I don't. Instead, I climb out of bed and pick up my discarded clothing, dressing and trying to mentally prepare myself for what comes next. This isn't going to be easy but at least we're together. I can't imagine how often he's had to face this type of situation alone and it guts me. If I have any control over our future, he'll never be alone again.

Neither one of us will be.

ALEX

CAN'T HELP FALLING IN LOVE BY SAYWHEN

I feel like a complete ass. Lumineux is lying, dead, on my sofa and all that's been on mind since the moment she stepped foot in my bedroom last night is Bella. I don't do it intentionally, but she monopolizes my thoughts. She's haunted me in my dreams and every waking moment since I found her in the woods. Every corner of my brain and every inch of my body is utterly and thoroughly enthralled by her. I want to know and explore every facet of her being. I want to know her and understand her on a level that's unlike any I've ever encountered before. It's more than flesh and words.

It's soul deep.

And what does that even mean? Like her words earlier, it doesn't make sense, and maybe that's why I knew exactly what she was saying. It's nothing words can describe and yet, it's everything. She's everything.

Unfortunately, I know how quickly the next sixty or seventy years will pass. It may be a lifetime for her but it's a blink of an eye to someone like me. This is why I want to escape into Bella with everything that I am. I want to be present and take advantage of every damn moment with her because I know how precious every single second is. Spending time with her doesn't make Lumineux any less dead.

Yes, I know how disgusting and uncaring that sounds. I don't mean it to be but it's the truth, nonetheless.

Still, Bella is right. We can't leave him on the sofa. He does deserve his peace, though I'm sure he's already found it. His soul may be at peace, but his body needs to be laid to rest, too.

As much as I wanted to shower with her, we decided it would be best to head our separate ways. We were able to stop anything from starting this morning even though it took all of my strength not to devour her again, but I don't think either of us are strong enough to say no a second time. Especially when naked, wet bodies are involved. Just the thought of her naked in my arms as my soap slicked hands glide over her body has my cock twitching in response.

This is going to be a long fucking night.

I head outside while she showers. The sun has dipped below the horizon but there's still a faint glow in the sky. I've become powerful enough that the light no longer hurts me unless I'm standing directly in the sun's rays, but even though the fading light no longer hurts me, I can still *feel* it. It's like an ache deep in my bones. A warning in my body that was instilled in me the night I became a vampire. It served me well in the beginning when I spent time mostly underground, hiding from the pain, *all* of the pain becoming a vampire caused.

I find a beautiful and peaceful spot on the mountain, just below one of the large cedar trees that lines the forest sprawled below. It will be close enough to visit but also far enough away to be left alone and peaceful. Not that there's anyone else out here to mess with his grave. Nonetheless, the thought of him being left in peace is still important.

I get to work digging his grave. I have to clear the space of snow before I start. The cold, frozen earth is difficult to penetrate and would be impossible to dig up if I was simply human. But I'm not. It doesn't take long for me to dig the hole, but night has completely fallen by the time I walk back to the castle. I find Bella standing just outside of the sitting room, hugging herself.

"Hey...," I gently stroke her arm, letting her know I'm here, "you ok?"

She nods her head yes but then shrugs like she's not sure. We stand in silence for a little while, both of us just staring into the room.

"I can't go in there," she finally whispers. "From here, I can pretend like he's still sleeping but if I go in there...." her voice breaks.

"Shh, it's ok." I pull her into my arms and hold her tightly, leaning my cheek on her head as she sobs into my chest. "You don't have to do anything."

I continue rubbing her back as she clings to me. I hate that she's sad and crying but God, I love that she needs me like this. I love that she comes to me for comfort. I love that she trusts me enough to be vulnerable in my arms. And fuck, I love the way it feels to hold her. Her body fits so perfectly against mine. I inhale the smell of her freshly shampooed hair and the jasmine scented soap on her skin, but nothing compares to the smell of her arousal. I engrained her scent into me so deeply last night that no other scent will ever cause it to fade.

Shit. Here I go again. Being consumed by completely inappropriate thoughts while she's mourning, and I'm supposed to be comforting her.

I clear my throat and step slightly away from her. "I just need to clean up and then we can finally put Lumineux's body to rest, ok?" She sniffs and wipes at her eyes, nodding in agreement. "Will you be ok here? Or would you like to wait for me in my room?"

"I, uh, I think I'll wait for you in the library. If that's ok?"

I cradle her face in my hands and wipe the last of her tears from her cheeks. "Whatever you want." I lean in and brush a kiss to her forehead before grabbing her hand and walking with her down the hallway, away from the sad truth of the sitting room, and up the stairs towards the library.

She walks with me to my bedroom where I provide her with a lantern before she heads off to the library, leaving me alone and longing for her once again. *Will the desire to simply be next to her ever fade? Or will I constantly crave her?* And I haven't even had her blood yet. Just the thought of what she'll taste like has my fangs aching to be set free and piercing her beautiful skin.

She made the choice to stay here with me. She said the words, *I'm yours*, but does she truly know what giving me everything really means? I know we've talked about it. She understands what I am and what I want from her, but I hope she knows that's not *all* I want. She's so much more to me than the blood pumping through her veins. Yes, her blood will sustain me and keep me alive, but simply being alive doesn't mean you're living. And I live for her, for her heart, for her soul, for every little gasp and whimper and moan, for every laugh and every tear. I've been drinking blood for centuries, but I haven't felt this alive since I was human.

Bella makes me feel like I'm capable of being who I once was. Maybe not in the flesh, I can never again be human, but in every other way that matters I can, and *I will*. For her.

I step under the lukewarm water, attempting to keep the flame inside of me tempered to embers so I can get through what needs to be done but it's futile. I could jump into a frozen lake and still feel my soul burning for her, desperate to feel her hands on my skin again and feel her body sticky with sweat and desire underneath mine. I shower in record time, leaving myself unfulfilled and unsatisfied, even by my own hand. If it's not her bringing me to release, then I don't want it. I'm on a mission to get this task completed, to say goodbye to Lumineux properly, and to keep moving forward with Bella with nothing to stop or distract us.

I pull on dark jeans, black boots, and a deep maroon sweater.

I even manage to find some gloves, more than likely they belonged to Lumineux or one of my other companions. The cold doesn't bother me, but I don't want my touch to be freezing again the next time I'm with Bella.

She's sitting on the chaise in front of the cold, empty fireplace, a blanket pulled over her, and her legs tucked underneath her. I've always kept the castle in darkness, only allowing Lumineux the use of lanterns and candles with an exception to the kitchen. The fire in the sitting room has always been kept small, leaving the smoke minimal and inconspicuous this high up the mountain for the fog and clouds to hide, for the most part. However, seeing her sitting here now in front of that cold fireplace makes me want to start the largest fire this library has ever seen. I want her to be comfortable here, not shivering in darkness, hiding away from the world.

Who fucking cares if they know I'm here? The legend is vicious enough to still keep the townspeople at bay even if the castle was lit up like a lighthouse. And if people get curious and venture into my woods, I have no qualms about scaring them right back down the mountain. The image of Bella's beautiful naked body illuminated by nothing but firelight only solidifies my decision.

Approaching her quietly, I notice that she has a book open in her lap, but she's once again lost in faraway thoughts. It's one of my favorite times to watch her. She's completely unaware of her surroundings and just...being. She always looks so serious when she's like this. She gets a little crease between her brows and her lips are set in a firm line. She *feels* everything so incredibly deeply and I don't think she even realizes how beautiful that is.

"Do you ever actually read the books?" I tease, as I stop a few feet away from where she's sitting, sliding my hands in my pockets to keep from reaching out for her. I know she said not to hold myself back from doing what I want, when I want, but I also know there's a time and place for everything.

She gives me a weak smile, looking only slightly embarrassed. "I'm going to pretend you didn't ask that question considering you *know* I do."

"Do I though?" I continue to pick on her, trying to lighten her mood. "I mean, I see your eyes moving and you flip through the pages but for all I know you don't *actually* know how to read."

She scoffs. "Well, the same could be said for you then, Mr. I Read Romance Novels."

"I do read them. Maybe one of these nights I'll read one aloud to you. One with especially *explicit* detail and you can show me exactly how it makes you feel."

Fuck. Here I go again, unable to be chill for even a second around her. But the blush on her cheeks and the quickening of her pulse tells me she's on the exact same page as I am.

I smirk and stalk toward her. Once I'm standing next to the chaise, I brace myself on the back and lean into her. "I can tell that this is something you want to explore, and I'd be happy to oblige."

Her head is forced back to look up at me, her eyes are heavy lidded and full of need, but it's when she licks her lips that I can't help capturing her mouth with mine. Once again, the only thing connecting us is our kiss and it only adds to our tension. I'm the damn gasoline and she is my match. Together we are nothing but combustible.

She sighs as I pull my mouth away from hers. "Keep that thought close by," I order, as I offer her my hand. "But right now, we have something important to finish."

She nods and takes my hand. We descend the stairs and head to the sitting room in silence. She waits for me while I wrap Lumineux in a blanket and then pick him up, carrying him outside. Bella holds a lantern, but a full moon has blessed us with its presence, giving us more than enough light to see by. It's an uncommonly clear night considering the last few days have been overcast with storm clouds. I wonder if Lumineux has anything to do with it. It makes me smile to think he does.

The snow looks blue under the glow of the moonlight, coating the ground and treetops as far as I can see. It makes everything look clean, untouched, and beautiful. Peaceful. The perfect night to say goodbye to my dear, dear friend.

I hop down into the hole and gently lay him down before lifting myself back out easily. "Would you like to say anything?" I ask quietly.

She wipes at her cheeks again and clears her throat. "Umm, yeah, of course. I, uh...well, I didn't really know you very long, Louie, but you made me feel so...normal. I know that sounds unimpressive, but for me, it was exactly what I needed. You took care of me and helped heal me in more ways than just some bruises and a sprained ankle. You truly became like family to me and, even though it was briefly, I loved you and I will forever cherish our moments together. As sad as I am to say goodbye, it makes me so incredibly happy to know you're finally with Claire and Chloe. Rest in peace, my friend."

I grab her hand and squeeze it. She looks up at me with tears in her eyes but a smile on her face. She needed this goodbye just as much as I did. I reach for the shovel next to the loose mound of dirt.

"Aren't you going to say anything?"

"I said everything I needed to say when he woke up. We had a few minutes before he passed."

"Oh, I didn't know. I wish I had been there."

"He knew how much you loved him, and he loved you just as much. I promise, he knew."

She nods her head and smiles again, only this time it's a little sadder. I don't blame her; this is a hard loss.

I begin to shovel the dirt. She stands beside the grave in silence as it slowly refills, securing Lumineux deep underneath where no animals will be able to dig him up. It doesn't take as long for the dirt to go back in as it did for me to get the dirt out, and far less messy, too. Once all the dirt has been replaced, I walk over to the side where I had laid down a single white rose, pick it up, and place it on the grave.

"How did you manage to find one still alive in this snow?" Bella asks in awe.

"I have a rosebush in my bedroom that I tend to personally. The blooms can last quite a while into winter if they're taken care of properly."

"I had no idea."

"Come on, let's get you back inside, it's cold out here."

As she turns to head back to the castle, I walk up beside her and scoop her into my arms. I'm rewarded with a beautiful, lighthearted laugh, which is why I did it. Plus, I like having her in my arms.

"Alex!" She playful swats at my chest. "I'm more than capable of walking on my own."

"Are you though?" I tease her again, adding to our conversation from earlier. "Since I've met you, you've needed assistance walking more than not." She looks only slightly offended but I'm pretty sure it's not genuine.

"Injuries don't count."

"Well, consider this my effort to minimize your chance of sustaining another injury."

She laughs and I can see the twinkle of playfulness in her eyes. "You can't carry me around everywhere."

"Can't I?"

This earns me an impressive eyeroll but she can't hide her beautiful smile. And I don't want her to. I realize I'm smiling back at her just as broadly. What a sight we must be, smiling uncontrollably at each other like two psychopaths walking away from a fresh grave.

She doesn't protest as I continue to carry her up the staircase and into the South Wing, toward my bedroom. Once inside, I gently sit her down on the edge of my bed. There's no light in here but the electricity between us is palpable. I know she feels it, too.

I move around the room, lighting a few candles but not nearly as many as I did last night. Once I'm done, I stand back in front of her. I can tell that something is bothering her and I'm hoping she's comfortable enough to tell me.

"Alex, I...," she hesitates, looking down into her lap before continuing, "I know what I said about you having my permission. I totally meant it. And still do!" she adds quickly. "I don't want to be alone, but I also don't want to...it's just that it doesn't feel right, you know, with Louie and everything and I—"

"Bella," I interrupt her rambling.

Her big, worried blue eyes pierce my fucking soul. I can feel how nervous she is, but I don't understand why. I've never pressured her for sex, and I never will. My hand finds her cheek. I'll never get tired of holding her face in my hands and having these incredible eyes hypnotize me from inches away.

"We never have to do anything you don't want to do. I'm perfectly satisfied if you let me fall asleep and wake up with you in my arms. You don't have to be alone, and it doesn't have to be more than that."

"You're not mad?"

My eyebrows furrow in confusion. "Why on earth would I be mad? Have I given you a reason to think all I want from you is sex? If I have, it was not at all my intention."

"No, no! You haven't, I swear. I guess it's just...old habits."

Old habits. More like old lovers. She's mentioned this piece of shit before, and every time she reveals another truth about how he hurt her, I want to rip a piece of flesh off his fucking bones and hear him scream in pain and fear. It takes all my effort to control my thoughts and not let the anger show. I don't want her to misinterpret it.

"I'm not him." I can't keep the words to myself. "You don't ever have to be scared to say what's on your mind, to tell me exactly what you think and what you want. I promise you; I will never hurt you physically or do anything to break your heart. It's far too precious."

She scoffs and rolls her eyes again.

"I'm serious, Bella. Your heart should be handled like the most exquisite and delicate piece of blown glass. You should entrust it only to the most capable and worthy of hands. Hands that will appreciate it, but most importantly, hands that will keep it safe."

"It's too late," she whispers. "My heart has already been mishandled. It's already been broken."

"Are you familiar with the Japanese philosophy of *wabi-sabi?*"

She looks confused. "No."

"They choose to embrace that which is flawed or imperfect. They even go as far as to repair broken objects with seams of gold. It's a technique called *kintsugi* and it's used to highlight the history of the item instead of trying to disguise it. Just because something has been broken, doesn't mean it's beyond repair. Often times, the broken item repaired with *kintsugi* becomes even more treasured and considered more valuable. Do you follow what I'm saying?"

"I think so."

"You had to suffer some cracks and breaks so that you could experience life and learn to appreciate the good that is otherwise overlooked or taken for granted until it is directly compared to something bad. Your broken heart has given you character and wisdom. All it needs is a little *kintsugi* and it will be even more beautiful and valuable than ever."

I'm not sure if the tears in her eyes are happy ones or sad ones until she pulls me down and thanks me with a kiss. It's a chaste kiss compared to our others, but I can feel her overwhelming gratitude.

The saltiness of tears has never tasted so sweet.

"Thank you," she breathes against my lips. "Now will you please take me to bed and hold my body...and my heart...in your capable and worthy hands?"

My own heart squeezes in my chest. When I lose her, and one day I will, my own heart will be crushed to dust beyond any type of *kintsugi* repair.

With no regard for my own damn heart, I whisper, "Yes."

ALEX

HERE WITH YOU BY SICK PUPPIES

Falling asleep to the sound of her steady breathing and the warmth of her naked body pressed to mine is my new favorite drug. She held my hand tightly to her body as it was wrapped around her, as if she couldn't get enough of me covering enough of her. I wanted to just hold her, and talk to her, like she had mentioned wanting to do, but she fell asleep almost instantly. So, I lay beside her and just soaked in the moment. I'm not sure how long I stayed awake, listening to her breathe, but it soothed me.

Like Lumineux, I've come to find my own sense of peace when I'm with her. That sense of peace is momentarily interrupted as I wake up to find its source missing. The bed is still warm, indicating that she hasn't been gone for long. I slip from beneath the covers and quickly get dressed. Her clothes are no longer discarded on the floor where we left them last night, so she has definitely left the room.

I start in the library, then check her old room before heading downstairs. The kitchen is also dark and quiet. I doubt she's in the sitting room, but I check anyways. When I don't find her anywhere inside, I know that she must be in the garden. It's the only other place she enjoys being.

There's a slight glow in the sky but the sun is still far below the horizon. I can always *feel* it. I have at least thirty minutes before it starts to climb into the sky, but it won't matter anyway since the sky is once again filled with big, fluffy storm clouds. The early morning hour brings a frigid chill to the air. Winter has come earlier than normal this year.

I find her exactly where I knew I would, sitting on the bench in the garden, eyes helplessly lost to the sky, as if she's incapable of looking away. Déjà vu rushes through me from the first night I approached her, only this time, her small body is almost lost to the enormous jacket engulfing her. A furred hood is pulled over her head and all I can see of her is her beautiful face, cheeks and nose tinted red from the cold.

God, she's adorable.

I watch her silently for a few minutes before the urge to be next to her overtakes my body and pulls me into her orbit. She looks my way when she hears me approaching and graces me with a smile more luminous than the sun. Her eyes are clear and crystal blue this morning, like sunlight sparkling on the surface of the ocean. I want to dive into those warm waters and never come up for air.

"Good morning," she says brightly.

I want to tell her how disappointed I was waking up without her in my arms, but the look on her face and the genuine happiness I feel radiating off her dissipates any disappointment I had.

"Good morning, Sunshine." I lean in and gently graze her lips with mine before I take a seat next to her and wrap my arm around her, tucking her into my side.

She lays her head on my shoulder and lets out a sigh. "The only thing that could make this moment any more perfect would be a hot cup of coffee."

"That can be easily taken care of. Would you like me to bring you one?"

"Mmm...," she contemplates my offer, "actually I lied. This

moment is already perfect. I wouldn't trade you for any cup of coffee in the world."

"Happy to hear it," I chuckle. "How'd you sleep?"

"Oh my, so good. I don't think I've ever slept as good as I did last night. What about you?" She pulls her head back to look at me with a smile that doesn't seem to want to leave her mouth. I don't blame it. I have a hard time leaving her mouth, too.

I move my eyes from her lips and give her my full attention. I've never seen her eyes this blue before. Or this…alive. And right now, they're directed at me. Her happiness is directed at me. And it's contagious. I brush a thumb over her flushed cheek. She doesn't seem to mind the cold.

"Never better," I say, as her eyes hold me captive.

If eyes are windows to the soul, then I can clearly see that this soul is mine. It belongs to me. Not because I want it. Not because I asked for it. Not because I have any say in the matter whatsoever. But because it just is. I knew it from the moment I heard her scream. Her soul is connected to mine. She is a piece of me just as much as I am a piece of her.

We stare at each other for what feels like hours but is really only seconds. A stare has never been so powerful. A stare has never felt this physical. A stare has never said so much. A stare has never *shown* so much. I see everything I'll ever need to see shining up at me. I see all the words she never has to say. And I pray that she sees mine.

I want to say the words out loud, but I don't want to ruin this moment with words that are unnecessary. There will be plenty of time for that later.

She finally breaks eye contact, but the smile doesn't leave her face. "I came out here to watch the sunrise. I feel like it's been too long since I sat to enjoy it. My sleep schedule is way off."

"I suppose that's my doing."

She laughs. "A little. I just kind of stuck to what Louie was doing. I don't mind it," she shrugs. "Though I probably shouldn't have slept through so much of the night last night. I'm going to have to stay up all day and all night now to get back on track."

"Well, I have some ideas that we could discuss to keep you awake."

I watch as she bites her lip, trying to hide her growing smile, but I see it. I also see that cute blush redden her cheeks even more. I love that she gets a little shy around me. I hope it never changes.

"I'm sure you do," she laughs heartily.

"But for now, we watch the sunrise."

She nods but then turns to face me, quickly a look of worry and devastation in her eyes. "But you can't watch the sunrise. Won't the sunlight be painful?"

"It might be a little uncomfortable, but the clouds will keep the direct rays at bay. I'll be ok." She doesn't look convinced. "I promise. I can watch the sunrise with you today. I won't always be able to, but today I can."

"Ok." She finally lets her smile come back.

"Ok." I kiss the tip of her nose before returning my eyes to the sky. She follows my lead.

About ten minutes later, when the sky is as bright as I think it's going to get, even though the sun hasn't quite peaked, huge snowflakes start to gently fall down around us.

Bella gasps, holding her palm upward to catch the flakes as they fall. "Look how *huge* these snowflakes are! I don't think I've ever seen any this big or...fluffy before!"

Next thing I know, she's stands and walks to the open space in front of us. She tilts her head up to the sky and closes her eyes, letting the snowflakes land on her. She spreads her arms wide and then begins spinning in a slow circle. The hood falls away from her face, but she doesn't seem to notice. Her pure and sweet innocent giggle pierces my chest the same way her scream had.

I watch her with rapture. I've never been happier or more fulfilled than I am in this moment, watching her unrestrained joy in something so simple. She finally stops spinning and fixes me with her jubilant stare. Snowflakes are stuck in her copper hair and cling to her lashes. I think the sun continued to hide today because it knew it couldn't compete with Bella. I'll never again be able to experience the sun the way she can, but I have something better. *I have her.*

Sunshine.

She is my sun.

She bites her bottom lip and I see a gleam of mischief flash in her eyes before she gives me her back and crouches down to the ground. A few seconds later, she stands back up and, as she spins around, a snowball comes flying towards my face. I could easily move to avoid it, but I don't. I let her think she caught me off-guard. Her laughter is worth a million snowballs to the face.

A slow, deadly smile creeps across my lips as I wipe snow off me. "Oh Sunshine, you're going to pay for that."

I get off the bench and reach for the snow at my feet. She laughs again and rushes to create another snowball but I'm faster. Mine catches her in the shoulder and her throw goes wide. I'm already making another one when she realizes this isn't a game she's going to win and starts running away from me.

"Oh no you don't!" I yell, as I release the snowball, catching her on her ass, before I start after her. "You don't get to start a snowball fight and then runaway."

I catch up to her easily. My arms wrap around her, lifting her up, and she squeals in delight as I take us both to the ground. I fall first, cradling her body against mine so I don't unintentionally hurt her, then I roll her onto her back, pinning her down.

She tries to fight me off playfully but we both know it's pointless, even if she wasn't pretending. My lower body presses into hers and I have both of her arms pinned out to the side. She's laughing and breathing heavily, letting me know she's enjoying this little fight as much as I am. God, I haven't smiled this much in ages, and I forgot how ridiculously *good* it feels to be happy.

Her laughter slowly fades, and we lay staring at each other with smiles plastered on our faces as snow continues to fall around us. The only sound in the entire world is her heavy breathing. Her eyes drop to my lips and my heart drops to my stomach. She licks her lips and I break.

My lips crash onto hers and they're so cold. I don't know how she's managed to stay out here for as long as she has. My concern is quickly forgotten as the warmth of her tongue seeks entry into my mouth. I part my lips and my tongue meets hers in a deliciously heated dance that stokes the ever-burning fire in my soul. I settle between her legs, and she spreads them wider making room for me. My hand leaves her wrist to travel down her body until I grip behind her knee and pull her leg up, giving me even more space to fit my body against hers. God, I want to feel her skin.

She pushes her hand against my chest, and I concede, allowing her to roll me into the snow and climb on top of me. She leans down to continue our kiss as she straddles me. She presses down on my already hard erection and rocks her hips against me, making me moan into her mouth. It's too much. Everything is too much. The pressure in my chest. The ache in my dick. And definitely too many fucking layers of clothing.

"Bella...," I manage to pull away from her kiss to speak, "we either need to go inside right fucking now or you're about to be really damn cold when I undress you and take you in the snow."

"Then hurry up and take me inside," she breathes against my

lips.

We get to our feet and then she's once again being held in my arms. "If I use some of my power to get us inside quicker, will it freak you out?"

"You mean like superspeed?"

I grin. "Yes Bella, like superspeed."

She grins back at me excitedly. "Do it."

She squeals again and wraps her hands around my neck tightly as the world flashes past us. Seconds later, I'm tossing her down onto my bed. Her joyful laughter fills up the quiet room. Her presence and her energy bring much needed life to this place. To my world. I once again move around the room lighting all the candles. I also quickly get a fire going in the fireplace. I can't remember the last time I used it, but Bella can't handle the cold as well as I can. Now that she's seen my vampire speed, I'm back beside the bed in minutes.

"Wow! Now *that* is impressive. It's almost easy to forget what you are until you do something like that."

"Did it bother you?"

She shakes her head. "Not at all. So, what did you have in mind for keeping me awake? I'm feeling a bit tired," she fakes a yawn. *Devious little angel.*

"First off, since I did the undressing last time, I believe it's your turn. You can start by getting undressed and then you can get over here and undress me."

She bites her lip and her cheeks flush. It's all I can do to hold my ground and not crawl on top of her and rip all her clothes to shreds.

Starting with her knee-high boots, she unzips them, slides them off her legs, and kicks them to the floor. She pushes up until she's standing on the bed, giving me the perfect view of what's to come as she starts unzipping her jacket next. Her eyes are blue flames burning through me as she holds my stare and throws the jacket to the floor.

Crossing her arms in front of her body, she grabs the bottom of her sweater and pulls it excruciatingly slowly up her stomach. Once it reaches her chest, she inches it up to reveal she's not wearing a bra. I groan at the sight of her bare breasts. My palms itch to caress them but I remain in place.

Her fingers slowly release the buttons on her jeans. *Why does one pair of jeans need so many fucking buttons!* My eyes are glued to her hands as they push the jeans down her thighs, over her knees, and then she's stepping out of them one leg at a time. She stands back up in nothing but red lace underwear. The color of blood. And I don't know if she made that choice on purpose or if I'm thinking too much into it.

She walks across the bed to where I'm standing beside it. The height difference puts her beautiful breasts right in front of my face. I bite the inside of my cheek, trying to maintain control, but it's quickly melting away to nothing under the assault of her flames.

She reaches for my sweater and slowly starts to lift, letting her fingers graze my skin as she does. I raise my arms above my head for her, but the shirt is quickly forgotten when she falls to her knees. Her hands are cold against my skin as she caresses my chest and then traces her fingertips softly down my abs. My muscles contract under her touch and she smiles.

"I don't think I'm ever going to get used to how sexy you are," she says in a quiet whisper, as she continues to let her eyes and fingertips roam over me.

She finds the tattoo on my ribs. "This is beautiful." She traces the stem of the rose down to where it meets my obliques, then lets her fingers trace the V until she reaches the button on my jeans. Thank fuck there's only one. She can only push my jeans down so far, so I help her and take them the rest of the way off. I'm now standing completely naked in front of her for the second time. This time she's more comfortable and confident and takes more control. Her hands wrap around my hard dick, and I hiss, partly because her hands are still a bit cold and partly because it just feels so fucking good.

She strokes me for a few seconds, all her attention focused on her hands while all of my attention is focused on her face. I love watching her. I love the way she looks at me. She must feel my eyes on her because her heated ones lift up to mine. She holds eye contact as she lowers her body to the bed. She angles my dick towards her mouth and then, with the same teasing slowness, she envelopes me.

The warmth and wetness of her mouth, in direct contrast to the cold of touch, has me shuddering. The sight of my dick disappearing into her mouth one slow inch at a time is so fucking hot and so fucking excruciating.

I groan. "Fuck, Bella."

I want to grab her head and push all the way inside her. All I do though is gently take up her hair and hold it firmly in my hand so I can watch her suck me. Her head bobs up and down as she abandons her slow teasing and finds a steady rhythm.

She uses her hand as an extension of her mouth to work the entire length of me with every stroke and pass of her mouth. Her eyes are closed now, and she moans as she takes me deeper down her throat. My head falls back and my own eyes close as I focus on every little stroke of her tongue, every press of her lips tighter around me, and every gentle suck. My own moans start to echo hers as I get lost in the intense pleasure.

I move my hips in rhythm with her strokes, holding her head a little firmer as I start to push a little further down her throat. My eyes open and I watch as I try to disappear inside of her. Her sparkling blue eyes flick up to me and I see the challenge in them. She wants to take all of me.

"Are you sure?"

She nods and moans again, letting me know how turned on she is. I pull her head down on me as I push my hips forward, feeling my dick slide down her throat, completely blocking off her air. Her mouth is opened wide, lips wrapped around the base of me when she gags on my dick. It's the sexiest thing I've ever seen.

"Goddamn," I moan.

I pull all the way out, letting her gasp for air. She catches the line of spit hanging from the tip of my cock and uses it to pump my dick as she takes a breather.

"Jesus Bella, it feels so fucking good."

Her eyes look up at me and she demands, "Again."

I only hesitate for a second before I slide back inside of her little mouth and push all the way down her throat a second time. I feel her reflexes trying to fight me, off but she manages it better this time, not gagging. I pull out and pump a couple of times into her mouth but have to stop. If I'm not careful I'm going to come down her throat before we've even gotten started.

I climb onto the bed and pull her away from the edge, flipping her onto her back. I hook my fingers into her panties, and she lifts her hips so I can take them off. I spread her legs to find her soaked and glistening. I use two fingers to slide up her center, massaging her clit, before sinking them inside of her.

"Fuck, you're so fucking wet. Did it turn you on that much giving me head?" She nods, no embarrassment whatsoever on her face. "Well let me return the favor."

I continue to stroke in and out of her with my fingers as my tongue finds her clit. She moans immediately and her hands fist into the comforter. Fuck. If sunshine had a taste, it would be her. She's so sweet and perfect. So responsive to every stroke and flick of my tongue, telling me exactly what she likes. I suck her clit into my mouth and her body jerks with pleasure.

"Oh fuck, Alex. That feels so good."

I continue eating her and fingering her, soaking the blanket beneath us and she hasn't even come yet. I can tell when she starts to get close to her release when her stomach starts to spasm and her thighs start to shake uncontrollably. Her hands move from the comforter to grip my hair instead. She's moaning and panting, holding her breath, and then gasping for air.

She starts to rock her hips, chasing her release, and I let her take control. "Right there. Don't stop. Holy shit, you're going to make me come. Please don't stop."

I can feel her pussy pulsing on my fingers, and I suck her clit into my mouth again as her body releases her orgasm and she screams my name to the ceiling, practically pulling my hair out and squeezing my head with her thighs at the same time.

Her legs and hands slowly release me as the pleasure floods through her. I climb up her body, her chest heaving, and I find her eyes dazed and a lazy smile spread across her face.

"I've never come as hard as you make me come in my life. Holy hell that mouth of yours is sinful."

I smile arrogantly, my ego one hundred percent inflated by her words. "I will live happily ever after giving you orgasm after orgasm if you'll let me."

"I don't think my body can physically handle another one."

"Let's find out."

She pleads and tries to stop me, but I hold her thighs hostage as I devour her again. She's much more sensitive now and it doesn't take long at all before I have her writhing in pleasure again.

"Stop, stop, stop!" Her hands are on my forehead, attempting to push me off as she comes again on my tongue. When she finally catches her breath, she looks down at me with a smile. "It's so good it almost hurts. How is that even possible?"

I just smile up at her as I climb her body once again, wiping her wetness off my chin. I'm about to slide into her when her hands come to my chest.

"Wait." Her tone is so serious that I stop, worried that something is wrong. Worried that maybe I took it too far. "I want to be on top. I want to feel you slide inside of me while I sink down on you."

I sigh in relief and chuckle. "You're not going to get any argument out of me."

I roll onto my back, and she climbs on top of me. She falls to one knee and leaves one leg up, allowing herself room to move more freely. Her hand grabs a hold of my cock and positions me at her opening. I'm impossibly fucking hard, and every little touch feels amazing. We lock eyes and then she starts to sink down onto me. Her eyes flutter closed, and she moans as my tip stretches her open.

I groan as my dick fights against the tightness of her pussy. I watch where our bodies meet, and she continues to slide down my length until I once again disappear inside of her.

Once she's seated all the way on top of me, she pauses for breath, letting her body adapt to me. "God, you're so fucking deep."

"Does it hurt?" I ask, worried.

She shakes her head. "No, it's just…a lot." She laughs.

And then she starts to move.

I feel like I've been repeating myself, but I swear, *this* is the sexiest thing I've ever seen. Her head is tipped back, eyes closed and mouth open, and she's moaning as she rides my cock. She lifts her hips all the way up, almost coming off, before sliding all the way down, taking all of me every single time.

I make a fist and bite down on my knuckles to keep the words I'm feeling right now locked inside of my treacherous mouth. I don't want to say the most important words I'll ever say to her while she's thoroughly fucking me, but goddamn it, I want to.

Her breasts bounce up and down with the rhythm of her body and I reach out to grab them. Her skin is so soft and perfect. I pinch her nipples, and she moans louder and falls down harder on my dick. Fucking hell. I lift up and wrap my arms around her, pulling her down on top of me. I replace my fingers with my mouth and teeth as I hold her ass up and thrust into her.

"Oh God, yes," she cries out. "Harder, Alex. Fuck me harder."

I growl around her nipple and pound into her. The wet slap of flesh against flesh accentuates her beautiful voice as she begs me to fuck her and not to stop.

"Shit, I'm gonna come again." Her voice is ragged and strained and so fucking sexy.

I'm close to coming too but I'm aching for something else. I release my fangs and let the tips scrape against the sensitive skin of her breast that is still in my mouth. She gasps and looks down at me. I'm terrified of what I'll see in her eyes but she doesn't look scared. She looks excited. But maybe it's just the rising orgasm.

Whatever it is, I don't question it when she whispers, "Do it."

My fangs pierce her flesh at the same time her orgasm pulses around my cock. Her eyes roll back, and her mouth falls open, but no sound comes out.

The first sweet taste of her blood is like a sucker punch to the gut. It's powerful and heady. It's rich and sweet and delectable. It's literally the life flowing through her veins and now, I get to have it. I get to have all of her. I've never felt so possessive in my life but, *She. Is. Mine.* Body, blood, heart, and fucking soul.

She is mine.

Her blood coats my tongue and I swallow down a mouthful before I let her breast go. My own orgasm hits and I slam into her one last time as we both come undone. She collapses on top of me, her body limp and heavy. We both struggle to catch our breath and slow our racing hearts. I can feel the beat of her heart pounding through her chest and into mine. It feels like we have one heartbeat.

My dick slides out of her as it softens but I continue to hold her to my chest, not wanting her to be anywhere else but right here on top of me. I brush her hair to the side and then softly start to stroke her back with my fingertips. Goosebumps erupt across her skin; she shivers and lets out a deep sigh against my chest. Her heartbeat starts to slow and settle into a normal rhythm.

"Alex?" Her voice is quiet.

"Yes, Sunshine?"

"Is this the way it's always going to feel?"

I'm not sure what she's asking, but if I had to guess, she's asking about my bite. "Do you mean my bite?"

"No," she mumbles. "Although, that was...."

I start to get a little nervous when she doesn't continue. "It was what?"

"I don't even know. Indescribable. I have no words for how it felt. Amazing just doesn't seem to cover it. Earth shattering, maybe?"

I chuckle, relieved that I didn't scare her. "Then what are you asking?"

"This. All of it. Me here with you. How you make me feel. Not just when we're having sex, although sex with you is definitely happening...*a lot*." She pauses, and I chuckle again. "I just mean... I don't know. I want to always feel this way. I don't ever want these feelings to go away."

Once again, she doesn't have to make sense for me to understand exactly what she's saying. She's talking about falling in love. I can't say for certain that's what she's feeling but it's damn sure what I'm feeling. But unlike her, this feeling will come to an end for me whether I want it to or not.

"There is one feeling I could do without though," she

continues.

"Oh yeah? What's that?"

"I'm **s t a r v i n g.**"

Yeah…me too, Sunshine. Me too.

"Well, we better get you some food then."

Bella

Alex was true to his word. He kept me up all day and all night, *effortlessly*. After the bedroom, we made it down to the kitchen where we made waffles together, even though he doesn't eat human food. He had no reservations about the syrup though which was eaten off *me*. That got very messy. It was fucking delicious…but messy which then led us to the shower. Who knew water, and soap, and his muscled body would be so damn sexy.

Jesus, save me.

My body and vagina have never been so sore from sex in my life. Then again, I only ever had sex with Gabriel, and it was nothing like sex with Alex. It was very vanilla and very one-sided. Not to mention the size difference. I don't care what anyone says, it does matter. If you would have asked before, if I considered myself to be a sexual person, I would have told you no. I would have told you that it didn't really matter to me one way or another.

HA! How wrong I was.

Turns out, I'm an insatiable little nympho when it comes to Alex. Even when my body is slightly protesting; one look, one kiss, one touch from the sexy vampire has me throwing my vagina in his face.

Vampire.

Fuck. Don't even get me started on his bite. Everything I've ever read in paranormal romance books is right. Their bites are beyond pleasurable.

"What random thought is passing through that pretty little head of yours this early in the evening?" His voice pulls me from my thoughts.

My head is rested on his chest and his fingertips have been drawing patterns on my skin since we woke up about twenty minutes ago. Neither one of us seem eager to get out of bed or out of each other's arms.

"I was just thinking about your bite."

"Oh yeah?" He grins, letting his canines grow into points and rubs his tongue back and forth under one. Why is that so fucking hot? Just the sight of them has my pulse speeding up and my core clenching.

"God, you're insufferable." I gently push his face away from me. He laughs and this time when I look, his teeth are the perfect straight white ones I've always seen.

"Tell me what you were thinking."

"Do you know why it feels good?"

"It's caused by a mix of two things happening. One, there's a non-lethal venom in the fangs designed to cause a certain kind of pleasure and two, simple blood loss. The venom also allows the blood to flow faster through our punctures, which leads to a lack of blood flow to the brain, which in turn causes the weightless and euphoric feeling."

My brows furrow as I contemplate his answer. "That's oddly very...National Geographic," I laugh.

He shrugs. "We're predators. The venom is designed to make our prey docile and with the quicker blood flow, we can drain a person within about forty seconds. And new vampires never have control, it's one of the reasons we're so dangerous."

"Am I your prey then?"

Faster than my poor tiny human brain can register, he has me on my back and is looking down at me with very serious eyes. The silver looks almost grey in this light, but I know better.

"You were never my prey and never will be."

"Alex, I was teasing. I didn't me—"

"I know you were. I know. But please, don't ever tease about that. I don't like those thoughts in your mind, not even as a joke."

"Ok. I didn't mean to upset you," I whisper.

"You didn't upset me, Sunshine. I don't think you could ever upset me."

He leans in and kisses me deeply. Everything he does, from a kiss to sex to the words he speaks to me, is more along the lines of worshipping me than using me. I never once thought I was his prey and I regret ever saying the words. I know his past will forever haunt him, the things he's done as The Beast. I don't want to remind him of his horrors, but I also want him to feel comfortable talking to me about everything without fear that I'll judge him.

Once he breaks the kiss, I bring up a topic I've wanted to discuss for a while. "Tell me about your tattoos."

I can see the hesitancy in his eyes.

"They obviously mean something very deeply or you wouldn't have gotten them. I want to know everything about you. Not to judge you but to understand you. To connect with you." I run my fingers through his hair, and he closes his eyes and sighs. "I umm...," it's my turn to hesitate. "I meant to tell you this a long time ago but I...I read your journals."

A small smile pulls at his lips. "I know you did."

My eyes widen in shock. "You do?!"

"I asked Lumineux to tell you about them."

"Why?"

"Because I wanted you to know about me. I wanted you to

make your decision knowing who, and what, I am."

"Well, I've made my decision. I'm here, with you, and I've never been happier. You don't have to hide anything from me, and I know I don't have to hide anything from you. Don't hide from me," I whisper.

He sighs but yields to me. He sits up and turns his back to me. The dim lighting barely allows me to see the tattoo, but I know from past glances that it's the face of a large animal, snarling, sprawled across his entire back from shoulders to the base of his spine. The application and detail are flawless.

"What do you see?" he asks.

I stroke my finger over the large canine of the animal. The entire tattoo is done in exceptional black and grey, but the eyes have been done in color. Silver. And they're so realistic it's actually a bit unsettling. Terrifyingly beautiful.

I move my hand to trace the spots on the big cat. "Leopard?"

"Close. It's a jaguar. I got it after Katherine all but destroyed me. I know it sounds strange, but I relate to it. I am after all *The Beast*. I may not be that version of myself anymore but at one point I was more animal than...." he trails off.

"Than human?"

"Than vampire. I haven't been human in a long time." He hangs his head but continues. "Jaguars are solitary animals, which suits me. They also have a very powerful name. It originated from the indigenous word, *yaguar*, which means *he who kills with one leap*. They also kill with their bite. A jaguar's bite is even more powerful than a lion's. And, like vampires, they're almost all but extinct. So, you can see why it fits."

"I know it represents a time you would rather not remember, but I think it's beautiful, both the artwork and the meaning. It's a part of who you are. You can't change your spots," I tease, with a smile he can't see. I hope he can hear the sincerity in my voice.

He scoffs.

I laugh a little. "I'm serious though. Look at me." He turns back around to face me, his handsome face set in serious and contemplative lines. "I can see the jaguar in you. The Beast is the one who saved me from the coyotes. And being solitary doesn't mean alone. Even jaguars have mates, do they not? I'm a solitary creature too, and I'd be the happiest girl alive to live out my days here, in the castle with you, never having to see another person."

"You really mean that," he says, almost in disbelief.

I smile. "More than anything."

He reaches out to caress my cheek, one of his favorite things to do I've noticed. He smirks. "You must really like me."

"Well…actually," I fake a grimace. "It has more to do with your library than you," I tease.

He laughs a deep throaty laugh that stirs up my insides and leans in to whisper, "Liar," before he kisses me breathless.

When he pulls away from me, I let out a heavy, shaky sigh. I don't think I'll ever stop being affected by this man's kiss. "That was almost, *almost,* enough to distract me. I'm on to you and your sorcery." I narrow my eyes at him. "But I want to know about the rose next."

"Hmm…guess I need to work on my spells. Next time I'll bring out my *wand.* That always seems to do the trick," he grins wide, dimple on full display. I feel the heat climb into my cheeks at the mention of his very magical dick.

He laughs and I playfully punch him in the arm. "So cocky!"

He lifts an eyebrow. "Why yes, yes I am."

"Oh my," I hide my burning face in my hands. "I didn't mean it like that!"

"You walked right into that one!" His laughter is contagious. I bust out laughing and it's just what this moment needed. It's what he needed.

He rolls onto his left side and holds his arm back, away from his body, so that the rose tattoo is fully displayed. Again, I let my fingertips trace over the ink. Another beautiful black and grey piece applied so...delicately.

"Whoever did these was immensely talented. They look so real. Like I should be able to feel the silkiness of the petals and the sting of the thorns." We're quiet for a while as I take the time to really appreciate the piece. "What does it mean?"

"Roses can mean different things but for me the white rose is a representation of a clean slate, so to speak. A new beginning. I know I can't ever escape the past, or change the things I did, that's why I chose to add the thorns, as a reminder that blood is always one decision away, but I can control my present self. I haven't taken a life since I got this tattoo."

"It's beautiful. The art and the meaning behind it."

I push him so he's lying on his back, and I drape myself over his stomach and look at him. He places an arm behind his head and the other on my thigh. Yet another normal and insignificant thing he does that makes my heart skip a beat.

"You're a good man, Alex. I'm sorry all of this happened to you. I'm sorry you never had a choice, but I'm not sorry because it made it possible for you to be here, right now, hundreds of years after you would have left this earth, and I never would have met you had it not happened. I can't imagine never meeting you."

"I would live it all again if you're the end result, Bella. It's all worth it if I get to spend my next lifetime with you."

His next lifetime. Not his only lifetime, his next one, which means he will continue living long after I'm gone, which means there will be someone after me. I know it's ridiculous to think about, but the thought makes me sad and jealous and pisses me off. It's not fair. It's not fair to either of us. He has to eventually watch me grow old and die. Will he even still want me once I start to age, and he doesn't?

"What's wrong? Why the tears?"

"Tell me about the curse."

A pained look enters his eyes and, once again, I hate that I'm bringing up such a hard topic for him, but I need to know.

"You read the journals. There's not much else to tell. I'm cursed to forever walk this earth alone, eventually losing everything and everyone I love to time."

"You're sure there's no way to break it? In all the books I've ever read, there's always a way to break curses. There has to be a way to break this one."

"This isn't a book, Bella. This is real life, and if there was a way to break the curse, I would have found it by now. Trust me, I searched for a long time. I sought out every witch and Voodoo Priestess I could find. They either didn't know how to break the curse or refused to tell me."

"This is all so unfair."

"Please don't cry." He wipes my tear-streaked cheeks. "I hate seeing you cry, and it won't do either of us any good. All we can do is live in each moment we're blessed to share together. I want you here with me, always. Not focused on the past and or on the future. *Here*. Ok?"

I nod and swallow down the rest of my tears. "Ok."

"Good. Now I have something special planned for us tonight. I left a gift for you on the bed in your old room. I need you to go get ready and wait there until I come for you."

I smile both nervously and excitedly. "That's awfully vague."

"It's meant to be. It's called a surprise. Now, go."

I bite my lip, trying to contain my excitement, but it's no use. I know anything he surprises me with is going to be spectacular and I can't wait to find out.

The hardest part is leaving his gorgeous, naked body in his large, comfortable, and warm bed, but I manage to pull myself away. I throw on a sweater, leggings, and slippers to walk to my old room. It's gotten quite cold in the castle outside of the rooms with fireplaces. Well, outside of his bedroom, really. We haven't left it much in the past couple of days…weeks? I don't even know. Not that I'm complaining.

I enter my old room to find the lights on and a large fire already roaring in the fireplace. He must have done this while I was sleeping, *sneaking vampire*. I walk over to the bed and gasp at what I see waiting for me.

I've never seen anything so breathtaking in my entire life. I can't imagine what on earth I would need something this beautiful for but I'm dying to find out.

ALEX

Beauty And The Beast by Angela Lansbury, Disney

I'm showered and dressed in record time. I'm eager to see her but I need to give her plenty of time to get ready, so I've been pacing my bedroom for the past thirty minutes like a damn caged animal. *If that isn't fucking accurate.* I'm a beast in a whole new way when it comes to Bella. I feel ferocious about protecting her, my feelings for her are feral, and I feel wildly untamed when it comes to my need to touch her. How I've managed to control myself is a testament to all the hard work I've done on controlling The Beast.

Unable to wait another minute, I finally leave my room in search of her. *What is that? Is that...nerves? Am I nervous?* I take a deep breath and slow my steps. "Calm down there, tiger. Nice and easy."

Once I'm standing in front of her door, I take another deep breath, hold it in for a count of ten, and then slowly blow it out. I shake out my hands, and then...I knock. Taking a few steps back, I wait with my heart pounding in my chest. I hear the click of her high heels against the floor as she approaches and then the door slowly swings open.

Sunshine.

She has the sweetest smile on her face and the lightest pink blush on her cheeks as she looks shyly up at me. "Wow, you look like a dream. I *must* be dreaming."

I barely hear her. My hand clutches my chest, I slowly release the air that's trapped there, and once I remember how to breathe, I wish I remembered how to speak. "Is it possible for a vampire to have arrythmia?"

Her eyebrows furrow in confusion. "Umm…what?"

"I think I just felt my heart stop in my chest before starting up again. You look…," I trail off as my eyes slowly roam over her.

She spins in a slow circle. Her back is completely bare, the satin gold dress clings to every delicious curve of her body. It's tight across her chest and stomach then flows to the ground. A slit in one side showcases her sexy leg from ankle to thigh, taunting me. Her hair has been pulled into a low bun and long loose strands frame her face. She's done something to make her blue eyes impossible to ignore, and there's a faint tint of pink to her luscious lips.

"You look…," I try again but words utterly fail me.

I finally remember how to walk, at least there's that, and close the distance between us. I gently tilt her chin up and then I'm lost. I fall hopelessly into her ocean eyes.

"I've been walking through the dark for so long, literally, and figuratively, that I don't even know what sunlight is anymore. What it looks like. What it feels like. But now I know. It feels like you, Bella. You are the sun in my eternal night sky, and I will revolve around you for as long as I'm able. You are, quite literally, the sunshine in my life."

Her eyes begin to water, and she bites her lip, trying to hide her smile. I reach for the lip. "What have I told you about doing that?" I lightly growl as my lips land softly on hers.

She melts into me. I wrap my arms around her, my fingertips exploring the smooth expanse of her back. She moans into me, and I back us towards the room, pushing her against the door. My cock starts to harden, and I press my body into hers so she can feel it. I need her to know how much she affects me. Everything in my body is begging me to devour her, to get lost in her both physically and emotionally, but this wasn't my intention for the night. I reluctantly step away from her, both of us breathless, happily willing to suffocate for each other.

I clear my throat and run my hands down my black dress shirt, trying to regain a semblance of control. "This is not at all what I had planned for tonight. If you'd kindly stop distracting me, I'd love to show you." I offer her my arm.

She smiles up at me and slips her arm through mine. "By all means, lead the way. I'm dying to know what it is you have planned."

We head down to the lower level of the castle, and I lead her down a hall I know she's never been before. The South Wing on the lower half. I haven't opened this part of the castle in centuries, but I've been slowly cleaning it up for the past couple of weeks. Yes, because of Bella. Because I want to give her everything.

While she was getting ready, I came down and prepared. I turned on all the lights and started fires in both of the fireplaces, but we're currently walking through a darkened hallway. I wanted to leave as much of the reveal until the end as possible. Two enormous doors come into view in front of us. There's not one crack or gap that reveals the bright lights hiding behind them.

"Are you ready?" I ask.

"I don't know!" She's squirming, practically jumping up and down. "I have no idea what to expect."

I can feel the excitement and anticipation rolling off her and I smile. This reaction alone is worth it. "Well, here we go."

I take my arm from hers and push both doors wide open, revealing the grand ballroom illuminated as if I lassoed the sun and hung it from the ceiling. She gasps, hand covering her mouth as she slowly steps inside. Her eyes are darting everywhere, taking in as much of the room as she can with every sweep of her gaze. I stand by the doors and watch as she walks further into the room and slowly spins and spins and spins, trying to take it all in.

"Oh, Alex," she whispers in awe. "This is stunning."

I look around the room, trying to see it through her eyes. I imagine what it must be like seeing something of this grandeur for the first time, especially if you're not used to it. The floor is all polished marble in creams, gold, and burnt orange. There are big, round marble pillars that support the ceiling, and a chandelier the size of a small house hangs from the center of it. It really is spectacular but still pales in comparison to her.

I follow slowly behind as she makes her way across the room and comes to a stop before the floor to ceiling windows. The entire outside wall is covered in them. I walk up behind her and wrap her in my arms. She leans against me but doesn't say a word as she continues to stare out the windows.

The moon is almost full, and the clouds have somewhat cleared, leaving parts of the night sky and the stars visible. Beyond the windows is a small lake reflecting the moonlight, and beyond that is nothing but trees. This is the opposite side of the castle from the garden, and I know she hasn't seen it.

"I had no idea there was a lake here. This is a dream. This is all a dream."

"Then let's never wake up," I whisper in her ear.

I hold her for several long minutes as we stand in beautiful silence appreciating the life around us. I don't know what she's thinking, but I'm only thinking about her. I'm always only thinking about her. How to make her happy. How to give her what she doesn't know how to ask for, what she doesn't even know she needs. How to spend every waking and sleeping moment by her side. How to stop time.

"Will you dance with me, Sunshine?"

She moves her head to the side and looks back at me with smile on her lips. "There isn't any music."

"There isn't any music...yet."

I leave her standing by the windows, and she watches as I walk towards the only source of music, an old record player. The last time this room was used, a live band played in it. It's not set up for modern day music streaming but I'm hoping that won't be an issue. I don't even know the record on the player, but I turn it on and move the needle over it anyways. The scratching sound of the needle on the record as it spins comes through the speaker. I turn the volume up as high as it will go and make my way back to her.

It's an instrumental song, one I don't actually know, but it's a slow waltz, something I think we can manage. I'm pulled back to my sunlight, a moth to a flame, only I'm completely aware of the deadly end that awaits me. Pushing those thoughts out of my head, I bow once I reach her and extend my hand out for her.

"May I have this dance, My Lady?"

She throws her head back and laughs but then manages a small curtsy. "It would be my pleasure, Good Sir."

I take her into my arms once again, way too close for a proper waltz and would have definitely caused a scandal back in my day, but I wouldn't have it any other way. I lead her around the huge ballroom floor, almost losing the music when we reach the far side of the room. Even if there wasn't any music, I'd dance with her anyway.

The smile on her face and the light in her eyes as we flow across the floor is magnetizing. I can't look away. I think back to the scared and insecure woman she was when I found her, and I still can't fathom why anyone would want to dim her light. How could anyone ever cause such a pure soul any type of pain or heartache? I vow to never let her spirit or her light dim. As long as I'm alive, and as long as she's mine, she will shine.

A much slower song starts next, and I keep her close to my body. She lays her head on my chest as we slowly move from side to side. We're more swaying now than dancing, but as long as she's in my arms, I don't care what we're doing. We dance song after song. She finally takes her heels off, but we keep dancing. Minutes tick by and all sense of time disappears. After five record changes, we finally decide to stop for the night.

"If I dance one more song, I won't be able to walk tomorrow."

I quickly scoop her up in my arms. "What did I tell you? You always need help walking. It's a good thing you have me to carry you around."

"You're such an ass," she says, with a smile. "Again, I'm perfectly capable of walking, but I have to admit, this is definitely *much* better. A girl could get used to this."

"Then let's get used to it."

She bites her lip and I'm suddenly starving. Having her pressed against me, touching her skin, and stealing kisses all night has me ready to snap.

"So, what's next on the agenda?"

"I'm so glad that you asked," I say, smiling widely because I know she loves my dimple. "You."

ALEX

BODY ON FIRE BY SLAVES

Back in my bedroom, I help her out of the dress. She's not wearing a single thing underneath and my body instantly responds. God, I crave her. I crave everything about her. This next part is going to be excruciating and will test just how much control I have.

"Here," I say, as I drape my discarded shirt over her shoulders. "Put this on for now."

"For now?" she questions, as she secures a couple of buttons to keep the shirt in place.

She's swimming in it. The bottom of the shirt hangs to right above her knees. There's just something about her wearing *my* shirt that turns me on and satisfies me immensely.

"Yes, for now. We both know it won't stay on for long, but I need you covered up if I'm going to see the rest of what I have planned through."

She grins up at me. "More surprises? I hope it involves something sweet."

"Mmmm, it does." I lean down to brush my lips against hers. "Let me change and I'll show you."

I leave her standing by the fireplace as I walk into the closet to get out of the dress pants and into something more comfortable. The look on her face as I walk back out and approach her is worthy of sketching. I can't help the arrogant smirk with how that look makes me feel.

"Oh, fuck me," she whispers.

"Is that a request, Sunshine?"

"Yes, please." She's practically speechless. Her eyes travel down my bare chest and stop below the waist for a few seconds before traveling back up.

"I get it now. I never believed it, in all the books I've read, I've never believed it, but seeing is believing. Grey sweatpants are superior."

I may have them hanging lower on my hips than necessary, and my cock may already be semi-hard, adding to the visual. I will never tire of seeing her look at me this way, and I will continue doing whatever it takes to keep it happening.

I stop in front of her and grab her wrist as she tries to reach out and stroke me over the sweats. If she touches me, I won't be able to see this night through. And I *really* want to see this night through.

"Uh-uh," I tsk. "Not yet."

"I never thought I'd say this to you, but you're cruel. You can't walk out like this and then not let me touch you."

"I promise, there will be touching soon. But first, we need to go up to the library." I intertwine my fingers with hers as I lead her out of my bedroom and to the library.

Once again, the room is already prepared. The lights are off though, leaving the room emblazoned by only firelight. As we approach the far end of the room, my plan comes into view.

"Oh, Alex! This is perfect! Absolutely perfect!" She releases my hand and rushes to the fireside, throwing herself down on the makeshift bed I've made with practically every blanket and pillow in the castle.

I pick up the serving tray from the desk and bring it over,

setting it on the floor next to her. "As promised, something sweet for you."

She gasps and kneels in front of the tray as I sit down next to her. It's filled with a variety of chocolate, fruit, and nuts. She immediately reaches for a piece of chocolate first and then the red wine.

"Mmmm," she licks her lips, slightly sucking on the bottom one as she savors the tastes. "Chocolate and wine, there's seriously nothing better than this."

"Oh, I can think of a few things I prefer."

Like her arousal. Like her blood. I'm dying to taste the flavors off her lips and tongue right now. No doubt, they are a hundred times better from her mouth than straight from the source. But if I kiss her now, it won't stop there, so I keep myself sprawled across the blankets as I watch her enjoy her treats.

She smiles. "Like my blood?"

"Amongst other things." Her cheeks are slightly flushed, and I don't know if it's a blush or the heat from the alcohol, but I love it either way. "Flushed and happy looks good on you, Sunshine."

She smiles wider and then picks up a strawberry. I can't take my eyes off her mouth as her lips wrap around the fruit and her teeth gently sink into it. *Is it possible to be jealous of a strawberry?*

"Are you truly happy here?"

"You're joking, right?" she chuckles. "That's not a serious question."

"It is. Could you see yourself being happy here for the rest of your life? In this big, lonely castle, just you and I? Forever?"

She sets her wine glass down on the tray and crawls over to me. Her hand runs through my hair, and I close my eyes briefly, living in the feel of her fingernails gently brushing against my scalp before her hand stops to rest on my cheek. Just one simple touch from her has my heart racing and my mind utterly reeling. Her touch excites me and brings me tranquility all at the same time. A peaceful chaos, that's what she is. She's the raging hurricane and the eye of the storm all at once.

Strong.

Forceful.

Terrifying.

Deadly.

"Alex." Her voice pulls me from my mind, and I look up at her. I'm always caught so easily in her earnest stare. "I've never been happier than I have been since you found me and brought me here. I haven't once wanted to go back, *not once.* Even when I ran from you the night I saw The Beast, I was scared and I ran, but I never *wanted* to go back. If I did, I wouldn't have come back with you. I don't need or want anything else other than this, right here, *ever.*"

I push myself up so I can finally claim her lightly wine-stained lips. My hand sinks into the hair at the back of her head and I hold her gingerly, yet tightly, against me. I've never felt such gentle power before, but when her tongue brushes against mine, and I taste the mix of sweet chocolate and bitter wine, along with the taste of her, I swear it rocks my entire world. Such a gentle kiss, with ultimate power.

Power to fulfill me.

Power to destroy me.

And still, I keep begging for more. Because she's worth it. Because this love that I feel devastatingly crushing my ribs is worth it. When she starts to crawl on top of me, I pull away.

"Now who's the one trying to distract who?"

"I'm sorry, but I don't see the problem. What else did you have planned if not making love to me by the fire?"

"Oh, that is one hundred percent part of the plan, but first...," I scoot back so my back is supported by the chaise, and I grab the book that I left on it, "I'm going to make good on another promise. Come here." I pat the spot between my legs.

She laughs. "You're not serious, are you? You're really going to read a...a *dirty* book to me?"

"Dead serious. One of us has to prove that we actually know how to read. Now. Get. Your. Sexy. Ass. Over. Here."

She hides her burning face behind her hands and shakes her head before laughing brightly. "Oh my God, okay. Okay! I can't believe you're actually doing this."

She settles between my legs, her back pressed against my stomach, head resting on my chest. I have the perfect view of her body and I can't wait to see this all unfold. I just pray that she trusts me and that she's not too shy to do what I ask.

"This book is called *Dark Temptations*. I thought it was rather appropriate as it is about a woman and a vampire." I open the book to the page I marked, clear my throat, and start to read.

She swallows down her fear and hangs onto my hand as she throws one leg over the ledge and then the other. Her legs are now dangling over the edge of the balcony, thirteen stories up, her back is pressed solidly against my chest as she leans back into me. There's nothing to interfere with the view of the mountains and the glowing moon. The storm clouds are over us now, but somehow, the moon still manages to avoid their cover.

I stop reading. "Undo the buttons on your shirt."

I can see and feel the rise and fall of her chest as her body responds to me, the story, and my command. Her fingers shake slightly as she releases the buttons.

"Open the shirt. Let me see you." She pulls it open and her naked body is now perfectly displayed before me. "Now I want you to do to yourself what he's doing to her in the story. Do you understand?"

I hear her hard swallow, before she whispers, "Yes." I begin to read again.

I'm holding her with one hand across her stomach as my other hand moves between her legs.

She hesitates for only a second before her hand trails a delicate line down her stomach and falls between her legs.

My fingers slide through her folds easily, her body is already soaking with desire. She leans her head back against my shoulder as she moans.

Bella's head tips back. I see her eyes are closed, lips parted, and she moans as her fingers continue to massage her clit.

I whisper in her ear, "I love how your body eagerly responds to my every touch."

I use the slickness of her own desire to coat her clit so I can glide my fingers across it effortlessly. I move in a slow, steady circle, feeling her clit swell under my touch.

"Do you like that?" I ask, as I pull her earlobe into my mouth.

Mimicing the story, I lean down and capture her earlobe with my lips, gently sucking on it before I ask, "Do you like that?"

"Yes."

"Let's see if you're following along with the girl in the book." I start to read again.

"Yes," she breathes out.

She starts to rock her hips to my touch, her breaths become heavier and I listen to every moan and whimper she makes.

Completely engrossed in the words spilling from my lips, she starts to rock her hips as she continues to touch herself, building herself up to a release. She's panting now, and moaning and whimpering, just like the story. I'm having a hard time focusing on the book in my hand as I watch her touch herself. My cock is hard and pressed against her. I move my own hips, trying to create some friction and pleasure of my own as I watch her. Back to the story.

I dip my finger inside of her, causing her to buck against my hand. All fear and thoughts of falling off the ledge are forgotten under the simple touch of my fingers.

I move my arm from around her waist, just long enough to turn her head towards me.

Bella doesn't hesitate and tilts her head back and to the side, looking up at me. Her beautiful blue eyes are so open and honest, she's so vulnerable with me, and I don't think I've ever *felt* so much in my life, like I do in this moment. I want to use my hand to make her come but there's something about seeing her touch herself so unabashedly, while she's sitting between my legs, that is hotter than anything I could do to her. Somehow I manage to continue to read.

"I want you to cum while you kiss me, Amarah Rey. I want to feel your desire, your breaths, and your moans, as they leave that beautiful mouth, and then I'm going to to make you cum again, so I can taste your desire as it rushes out of your body and onto my tongue. I want to taste and experience all of you, in every way."

"Alex," she breathes out. "I'm close."

I take her mouth, as I continue to hold her body against mine, and I move my slick fingers back to her clit. I move my finger up and down and gently use my fingernail to add some friction. Her moans are non-stop as she continues to recklessly kiss me and rock her hips frantically against my fingers. I increase my speed, her moans turn into whimpers, and I know she's close. A scream erupts from her throat and her body starts to shake as she cums. I swallow down her scream, as I start to tap her clit, drawing out her orgasm.

Tap. Tap. Tap.

"Alex!" She yells my name as her body jerks against me.

I toss the book aside and cover her mouth with mine, swallowing down her screams of pleasure, just like in the story. The kiss is reckless with passion and need as her body continues to rock against me. Once her body has stopped shivering, I climb out from behind her and move to kneel between her legs.

I gently pull her body down so she's lying flat and comfortable on the blankets. The firelight dancing on her skin is just as magical as I knew it would be. I take a few seconds to take in the sight of her and then I lower myself between her legs.

"Mmmm," I groan, as I get the first taste of her arousal on my tongue.

I grab her thighs and push them up and wider so I can see more of her and have better access to her center as I plunge my tongue inside of her, drinking down as much of her as I can. I replace my tongue with two fingers, and I start to slowly and softly caress her swollen and sensitive clit. Her hands immediately sink into my hair, holding me gently but firmly against her.

Gentle power.

"Oh fuck. That feels so good."

Her voice is airy, her words are beautiful, and she's ever so slowly rocking her hips in motion to my tongue. Fuck, it's a slow dance of another kind and we are perfectly in sync. She pulls on my head, and I give her more pressure on her clit but not increasing my slow strokes. Slow and steady, a little more pressure, a little more, listening to her tell me exactly what she wants.

"Yeah, right there. You're gonna make me come. Just like that, don't stop. Oh God, Alex, please don't stop. I'm coming! I'm coming!"

I grip her thighs tightly, holding them wide as they shake and fight against me. Her pussy spasms and squeezes my fingers as she soaks them with her release, and I moan my satisfaction into her core. I stop licking her clit but continue to pump my fingers inside of her as she rides out the last waves of her orgasm.

I push the sweatpants down my legs and kick them off. "Take

off the shirt and lie on your stomach."

She struggles to move her limp body but finally manages to get free of my shirt and then rolls onto her stomach, never once questioning me.

I gently push her hair aside, leaving her back completely exposed to the firelight. It dances across her skin. I follow the flames and trail my hands down each side, meeting the sexy curve of her back as it dips before climbing back up to a tight, round ass. I straddle her thighs and lean over her, letting my lips and tongue taste and explore from her neck all the way down her spine.

I smile as she shivers and goosebumps erupt across her flawless skin. The moans she's making now are sweet and loving, not breathy and filled with passion, yet they still fucking move me just as deeply. I live for every reaction this woman has to me, to life, just fucking everything. When I'm done thoroughly kissing every inch of her back, I sit up and slide my fingers up and down her drenched core. She subtly lifts her hips, asking for more, and I love that she wants me as badly as I want her.

"Tell me what you want, Sunshine."

"I want you. I want to feel you inside of me."

I grab my dick and rub it against her slit, teasing her. "Is this what you want?"

"Yes, please," she begs, lifting her hips higher.

I grab one ass cheek in my hand and line myself up to her entrance with the other and slowly start to slip inside of her. She gasps and I groan as the tip sinks into her warm tight pussy. I grab her other ass cheek and spread her wide so I can watch my dick disappear inside of her.

"Fuck," I growl.

This position makes her feel even tighter and I have to work my way into her, fighting for every delectable inch. Once I'm all the way inside her, I watch again as her body grips my cock when I slide out. Pumping my hips, I start to thrust into her slowly.

"Oh God." Her voice is raspy and sexy. "You feel so good."

"You're so sexy, Bella. I wish you could see the way your body greedily takes my cock."

She lifts her hips higher. "Give me more."

I slide all the way in, sinking deep and then I keep thrusting deep inside of her as she continues to push back into me. She's pushing hard and I know she wants more. I push her legs wide with my knees as I kneel behind her.

"Get up," I order.

She pushes up to her hands until she's on all fours in front of me. I grip her hips tightly as I slam everything I have into her. It's her turn to let out a beautiful, animalistic growl as she says, "Yes, yes, yes." Over and over again as I continue to hit deep inside of her.

I lean forward and wrap her silky hair around my fist and pull, eliciting a deep guttural moan of approval.

"You like it hard, don't you?"

"Yes." Her voice is breathy and tight. She's barely able to speak with the strain I have on her neck.

I can feel her pussy getting slicker as I continue to give her every inch of me with hard thrusts. "Yeah, you do. You're going to come all over my dick, aren't you?"

"Yes," she pants, her breath coming out hard every time I thrust. "Bite me."

Those two words practically wreck me. I almost lose my rhythm as the thought of sinking my fangs into her and tasting her glorious blood overwhelms me. I release my hold on her hair and wrap my arms around her waist, pulling her up, her back arched beautifully as I continue to slide into her.

I hold my right hand in front of her face. "Spit." She never hesitates or questions me and God, I love that about her. I love that she's so open and confident when we're having sex. It's so different than how she is when she's being all shy and rambling. I love both versions of her.

I hold her tightly with one arm and the other I drop between her legs, using her spit as lube as I rub her clit back and forth.

"Oh shit. Oh fuck. Fuck, fuck, fuck I'm com—"

Her words get stuck in her chest as I sink my fangs into her neck and her body practically goes limp in my arms as her beautiful pussy pulses and soaks my dick with her orgasm. We ride the high together as she utterly fills me up.

I gently lay her back onto her stomach, my own release building quickly as her intoxicating blood slides down my throat and heats my chest and gut like a shot of fucking whiskey.

I look down to where I'm sliding in and out of her. The sight of her creamy orgasm on my dick is all it takes for me to fall over the edge. I push inside of her one last time as my own cock pulses and releases my cum deep inside of her. It's my turn to go limp, crashing to the blankets beside her. I come face to face with her and gently brush her hair away from her face.

Her bedroom eyes look at me with so much love shining through them it makes me lose my damn breath. A lazy smile pulls at her lips.

"I don't think you're a vampire," she mumbles. "I think you're a God."

Again, my ego is in serious trouble when it comes to this woman. If she keeps this up, I might actually start to believe I'm worth it. That I do deserve her when clearly, I don't.

I grin. "Well, a sex God at least."

"Indeed."

I fall to my back and reach for her. She scoots over until her head is resting in the crook of my neck, her arm and leg draped over me. I hold her close as we both remember how to breathe.

I could repeat this night over and over again for eternity and never once tire of this dance. I will never tire of the way she moves her body against me. I will never tire of the beautiful music her body makes and the profound lyrics her voice sings as she loses herself in her pleasure.

In me.

And I will never tire of this. Afterwards. When we're both satiated and spent, completely relaxed and comfortable in each other's arms. No words need to be said because our souls literally just touched.

Her soul speaks to mine and mine to hers.

Words that have not been invented.

Words will never be enough, but I feel like I need to say them anyway. I need to get them out of my chest before my heart explodes.

"I am hopelessly, devastatingly, deeply in love with you, Bella."

I hold my breath and wait for a response.

Only silence surrounds us.

Then, a quiet snore.

I smile and kiss her head, hugging her closer to me. There will be plenty of time for me to say the words again. And, even if she doesn't quite feel the same way I do, even if she can't say them back just yet, I'll continue telling her until she does. Because there's no way she doesn't feel the same way I do.

Right?

A little sliver of doubt pricks my mind. She's young. She hasn't experienced life the way I have. What if this is just...*new* to her? Something different and exciting. A distraction from her life and nothing more. What if I'm projecting how I feel onto her, thinking I see it reflected back in her eyes because it's what *I* want to see?

I let out a heavy sigh and focus on her warm, soft body pressed against mine. No, I refuse to believe she doesn't love me, too.

"You're mine, Sunshine. You have to be. Because I don't think I can live without you."

Bella

Can You Hold Me by NF, Britt Nicole

I jerk awake with a gasp, clutching the blanket to my chest. It takes me a few seconds to ground myself, to remember where I am. The fire has died down to glowing embers next to us and I can feel the chill in the air as it's trying to creep in against the fading warmth. Or maybe the chill I feel is coming from inside me. Something woke me up. Something is causing me to feel nauseous. I can feel the panic slowly gripping me.

"Alex." I reach down to gently shake him. "Alex, wake up."

His eyes crack open, and a small smile starts to pull at his lips, and then he sees me. I watch as his eyes go from sleepy and content to alert and laser focused.

He's up in an instant, hands cupping my face and eyes assessing me. "What is it? What's wrong?"

I shake my head. "I don't know…exactly, but…something isn't right, something's wrong. I know it sounds crazy, but I can *feel* it."

"What do you feel?"

"I don't…I'm not sure." I squeeze my eyes shut, trying to focus on this weird sixth sense taking over my body and mind. "It's my mother. I don't know how or why but I know something's wrong. I need to go to her."

"Ok, I believe you. Sunshine, look at me." I focus on his silver eyes, his calmness and focus slowly helping me to feel a little better. "It's going to be ok." I nod. "The sun is still out. Let's get up and get dressed, then we can head down to her once the sun has set."

"No!" The panic starts to rise inside me again. "I need to go to her now! I can't wait."

"Bella—"

"No, Alex! Please. I know you don't understand but I need you to trust me. I have to go, now." I climb out of the makeshift bed, taking one of the covers and wrapping it around my naked body.

"Ok"

He climbs to his feet next to me, finds the discarded sweatpants and slides them on before he grabs my hand, and starts to lead me across the darkened library. When we get to the stairs, he picks me up in his arms and carries me down. He doesn't set me down until we're inside my room.

I rush to the wardrobe and throw it open, struggling to see what's inside because of the darkness of the room. Then a light illuminates behind me as he comes to stand beside me with a lantern in hand.

"Thank you," I mutter, as I start to pull clothes out of the wardrobe.

"I don't like the thought of you traveling back through the woods alone."

"You said the sun is still up, right? I'll be fine. I'll go slow, and I'll head straight down."

"I really wish you would wait—"

"I can't! She's my mother, Alex! And something is wrong. I have to go," I say quickly, as I lace up some winter boots. I can feel the unease radiating off him and I feel badly for making him feel this way but this feeling inside me is…urgent. I can't shake it and I won't be ok until I know my mother is safe.

"I'd never forgive myself if something was wrong, and I waited to go to her only to find I was too late. Please understand," I plead.

I throw on my large winter coat and zip it up. I'm dressed and ready to go. Alex once again finds my face, pulling my focus to him.

"As soon as the sun drops from the sky, I will come find you. I promise."

I nod and try to smile but I know it's forced. The thought of leaving the safety of this castle and Alex's arms starts to add to my anxiety. I don't want to go back. What happens if I run into Gabriel? What will he say? What will he do? And Alex, God I don't want to leave him! But I have to.

I know he can see the conflict in my eyes. He leans down and gently brushes his lips against mine, then leans his forehead on mine for a couple of seconds before he whispers, "Go."

I look up at him through tears and desperately fight them back. I can't do that right now. I can't fall apart. I can't be weak.

"Go," he repeats. "I'll be right behind you."

I nod, and before I can lose my nerve, I turn and run. I run down the hallway, down stairs, and burst outside. I immediately have to slow down due to the snow, and no doubt ice, lingering on the front stone steps. An image of Louie sprawled in a puddle of blood flashes through my eyes and that godawful gut-wrenching feeling is back full force.

I make it unscathed down the steps, across the front lawn and down the sprawling hillside until I'm lost in the cover of trees. Even though the sun is still out, and no clouds cover it, it's still impossible for the light to penetrate the thickness of these trees. Only the sound of my ragged breath and the crunching of frozen snow underneath my feet accompany me. It's eerily quiet in the forest of trees and I try not to think about why. It could just be that I am the one traipsing through, causing animals and birds to hide, or it could be something else.

Coyotes. There's no rule that states coyotes only hunt at night. I push that thought away and focus on my feet and the path I can see in front of me. I need my focus and my nerve. My mother is counting on it.

It feels like hours pass by before I'm finally breaking through the tree line. Our cabin sits forlorn in the clearing. A place that once used to be my safe haven, my only place of solace, now looks like my prison. I do have happy memories here, as a child, but now that I know what true happiness and contentment feels like, now that I know what it feels like to truly love and be loved, this life isn't it. But right now, none of that matters. This isn't about me.

I rush across the clearing and barge inside. "Momma!" I cry, as I run to her.

She's tied to a chair next to the small fireplace, a gag in her mouth. I remove the gag. "Bella!" she yells in a quiet whisper. "You need to go. You shouldn't be here."

"What?! I'm exactly where I should be," I argue, as I start to undo the knots on the rope that binds her wrists. I'm once again having to fight back tears so I can see what I'm doing, but my hands are shaking, making it almost impossible to untie them. "What happened? Who did this to you? Why?" I take a deep breath, steady myself, and try again.

"He's been looking for you. He got tired of waiting for you to come back and said he knew that I knew where you were and that he'd get the answer out of me one way or another."

I look up into her tear-stained face. Her right cheek is swollen, and blood is drying on her lips and chin. She's the spitting image of me a month ago.

"Gabriel."

She nods. I finally manage to untie both of her wrists and move on to her ankles. "Momma, I'm so sorry this happened to you. I'm so sorry I left. I should have come back." The tears are rolling down my cheeks now, there's no holding them back as I fumble with the last knot on the rope. "If I had come back this wouldn't have happened to you. I would have been here and he—"

"Oh, baby girl." Her hands grip my arms, and she brings us both to our feet. Her gentle hands cup my face as she looks at me so lovingly and says, "I'm glad you weren't here. You shouldn't have come back, it's not safe."

"Momma, I—"

"I can handle this now. I wasn't prepared before. I didn't think he'd actually hurt me, but I can guarantee he won't do it again."

"I am not leaving you! Get your things, whatever you need, and come back with me to the castle. Alex will—"

"So that's where you've been." His deep voice makes me shiver with dread as he steps into the cabin. "Hiding out in an abandoned castle. I never considered that's where you'd be. I thought you had run off to another town. Lucky for me, here you are."

I move to stand in front of my mother. "How dare you put your hands on my mother. You're a sick piece of shit! I can't believe I ever thought I could love you!"

"Oh, Bella," he chides. "I know you love me, just like I love you. That's why you came back, isn't it? To be with me."

"Never! You're fucking delusional."

I see his jaw twitch and his nostrils flare as he storms towards us. I tilt my chin in defiance, refusing to cower in front of him or play into his insanity. His strong hands wrap around my upper arms, and he pulls me into him.

"You watch your tone when you're—"

I spit in his face. The shock I see alone is worth it, but the shock quickly turns into anger, and a large hand clamps down on the bottom half of my face, squeezing tightly.

"You're going to pay for that. And then we're going to work on fixing this attitude until you realize there's no other option for you. I am your only option and you will fucking love me."

A loud crack sounds in the air and Gabriel stumbles to his knees, taking me down with him. "You get your fucking hands off my daughter you piece of shit!" my mother yells, a cast iron pan gripped in both hands, held up like a sword in front of her.

Gabriel touches the back of his head and his fingertips come away with blood. Unfortunately, the hit wasn't strong enough to knock him out or do any real damage. He's on his feet and stalking toward my mom before I can scramble to mine. She tries to swing again but he catches her arms easily and then backhands her across the face, sending her sprawling to the floor.

"No!" I scream, and rush toward her.

Gabriel's arms catch me around the middle, and I fight as hard as I can, legs kicking and arms flailing as I try to land any sort of punch or kick to his body. It's absolutely useless. A large hand wraps around my throat and starts to squeeze.

"I wanted to do this the easy way but if you want to do it the hard way then the hard way it is," he growls, as his hand continues to block my air.

I frantically scratch at his fingers, but I know nothing I do will make a difference. My vision starts to spot, and I can feel the blackness creeping in around the edges. I try to fight as long as I can, but I'm quickly pulled under the weight of unconsciousness.

When I slowly start to come to, my mind starts piecing together my surroundings. The bed, the room, the smell of *him*. I'm lying on the bed I woke up in more times than I care to remember. The panic immediately takes hold of me, and I try to get up only to find that I'm the one now tied up. My wrists have been tied above my head to the headboard. I yank at them, only managing to tighten the rope as it burns into my skin.

"It's no use fighting." My eyes glance up to where he's leaning in the doorway, arms crossed and perfectly at ease. "You're not getting away from me this time and I'll keep you here until you realize that there's no other place for you but with me."

All I can manage is to glare at him. I know that nothing I say is going to sink into that thick skull of his. He believes he loves me. He believes he's entitled to have me, and nothing is going to change his narcissistic mind. So, I'll just refuse to play his game.

"Your mother is fine, by the way," he says, as he pushes off the doorframe and enters the bedroom. The room immediately feels too small, and I want nothing more than to be able to run away from him. "I had to tie her back up, to keep her from doing anything...*stupid* but she's fine."

I seethe as I stare at him, hoping he sees just how much I fucking hate him. When he sits on the edge of the bed, I pull my legs up and underneath me, trying my hardest to crawl into a little ball and get as far away from him as possible.

"I hate seeing you like this, Bella," he says in a soft, almost caring tone. God, he's so fucking good at playing the innocent, charming fucking hero. "It was never supposed to be this way between us. You just couldn't mind your business and let me love you."

He slides further onto the bed and my entire body tenses, but I refuse to show him any kind of fear. His hand softly caresses my cheek but there's nothing affectionate about his touch. He doesn't love me, he covets me. He wants to own me and admire me like a trophy. I don't think he's capable of loving anyone else but himself.

"And I do love you. And once you stop fighting this, stop fighting us, you'll see that you love me, too."

I jerk my face away from his touch and still refuse to speak to him. I see the anger flash in his eyes as he reaches for me again, this time grabbing my face in that vice grip he loves to use on me. He climbs to his knees and leans into me.

His lips land on mine in a crushing kiss, his hands still on my jaw holding me firmly in place. "You're only making this worse. It doesn't have to be this way. I don't want to break you, Bella, but I will. If that's what it takes."

His hands wrap around my ankles, and he pulls them from under me until I'm stretched out before him and he's kneeling between my legs. I buck and twist my body, but he pins me down easily. I realize that no amount of fighting will dissuade him. In fact, his sick and twisted mind might actually enjoy it. So, instead I lay still. I close my eyes and tilt my head away from him, refusing to acknowledge him and what he's clearly about to do.

His hand is back on my face, jerking my head forward. "Look at me, Bella." I squeeze my eyes shut. "Look at me!" he bellows.

I scream. I scream my hatred as loud as I possibly can. I scream and scream and scream until his hand clamps down on my mouth, suffocating me. His other hand unbuttons my jeans and my self-preservation kicks in, and I start to fight again. I can't let him take me against my will. Not again.

I have to fight not only for myself, but for Alex too. I don't know that I'll be the same if Gabriel rapes me. Not now, not when I know better. When he took me before, I still believed we were together. I didn't necessarily want it, but I didn't fight or tell him no either. I thought there was still hope for us. But I'm not in denial anymore. I'm not the same person I was. I'm stronger. I'm stronger because of Alex. Because of the love he's given me. Because he's shown me what it's like to be respected, valued…loved. No, I refuse to let Gabriel take this away from me. Not when I have something, *someone*, worth fighting for.

As if my will brought him to my side, I hear his beautiful, haunting voice rip through my muffled screams. "Get the fuck off of her!"

Gabriel's body is pulled off me as if he weighs nothing as Alex launches him across the room. His back slams into the wall and then he crumples to the floor.

"Bella!"

Alex is next to me, breaking the rope like it's a piece of string. As soon as I'm free, I throw myself into his arms.

"I'm sorry," I cry into his neck. "I'm sorry! I should have waited for you. I'm sorry."

"Shh, Sunshine. It's ok. You're ok."

"Who the fuck are you?" Gabriel's voice booms in the room as he gets to his feet, clearly ready to fight.

Alex releases me. We both slide off the bed and Alex pushes me behind him. "I'm the one who's been keeping Bella safe, away from you, you abusive waste of fucking life."

"Keeping her safe? She's safe with me if she just stops fighting the truth. She loves ME. She's been playing games and you fell for them. You're insane if you think she actually loves you. Whoever you are."

"I'm insane!? You had to tie her to your bed to keep her from running away from you! Again!"

"I'm not letting you take her."

Alex steps forward. His body is tense with anger, but his hands remain loose at his sides unlike Gabriel who has his hands clenched in fists, chest heaving with his own anger. They're about the same height but Gabriel has bulkier muscle. If I didn't know any better, I might be worried for Alex facing off with Gabriel, but I *do* know better. Gabriel doesn't have a chance in hell beating Alex because Alex isn't human. He can rip Gabriel apart with his bare fucking hands.

"Don't kill him," I whisper from behind him. I know that Alex hasn't taken a life in a long time, and I don't want him to start now. Not because of me.

"You can try to stop me, but I *am* taking her with me, and you will never lay eyes on her ever again much less a disgusting finger, or I swear to God, I will break it the fuck off."

Gabriel growls and lunges, swinging his fist towards Alex's face. Alex stands still, allowing Gabriel's fist to connect with his cheek. The sound of knuckles on bone cracks through the air and I wince in pain just from the sound and sight. Alex's head barely even moves under the vicious strike.

I step to the side, trying to see his face, wanting to make sure he's ok. His tongue runs along his bottom lip, tasting the blood that's now trickling from the side of his mouth. He wipes at it with his thumb and then he grins. I've never seen him look more dangerous than he does right now.

He launches himself at Gabriel, wrapping his arms around him and crashing him into the already damaged wall. The force of their bodies breaks through the drywall, and I hear the sound of wood splitting. Gabriel cries out in pain and Alex backhands him, hard.

"How do you like that? Do you feel powerful now? Now that you're fighting someone that can fight back." He backhands him with the other hand, and then again, and again, until blood is running from Gabriel's nose and mouth.

Gabriel rallies and punches Alex in the side. Another cracking sound and Alex growls. I think Gabriel just broke his ribs with that punch.

"Alex!" I scream in concern, as he grabs at his side and winces.

Gabriel uses Alex's slight distraction to push off the wall. They stumble back into the dresser and then fall to the ground. Gabriel manages to hit him in the face again before Alex finally uses more of his strength to get on top of him and hold him down.

He punches Gabriel in the face repeatedly until his arms fall limp to his sides and he stops fighting. He sighs, chest heaving with his heavy breaths as he climbs off Gabriel's prone body.

"If I ever see your face again, I will not hold back and I will fucking kill you." Alex takes his eyes off Gabriel and looks at me, offering his hand. "Come on. Let's get your mother and let's go home."

I run to him, taking his hand in mine. I kick Gabriel between the legs as I step over him. He grunts and curls onto his side, cradling his junk.

"You're lucky I didn't ask him to cut off your small dick, you piece of shit."

I follow Alex out of the bedroom and into the living room. I pull him to a stop before we reach the door. My hand gently touches his face where it's starting to swell, and blood is still trickling out of his busted lip.

"You're hurt."

He grabs my wrist and brings my hand to his lips, kissing it before lowering it and holding it between us. "I'm fine, Sunshine. It will be healed in a couple of hours. I promise, I'll be good as new before the sun is up again tomorrow."

"Thank you for saving me...again."

He shakes his head. "I should have come with you and none of this would have happened. I'm sorry." He brushes my cheek with his thumb. His caress is everything Gabriel's is not. It's affectionate and loving.

I smile because it's perfect. He's perfect. "It's not your fault. It's no one's fault. Now let's go get my mother and let's go home," I repeat his earlier words as I start to pull him to the front door.

Then I hear the familiar click of a gun. I look around Alex to see Gabriel propped against the hallway wall, gun in hand, and it's pointed straight at Alex's chest.

"You don't get to have him, Bella. Only me," he says, as he pulls the trigger and falls to the floor.

I don't know how I manage to move as quickly as I do, but I push Alex out of the way as the gun goes off, sounding like a bomb in the small living room. My ears start to buzz and then I feel wetness soaking my shirt. I look down to see a glistening red spot quickly expanding right between my breasts.

"Oh shit," I whisper. "That's not good."

"Bella!" Alex's arms catch me as I start to fall to the ground. "No, no, no! This can't be happening. Bella, no, why did you do that?"

"I don't know," I whisper, as the burning and intense pain starts to sink into my chest. "I was…trying to…save…you." It's hard to speak around the pain and the wetness I feel rising up my throat. I cough, trying to clear my throat, only to spew blood everywhere.

"I can't lose you. I can't! We haven't even started. We need more time, please don't die, I won't survive. Nothing good in me will survive."

"Alex, I…I love you. I love you so---"

He silences any more words with his lips on mine. His blood and his tears mingle with my own as he cradles me to his body and tries to kiss life back into my drowning lungs.

He breaks the kiss and there's a wild look in his eyes. "I'm going to bite you. It will only drain your life faster, but I need to try, Bella. I need to try to turn you. Please forgive me. I love you."

The familiar pleasure of his bite washes over me, taking away all the pain with it. I sigh and feel my body go limp in his arms. If I'm going to die, this is not a bad way to go.

The warmth of his bite slowly fades as the cold seeps in. Cold. So cold. I can feel it settle into my bones. The last thing I see are two shining silver stars looking down on me.

ALEX

This is not the way we end. It can't be. Life can't be so cruel as to allow me to find my soulmate after four hundred fucking years only to take her away from me after one month. But as I hold her body, I can hear the beat of her heart faltering.

"I can't lose you. I can't! We haven't even started. We need more time, please don't die, I won't survive. Nothing good in me will survive."

"Alex, I...I love you. I love you so---"

She loves me. I didn't think I'd ever hear her say the words. I wasn't even sure if they were in there, but she loves me. I feel my heart break inside of my chest, the collapse of everything I hoped to be with her, for her is crashing down around us.

I silence her words with my mouth. The taste of her blood is tainted with the taste of the bullet poisoning her system. Stealing her life. This can't be the way it ends. She's dying and I have to try. I have to try one last time because if I don't, I'll always wonder.

I pull away from her lips and I feel manic. We've passed through the eye of the storm and the hurricane has landed. It's a wild force swirling inside me.

"I'm going to bite you. It will only drain your life faster, but I need to try, Bella. I need to try to turn you. Please forgive me. I love you."

I sink my fangs into her neck and drink down the polluted blood, praying to anyone who's out there, praying to the one who made her for me, my fucking soulmate, to please save her. Please have mercy on my imperfect and damaged soul and save her. Save me.

I release her vein and bite my own at the wrist and trickle my blood into her mouth. "Drink it, Bella, please drink it."

It only pools in her mouth and starts to trickle out as her once lively blue eyes lock with mine, holding them in their trance one last time, as I watch the life drain away. Her eyes are still on mine but they're no longer seeing me.

I hug her closer to my body and I scream my hatred for the world as loud as I can. I scream myself hoarse and then I scream some more, until I'm left with nothing else to give. Nothing left inside of me as I rock back and forth with Bella's lifeless body in my arms. I feel every single piece of Alex slowly start to fade away as The Beast rises in his place.

I curse Katherine and her fucking curse.

I curse Louie for leaving me.

I curse that stupid empty castle.

I curse the entire goddamn world.

But most of all, I curse the man who took my Sunshine, my heart, the only good thing in my life, my entire world, away from me.

I slowly lower Bella's body to the floor and stand up. I turn around to face the demon that's two seconds away from being sent to Hell.

"I didn't...that wasn't...I wouldn't...." He's clearly in shock, eyes glued to where Bella now lays, dead, by his hand.

"You're going to wish you had killed me when you had the chance because I'm going to make you feel all the pain I feel in here...," I point to my now empty chest, "on every inch of your body."

His eyes widen in fear and he points the gun at me. I'm by his side in an instant and yank the gun out of his hand and break it in two, tossing the pieces to the floor. I lean down and grab him by his throat and lift him off the floor until his feet are dangling in the air. Then, I let him see The Beast. My eyes go red, my fangs drop, and my nails turn into claws. I rake them down his arm, making deep trenches in his skin, letting the blood flow like a river. He tries to yell but I'm still holding him up by the throat.

"All the pain you're going to feel and it still won't be enough. It will never be enough."

I drop him and his feet crumple underneath him, sending him once again to the floor. He's gasping for air and trying to stop the bleeding on his arm with his other hand.

I pull his hand away. "This is the hand that strangled her, isn't it? This is the hand that hit her. This is the hand that she feared. Well…," I chuckle, "no one is ever going to fear it again."

I snap his wrist in half until the bone breaks through the skin. Then, I grab the bone and continue pulling, tearing at the skin and tendons until his hand is ripped clean off his arm. His scream is loud and deafening. I can almost hear her beautiful voice speak out in triumph at his agony.

"Alex."

I close my eyes. Her voice will haunt me for the rest of my days.

"Alex." I hear it again, louder this time.

I turn around but don't believe my eyes. "It can't be. I watched you die. You didn't drink my blood…." I trail off in disbelief. "Sunshine?"

"I feel…different."

Epilogue

Bella

BEAUTIFUL MESS BY KRISTIAN KOSTOV

I am a vampire.

Four words I never thought I'd say. A year ago, I didn't even know vampires existed outside of fairytales and books, much less that I would fall in love with one or become one.

When I woke up in Gabriel's living room, both Alex and I were beyond shocked. That shock quickly got pushed aside as the intense hunger struck me with the force of a fucking lightning bolt. Son of a bitch, I've never felt anything so sharp and so severe as the craving for blood. Needless to say, Gabriel didn't live much longer after I awoke. My only regret is that I didn't allow Alex the chance to continue making him suffer for everything he did to me.

Once I was somewhat satiated from draining Gabriel of his life, we went to see my mother. We made sure she was safe. Other than being tied up, with some bruises and sore muscles from Gabriel's attack, she was fine. She took the news about me and about vampires better than I would have imagined. She also understood when I told her I couldn't stay. Not in the castle, not in New Haven. Alex had to take me somewhere where I could learn to control the hunger, somewhere where I could feed without notice until that happened.

Tokyo is where we ended up. A literal sea of people to choose from though I did try to focus on those that deserved death. I especially targeted men who raped, or rather *tried* to rape women. I couldn't kill them all but you bet your ass I tried. I wasn't always able to control it in the beginning, but Alex never let me hurt a child, and for that, I'm forever grateful.

Now we're back at Knightwell Castle, where it all started. I've gained control over the hunger, for the most part, but I still have a long way to go. A year is nothing in the life of a vampire, and most never even gain control until years and years later, but I have Alex. He's been with me every step of the way. He grounds me. He keeps me safe. And as my Mèt Nan San, he can lend me his strength to control it.

I've always felt connected to Alex in a way I never was with anyone else before. He says we're soulmates. I have to agree. Still, that bond is nothing compared to what I feel now. It's only intensified, for both of us. We've agreed that he won't attempt to sire any other vampires, even though the curse seems to have been broken. We don't know if it truly has been or if it was just our love for each other that trumped the curse for *us*. We've talked about it at length, gone over Katherine's words again and again, and one thing stood out.

You are incapable of loving anyone but yourself.

Her words had been true, until he met me.

The doors to the castle slowly push open and we walk inside. The chandelier is a brilliant flood of light as hundreds of candles flicker above us. My mother has been living here in the castle since we left, along with a few others that have strayed into its path along the way. Others like Louie. The castle is no longer kept in darkness but the legend of The Beast is stronger than ever after Gabriel's mutilated body was discovered. We prefer it this way.

Alex scoops me up in his arms, dispelling my thoughts, as he climbs the old familiar steps of the entryway leading up to the second floor. I laugh heartily and wrap my arms around his neck.

"What are you doing?"

"If I remember correctly, these steps can be quite dangerous, and you had quite the issue with walking last time we were here."

"Last time we were here, I was human. I can't get a sprained ankle anymore."

"Well, best to not take any chances," he grins at me, giving me his gorgeous smile and devastating dimple.

He's no longer able to compel me, not that he did before, but being a vampire has done nothing to protect me from his charm. Or his devious tongue and sexy body. No amount of time is ever going to quench my need or my love for him. An eternity with this man is only adding gasoline to an already blazing wildfire.

He lets out a playful growl. "You keep biting that lip and it's going to get you in trouble."

"Maybe I want trouble." My voice is already breathy with desire.

"That mouth is definitely going to get you into trouble."

"I can think of another use for this mouth."

He groans, and then the walls of the castle whoosh by as he takes us to his bedroom. My back hits the familiar bed and then his weight is on top of me a second later. I can feel the urgent need in his touch, but his kiss is slow and deep, the same intoxicating kiss it's always been, leaving me craving more and more. No matter how many times we give in to our need for one another, it's never enough.

I've never been happier. I never thought my life would ever be perfect, yet here I am, living it. Will it always be this way? No, probably not. But as long as I have Alex by my side, nothing else matters.

AUTHOR NOTE & ACKNOWLEDGMENTS

It's always surreal when I find myself here, again. At the end of another story that has lived in my head that I finally get to bring to life. I honestly don't know how it's possible some days. I've written six books…SIX!!! It's so crazy to think about but I couldn't be happier.

I wouldn't be as successful on this writing journey if I didn't have my husband by my side. He's my biggest cheerleader and my sounding board. He has to deal with all of my crazy, my book obsession, and my emotions. Let's be honest, that is *not* an easy task. It takes a lot of time, not only to write a book, but all the behind-the-scenes stuff takes so much time away from us. One of these days, I will be a full-time author and retire you! Then it will all be worth it.

Of course, I won't ever become a full-time author without you, the reader. I see so much debate and conflict on social media between readers and authors, talking about whose space is whose and what should and shouldn't be done by each group. I HATE IT. We would not have a book world without the author writing the books and the readers reading them. This community is one and the same. It shouldn't be segregated. I understand why it has become this way, with disrespect happening on both fronts, but that doesn't mean I have to like it or agree with it. So, if you're reading this, author or reader, DO BETTER! BE BETTER! I will continue to read reviews, comment on reviews, and engage with my readers as much and as often as possible. That's why I am here. So please, don't ever hesitate reaching out to me. Respectfully.

Now that my rant is over, I want to thank a select group of people. This group tends to remain the same from book to book because I have the most loyal group of friends in my corner!

Miss Jenny, my Alpha reader, who always provides the best story feedback. Thank you for your time and all the support you continue to give me outside of Alpha reading. I adore you.

To my Beta reader, Kara, who makes me feel like a terrible writer (sorry you bear this burden!) but who I appreciate the most. I wouldn't be able to publish such a well-developed/constructed book without you. I've come to terms with the fact that I'll never put a comma in the right place or understand the English language. My appreciation for your ability to do so is beyond words!

To all the lovely souls on bookstagram, all 20 of you haha, who continue to like, comment, and support me...THANK YOU! I see you. I appreciate you.

As always, please don't forget to leave your review on Amazon and any other social media platform you use. Even if it's just a rating and not a written review, it helps immensely.

I know I'm probably forgetting to say something here... but the only thing that really matters is, thank you. Thank you for being on this journey with me and being an integral part of my dream to become a full-time author.

XOXO,
Harmony

MORE FROM THE AUTHOR

If you enjoyed this read, check out my dark romance Peter Pan reimagining! It's nothing like the Disney story you know, I promise.

Unforgivable Sins

Also, check out my complete urban/paranormal fantasy series, The Amarah Rey, Fey Warrior Series.

Awaken
Fey Blood
Dark Temptations
Divine Destiny

You can find them on Amazon here: Amazon Author page or the kindle version here: Amazon Ebooks/Kindle

Stay up to date on news and exclusive content and follow me on social media! Who knows what will come next!

Instagram
TikTok
Newsletter

Thank you for being here and all of your support! Again, I could not do this without You. Leave those reviews 😊

www.ingramcontent.com/pod-product-compliance
Lightning Source LLC
Chambersburg PA
CBHW030650260626
47157CB00007B/2584